THEIR TEMPORA

The Doms of Club Mystique 3

Mardi Maxwell

MENAGE AMOUR

Siren Publishing, Inc.
www.SirenPublishing.com

A SIREN PUBLISHING BOOK
IMPRINT: Ménage Amour

THEIR TEMPORARY SUB
Copyright © 2014 by Mardi Maxwell

ISBN: 978-1-62741-950-5

First Printing: September 2014

Cover design by Harris Channing
All art and logo copyright © 2014 by Siren Publishing, Inc.

Printed in the U.S.A.

PUBLISHER
Siren Publishing, Inc.
www.SirenPublishing.com

DEDICATION

For my BFF, so many years of friendship and love. Thanks.

For my editor…you rock. Thanks.

THEIR TEMPORARY SUB

The Doms of Club Mystique 3

MARDI MAXWELL

Chapter One

Cassie Edwards wondered how much longer she could avoid the punishment she had coming for her sneak attack on Luc and Logan Ramsey. Sure, she had used ice cream instead of bullets, and chocolate sauce instead of knives, but within moments she had taken them down. Then, to make matters worse, she'd zip-tied their arms behind their backs, gagged Luc and then covered his face with whipped cream. That had really pissed him off and she figured he wouldn't stop spanking her until her ass was a bright rosy red. She was dreading the punishment but also looking forward to it—and that was the problem.

Sighing, she rinsed the glass she had just washed and reached for another. How had she let herself get so tangled up with the Ramsey family? She never formed bonds with people. Not since she was seventeen and her actions had gotten her father killed. Of course, the Ramsey's didn't know the truth about that, and neither did her boss, Thor Larkin, whom she'd known most of her life. Thor had been a member of her father's Marine recon team, then years later Jackson Ramsey had joined the team and she had met him, and through him his older brother, Cade Ramsey. Jackson and Cade had become surrogate brothers to her, and Thor had become her guardian after her father's death eight years ago. Now Thor owned a much sought after security company, The Larkin Agency, and she and Cade worked for him.

One thing about these people—there was never a boring moment around them. In the last three months, Cade's fiancé Addison Matthews had been attacked and kidnapped by Carlos Mendez, the head of a Columbian drug cartel. Then, she had been rescued and returned to Cade by Juan Rios, the head of a competing Columbian drug cartel and Carlos Mendez's bitter enemy. The Ramsey brothers had barely recovered from Addison's ordeal when an old enemy of their father's had decided to go after Jackson and his sub, Jenna Parnelle. Now, Jackson and Jenna were engaged and planning a winter wedding while Addison and Cade's wedding was next week. It had been pared down from a huge event to a surprise wedding disguised as a backyard barbecue for close friends and family. The wedding plans had been changed to mislead the paparazzi and to conceal Addison's pregnancy.

And that's where her problem became more complicated. Cade had decided to leave fieldwork, and he and Thor had formed a partnership. They'd decided to open a new branch of The Larkin Agency here in Rendezvous, Texas, and she had a terrible feeling she knew who was going to get stuck helping them do that—her. A task she would have enjoyed under normal circumstances, but there wasn't anything sane about staying at the Ramsey Ranch within reach of Luc and Logan. The temptation of being this close to them was overwhelming, and there wasn't a moment in the day she didn't want to run her hands, and her lips, all over their bodies. They were twins and double trouble, and there was no way she was going to be able to hold out against their pursuit.

Logan had already let her know he was interested in getting down and dirty with her. He was always popping up near her with a grin and an offer to spend time with him. Luc, on the other hand, kept his distance, Although he was always somewhere near when Logan cornered her. They were like the positive and negative posts on a battery, and she just knew touching them at the same time would be the most electrifying experience of her life. *If* she was brave enough to take that last step, and that was the root of the problem—she wasn't brave at all. In fact, she considered herself a coward of the first order.

Frowning, Cassie scrubbed at a spot on a plate. She hadn't realized she'd forgotten so many details about her friend, Julia, until recently, when her memory had started coming back. At first, when the nightmares had begun about a year ago, she'd thought she was going crazy. Then, the flashes of people, places, and incidents came. The memories began to form a picture of how she'd met Julia, and how Julia had gotten her involved with her drug-dealing boyfriend Jimmy. Eventually the memory of Jimmy threatening her with a fake video of her delivering a box of drugs for him had returned to her. As bad as those memories had been the flashes of memories she was beginning to have of more than one man raping her were the most frightening.

Every time she'd tried to date over the last eight years fear had overwhelmed her and she'd always ended up withdrawing from the relationship. Her last attempt had been a few months ago, when she had tried again at Club Mystique's masquerade party. She still cringed when she thought about poor Sir Thompson's reaction when he had put a cuff on her wrist and she'd turned into a raving maniac. He, of course, had maintained his control and had talked to her about getting some counseling. He'd even made her promise to see a therapist friend of his who specialized in working with victims of rape.

Cassie had kept her promise to Sir Thompson. After three months of two sessions a week and proper medication she was at least sleeping again, mostly. She'd told her therapist she had been raped, but she hadn't told her she was beginning to remember being abducted then held captive for two days, or that she was having flashes of being beaten and raped by several men. Two of the men had wanted to kill her, but another man had returned her to her Aunt Velma's home along with a warning that anyone she told would be killed.

By the time her father returned from his overseas mission, she'd been healed and she could have kept her secret. Her father had been her hero, though, and she'd believed he was invincible. So she'd told him, believing he would find the men who had hurt her. Instead, her father had been killed that same night, and she knew it was because of her. She wouldn't risk putting anyone else in harm's way by getting close to them or telling them what had happened to her. Which brought her back to her problem with Luc and Logan.

She wanted them, but she knew she shouldn't take the risk of getting close to them. Lately, strange things had begun happening around her, and she was pretty sure she was being followed by someone. Then there was the fact that Luc and Logan ran Club Mystique, the Ramseys' very expensive and exclusive BDSM club, and they were known for being no-nonsense Doms. She knew for a fact she couldn't give them what they needed. She simply wasn't capable of opening herself up to another person like that. She'd believed she was frigid until she'd visited Club Elysium in Dallas two years ago and been aroused while watching other people play. Since then she'd spent a lot of time in the local BDSM clubs as a spectator but never a player. Thank god she lived in the age of electronics and had access to a wide variety of sex toys, although she was beginning to wonder what it would be like to just once let go and let someone else take care of her needs.

Sighing, Cassie wondered where Luc and Logan were as she rinsed the last glass, set it on the drying rack, then turned, screamed, and jumped back. Logan stood a couple feet from her, his beautiful hazel eyes with their thick, straight lashes looking down at her. He stepped closer and she felt the heat of his body against her bare arm. Her first instinct was to put a few more inches between them but she held her ground and glanced over her shoulder. Just as she thought, Luc stood a couple feet behind her.

Logan smiled. "Sorry, I didn't mean to startle you."

Like hell, she thought, but said, "That's okay, Logan. I just didn't realize you were there."

"So, Cassie, I was thinking about your problem," Logan said as he moved another step closer.

Feeling stalked, she forced herself to meet his eyes and noticed that his right eye was slightly darker than his left. She inched toward him, her eyes locked on his, as she checked to make sure. She would bet good money Luc's left eye would be darker as the two of them were mirror-image twins.

"Cassie?" Logan asked, a hint of warning in his voice.

She pulled herself back into the moment. She knew how to deal with men like Logan and Luc as she dealt with men like them every day at the Larkin Agency. Men like Thor and Cade and so many others. Most of the Doms who tended to gather in the same places and gravitate toward the same kind of high-risk, dangerous jobs. Blinking, she reminded herself that showing weakness of any kind in front of these two would be a huge mistake and asked, "What makes you think I have a problem, Logan?"

"You and Jenna and Addison signed up for the amateur talent show at the club. Now, Jenna has a broken wrist and the doctor has ordered Addison to rest for three weeks." Cassie watched Logan's face and saw him glance over her head at Luc. One of his dark brows flicked up then down as he frowned at Luc, and she was almost sure his right ear twitched before he looked back at her. "Are you going to perform by yourself now?"

"I haven't really thought about it," Cassie said, wondering what they were up to as she sensed Luc inching up closer behind her.

"What were the three of you going to do?" Logan asked.

Cassie caught him glancing at Luc again and watched as another silent message passed between them. Fascinated by the brow flicks, eyes squints, and other subtle facial gestures, she forgot for a moment that he had asked her a question.

"Cassandra, Logan asked you a question," Luc said from right behind her, his breath hot on the back of her neck.

A little ripple of arousal fluttered the muscles of her belly as she shivered, and goose bumps flashed over her shoulders. She glanced over her shoulder at Luc before turning back to Logan. She loved it when a man's voice went from casual and friendly to what she termed "Demanding Dom," so before she could stop herself she responded, "We talked about dancing but we hadn't decided yet, Sir."

Logan looked down at her and smiled then moved so quickly she didn't have time to step away. He embraced her, his arm around her waist as he twirled her around then led her into the opening steps of the tango. "You can still dance," he said as he turned her again, and she followed his lead then stepped forward and wrapped her right leg around his left hip. Her left leg was extended behind her, lying along his right leg, her weight resting on him, their torsos together. "With me and Luc," he said as he looked down at her. Their lips were almost touching, their breaths mingling. She wanted to lift her lips to his, but before she could, Logan threaded his fingers into her hair, then brushed his lips over hers, teasing her. "What do you say, Luc?" he asked, his hazel eyes focused on her lips. "You want to tango with Cassie at Club Mystique?"

"No," Luc said, his voice blunt.

Cassie pushed her hands against Logan's chest and struggled to rise. Logan tightened his hold on her, forcing her to maintain the position. "Logan, up."

His hazel eyes drilled into hers and a flutter of excitement followed by sensual anticipation rolled through her at the unspoken warning. He smiled at her, and she lowered her eyes, focusing on his throat. Another mistake on her part, she thought as she licked her bottom lip. She really wanted to lick his neck and taste him. As if he read her mind, he chuckled and offered his neck. She gave him a little lick, then frowned, and she decided these two were too damn smart for her own good. "Please, Sir, I would like to stand up."

"Better, sugar," Logan told her as he rose, pulling her up with him. Before she could move away, he pulled her in toward him, tightened his arm around her waist, and swayed her back and forth before twirling her around then leading her in Luc's direction and releasing her at the last moment.

Luc had to catch her or let her fall. He chose to catch her. She landed against him and he used the momentum to lift her. She curled her leg around his waist as he slid her down his body. The skirt of her dress caught on his belt buckle and the bulge of his jean-covered cock pressed between her legs. He held her there, his hazel eyes staring into hers as he lowered his mouth to hers. He brushed his lips over her lips. His tongue flicked out then pressed against the seam of her lips until she opened and gave him access to her mouth.

Cassie moaned with pleasure as Luc swept the inside of her mouth with his tongue. He tasted her and drew her into the kiss. She wrapped her arms and her other leg around him and pulled herself up his body. His palm slid under her thong-covered bottom, supporting her as he held her against him. The fist in her hair tightened, holding her in place as he took the kiss from soft to hard and back to soft. When he lifted his mouth, she was panting, her lips wet and swollen, her amber eyes dilated. Luc took a deep breath and she realized the scent of her arousal surrounded them.

"I expect you in the playroom at nine," Luc said before he unwrapped her arms and legs from around him and then set her on her bare feet away from him. He glanced at Logan then left the room.

Logan did a fist pump then smiled at her. "We're going to win, sugar."

Panting, Cassie clutched the edge of the center island. Brows raised, she looked at Logan. "Luc's not interested."

"He's interested. If he wasn't he wouldn't be thinking about spanking your ass tonight." Logan smiled.

"Logan, I like you and I'd like to play with you sometime but I won't get involved with you."

Logan gave her an aggravatingly understanding smile before he framed her face with his warm hands. Looking into her eyes, he leaned down and kissed her. "I don't know who hurt you, sugar, but we're going to love you so much that you won't ever want to leave us."

"I don't want you to get hurt, Logan."

"I'll see you at nine." He gave her another quick kiss then walked out, whistling.

Behind her the pantry door swung open and a feminine voice asked, "Is it okay to come out now?"

Cassie screamed and spun around, one hand over her pounding heart. "Damn, you scared the hell out of me, Addison! Don't do that!"

"Hi, Cassie," Addison said as she walked out of the pantry followed by Jenna.

"What the hell is it with you people always sneaking up on a person?" Cassie asked, while she wondered if the entire family was hiding in the pantry for some unknown reason. "What were you two doing in there?"

"Addison was looking for a can of spinach," Jenna said.

"We're out," Addison said, then giggled. "Of spinach, not the closet."

"So, Luc's decided tonight's the night to discipline you for the ice cream attack," Jenna said. "Dang, that was fun. Even though we had to clean up the mess."

Cassie laughed then nodded, her mind already on the coming evening. She shrugged. "Yeah. I probably should be worried about what the dominating duo have planned but no matter what they do it will have been worth it." She took a deep breath. "Even though I've only know Luc a few days, it was somehow satisfying to see him tied up and gagged. Maybe I'm a Domme rather than a sub."

"No," Addison said, "you're not a Domme—Luc's just annoying."

Addison and Jenna laughed then high-fived Cassie. Jenna looked at the clock, then said, "I've got to go. Jackson's waiting for me in the gym."

"Remember in this house a sub gets a swat for every minute she keeps her Dom waiting," Addison said, then turned to Cassie. "I like it."

Cassie cocked a silky brow, silently asking Addison what she meant.

"Your name for them—the dominating duo," Addison said, then laughed. "Don't be fooled by the act they put on, though. Logan isn't as easygoing as he pretends to be. It's just their version of 'good cop, bad cop.' I can hardly wait to hear what they do tonight."

Cassie leaned closer to Addison and examined her eyes. "Why are your eyes that color? Sort of silvery blue?"

"They get this way when I'm getting information."

"You mean gossip?"

"No, not gossip. Information." Addison lowered her voice. "Jenna and I both want to know if they use those odd blinking and brow twitching gestures when they're playing."

"Don't forget those strange little smiles and frowns, and I think they can twitch their ears," Cassie said.

"You can tell us about it tomorrow if we can get away from the guys. Cade hates it when I go—ur, gather information."

Before Cassie could answer, Cade and Thor strolled in and straddled the stools on either side of Addison. "Gossiping?" Cade asked. "Do you remember the rule about gossiping, baby?"

"Yes, Cade," Addison said.

"Where're the brownies?" Thor asked.

Addison pointed over her shoulder to a cabinet behind them. Thor retrieved the brownies then got the vanilla ice cream from the freezer before sitting back down.

Cade got up and grabbed a spoon and the strawberry ice cream from the freezer. He opened the carton then frowned at Addison. "We need to buy more strawberry ice cream." He scraped a bite from the bottom of the carton and ate it, almost humming with pleasure. "So, Cassie, are you dancing with Luc and Logan or just Logan?"

"Both of them," Addison said.

"Neither," Cassie said adamantly. "I'm not interested and how do you know about that?"

"Bugs," Addison said, pointing to the ceiling.

Cade smiled and took another bite. "I'll be interested to see how that works out." Chuckling, he finished the ice cream in the carton. "Are you going to the club, Thor?"

"Yeah. Ben, Mac, and I are going over for a while. We'll be leaving for Dallas first thing in the morning. Around five."

"Then we'll see you when you return for our wedding," Cade said as he led Addison from the room.

Thor stopped Cassie before she could escape. "You know Cade and I are planning to set up a second office here on the ranch. I told him you would stay and act as a liaison between him and the Dallas office."

"I thought I would be going back with you. I didn't bring enough clothes for a long stay." Damn, she thought. *Staying here with Luc and Logan is going to either be heaven or hell. Maybe both.*

"It's only an hour drive to Dallas. If you need to you can drive home and pack what you need and get back here in a few hours. Otherwise, I can bring you some things when I return in a few days with Marisol Rios for the wedding."

"Why don't you have Harley's assistant help Cade? She knows a lot more than I do."

"I need Dania in Dallas," Thor said, narrowing his glacier-blue eyes. "Is there a reason you don't want to stay?"

Shaking her head, Cassie forced herself to appear relaxed. Further protesting would trigger Thor's notorious curiosity and she didn't want him asking her questions. "No. I just hadn't planned on staying but that's okay. I'll stay." She glanced at the clock on the wall. "I'm late. I've got to go."

Thor stopped her again before she could slip through the door. "Cassandra, are you ever going to tell me what happened the night your dad died?"

Cassie turned back to him but dropped her eyes then shrugged. "There's nothing to tell." She heard a growl of impatience rumble from Thor and risked a glance. He was watching her, and he looked disappointed.

"You know better than to lie to me."

"I'm sorry, Thor," she said. "It's...complicated."

"Your dad was on his way to meet me the night he died, baby girl. He'd called me raging about something you'd told him."

Cassie took a deep breath, bit her trembling lower lip, and forced the tears away. If she told Thor the truth, he and Jackson would try to find the men who'd hurt her and they would die, too. "Luc and Logan are waiting for me. I have to go," Cassie said before rushing from the room and toward the playroom on the second floor.

Blinded by the unexpected tears in her eyes, she saw Logan standing in the open door and she ran to him. His arms wrapped around her and held her tightly as she buried her face against his chest, quietly sobbing. He picked her up and she wrapped her legs around him as he carried her into the playroom. The door slammed behind them and then Luc was pressed against her back and his arms slid around her too.

"What the hell happened?" Luc asked.

"I don't know. She was like this when she arrived," Logan said.

"Cassandra, stop that crying right now and tell us what's happened," Luc demanded.

Logan grimaced, then frowned at Luc as Cassie froze for a moment. Then her quiet sobs turned into hiccupping mumbling. He tightened his arms around her. "Damn it, Luc. You don't ever tell a woman to stop crying. It just makes it worse. I'll take care of Cassie and you can get a wet washcloth."

Logan set Cassie on the edge of the bed and ran his hands up and down her legs until Luc returned and handed him a dripping washcloth. "You're supposed to ring it out." He slapped it against Luc's jeans and let the material soak up the extra water.

"I was in a hurry." Luc cursed and stepped back while Logan began to wash Cassie's face.

Cassie opened her eyes.

"Sugar, can you tell us what happened?" Logan asked.

Cassie shook her head and another tear fell. Never, never, never, she thought.

Luc shifted from one foot to the other. His hands clenched and relaxed, then finally he stepped forward, picked her up, and sat down with her on his lap. He surrounded her with his arms and signaled Logan to continue.

"Sugar, can you tell me who made you cry?" Logan asked. "We'll have Thor and Jackson kill them for you."

"No. I'll kill them," Luc said, his voice deadly.

Logan dabbed at Cassie's face. He caught a tear on her left cheek and then a tear on her right cheek. "I'll help you." Logan wiped away another tear. "How do you want to do it? Guns? Knives?"

"I was thinking more along the lines of tampering with their car. You know, all covert like Cade and Thor—make it look like an accident."

Logan nodded his head. "That would work. We could cut the brake line."

"Do you know where the brake line is located?" Luc asked.

"No, but you can google it," Logan said.

Cassie snorted, then giggled. Logan smiled at her. "There you are, sugar. Better now?"

Cassie nodded, then sniffled. "I'm sorry. I never cry," She shrugged. "Well, unless someone spanks me." She sniffled again and looked up at Luc through her lashes. "Then, I cry a lot."

"We've got gags." Luc slid her off his lap and patted her bottom. "You've got two minutes to clean up."

Cassie nodded then fled to the bathroom.

Logan propped himself up against the headboard, one leg bent at the knee and resting on the bed, the other on the floor.

Luc copied Logan's posture with his back against the post at the end of the bed.

"So, what do you think is going on?" Logan tossed the washcloth back and forth between his hands then tossed it to Luc.

Luc snatched the cloth out of the air then tossed it back. "I think whatever it is she's not going to tell us."

"The other night when we were in here with her and had her list her limits, she tried to keep some distance between us." Logan nodded at the bathroom door. "Just now she locked the door."

Luc nodded. "I watched her at the May Day Masquerade at the club. She seemed okay then." He frowned, his black brows drawn down in a fierce frown. "I didn't like her playing with Dan Thompson."

Logan hid his grin. Cassie was beginning to get to Luc. "I think someone hurt her."

Luc nodded. "I'm not willing to play unless she's willing to open up to us."

"We have to give her a chance to learn to trust us. She's not like Linda." Logan could see Luc drawing back.

"I like Linda. She's straightforward. She approached us and set the limits of our relationship with her and she's stuck to them," Luc said.

"You like Linda because she doesn't expect anything from you. No contract. No emotions. No connection. Nothing but sex."

"I like our arrangement with Linda. So do you."

Hazel eyes looked into hazel eyes and a silent message flew between them. Logan sighed. "Are you sure?"

Luc glanced at his watch then at the bathroom door. "We need to get this punishment over with tonight. Linda said she wanted to talk to us. I told her we'd meet her at the club."

"I want Cassie."

"If you want Cassandra," Luc stressed her name, "then help yourself. Just leave me out of it."

"Is it just the agreement about waiting until we're thirty-two to settle down?"

"No. She's hiding something and I don't trust her. She's going to hurt you, and then I'll have to deal with your moping."

"I don't mope," Logan said.

"Yes, you do. Every time you get mushy about something and it goes wrong you mope."

"Name one time when I moped." Logan rose onto his size-fourteen boots and faced his twin.

"What about when Katherine wouldn't let you keep that baby raccoon you found?" Luc rose to face Logan, a smirk on his bronze face.

"I was ten! Besides, I wanted that baby raccoon, and why can't you call Katherine *Mom* like the rest of us?"

"She didn't care that I called her Katherine," Luc said, as they stood nose to nose, mirror images of each other. "Why do you have to be so emo? It makes me want to barf."

Logan smirked. "What? Are you twelve? Emo? Why can't you ever admit you have feelings?"

"Because I don't." Luc fisted his hands. "I'm going to kick your ass, you big crybaby." He mocked Logan. "I want Cassie. Booho—"

Logan slugged him, his fist striking Luc's hard belly and doubling him over. Luc looked up, black brows drawn down over disbelieving eyes as he rubbed his belly. He came up swinging. His fist caught Logan on the right cheek as Logan swung and caught him on the left cheek. They reached for each other at the same time. Two six-foot-four men in the prime of their lives. Equally strong and evenly matched. Their movements were synchronized, neither one of them capable of winning against the other.

Cassie opened the bathroom door and walked out just as Luc and Logan drew their fists back after landing another pair of punches to each other's bellies. Without thinking she ran between them with her hands up. They both swung and she screamed as she felt the air swirl by her bare arms as they pulled their punches. She scrunched her shoulders together, screamed again, and then fainted. Luc and Logan caught her, their arms under her legs and upper back.

"This is your fault," Logan said, glaring at Luc.

Luc glared back. "Fuck you."

"Let go."

"You let go."

"You both let go," Cassie mumbled.

Two pairs of hazel eyes looked down at her.

"You okay, Cassie?" Logan asked.

Cassie blinked then lifted her hand to her forehead and rubbed it. "Yes, I'm fine. Let me up."

Luc's eyes turned fierce. "Have you forgotten where you are and why you're here, Cassandra?"

Cassie shook her head. "No, Sir."

Luc nodded then glanced at Logan and they swung her up onto her feet, made sure she was steady, then released her and stepped back.

Cassie turned to face them. Logan was smiling at her. Luc was expressionless. She lowered her eyes then slowly sank to her knees, thinking, what the hell? *Luc never gives an inch.*

Several minutes of silence went by before Luc said, "We're postponing tonight."

"No, please don't, Sir." Cassie wanted to get the punishment over with tonight. "I'm okay. Really. You just scared me."

Logan squatted down in front of her and stared into her eyes, then nodded and stood up. "Okay, then, we'll go on but Luc and I expect you to use your safeword if you need to and we'll be very upset if you don't. Understand?"

"Yes, Sir."

Luc stood over her. "So, Cassie, I've read your hard limits. No restraints. Is that correct?"

"Yes, Sir."

"No fucking. Is that right?"

"Yes, Sir." Cassie shifted on her knees and slid her hands down a little farther, her eyes on her open palms. She should have put her hands palms down so she could grip her knees. For a moment she wondered if they would notice if she flipped them over.

"Let's see," Luc said. "No getting completely naked. No fingering. No breast play. Is that correct?"

"Yes, Sir."

"Maybe it would be easier if I just read what you said *yes* to," Luc said. "Let's see. No. No. No—ah, here it is. Yes to spanking. Is that correct?"

Cassie licked her lip then swallowed. Luc sounded angry. "Yes, Sir."

"This is a punishment, Cassandra," Luc said.

"That means we get to push your boundaries a little, sugar," Logan said. "We've decided to give you a choice, nudity or oral. You have one minute to choose or use your safeword."

Cassie remembered the scars on her back and knew if they saw them they would ask questions she didn't want to answer. That meant nudity was out. But, could she let them spank her and touch her while they were alone in a room without a monitor to protect her? She trembled, then broke a rule by looking up at them. "No restraints, Sir?"

Luc slid his fingers over her cheek and she flinched away from his hand as if she had been expecting a blow. "No restraints, Cassandra."

Cassie nodded her head. "Okay, then I choose oral."

"Excellent, Cassie," Logan said, reaching down and lifting her to her feet then moving to her right side. "You've made us very happy."

Cassie smiled. Knowing she had pleased Logan was like a rush of sugar in her veins and for the first time in years she felt a moment of pure joy in just being. Luc moved up on her left side and two pairs of hands reached under her skirt, grabbed the waistband of her thong, and tugged until the thin strap broke. A moment of fear rose until Logan ran his hand down her leg, calming her as he sniffed the crotch of her panties before he handed them to Luc. He sniffed them, then tossed them on the foot of the bed before picking her up and carrying her to the spanking bench. He set her on her feet next to it.

"Climb on." Luc tapped the padded bench while little lines appeared at the outer corners of his eyes—his version of a grin.

Cassie looked at the bench and saw that it was like the spanking bench at Club Mystique. It was a large sawhorse with places on each side for her knees and arms. Behind it was a mirror-covered wall and she could see the three of them reflected in it.

She had never been so drawn to a man, or rather two men, in her life, and in that moment, she knew she was going to fight her fear to have them. Determined, she drew on her observations of submissive behavior and began the performance of a lifetime. Fluttering her lashes down over her eyes, she wiggled her hips and pulled her skirt up until the hem brushed the top of her mound, then moved to the side of the bench. She gracefully straddled the padded bench and raised her knees to the knee rest. Then she balanced her weight and curved her shoulders back in a deep arch, and humped the bench. Feeling free for the first time in years, she shook her head, and felt her long hair brush back and forth over the thin material of her shirt. She stroked her braless breasts and gave each nipple a little pinch before dropping onto her belly and placing her forearms on the padded rests. The padded bench was cool beneath her left cheek as she opened her eyes and saw Luc and Logan reflected in the mirrored wall.

Logan's eyes were locked on her, his expression dark with lust. Luc's eyes were locked on her, too. She didn't know what his expression meant but it was definitely no longer blank. They both reached for their shirts and whipped them off then dropped them to the floor before moving toward her. A heated wave of lust flooded her body and her hormones woke up and screamed, "yes, yes, yes." They were gorgeous. Two bronze warriors with black hair, square jaws, and beautifully sculpted lips. Their arms were just the way she liked them, strong with well-defined muscles, and their bellies had sharply sculpted washboard abs that she ached to explore.

Luc moved to her left side as Logan moved to her right and she took note that this was their usual pattern. Looking in the mirror and seeing Logan's feelings on his face, she realized he didn't care if people knew what he was feeling, but Luc hid his emotions behind a blank mask. She smiled, wiggled her ass, and then relaxed. Logan flashed her a smile as Luc moved to her head and crouched down until his gleaming eyes met hers. God, she loved his eyes with their thick, straight, black lashes and sharply arching brows. When she looked closely enough, she thought she could see what he was feeling hidden deep within them.

"I expect you to stay in position. If you move I'll add ten swats." Luc smoothed her hair and arranged it over her left shoulder. "Do you understand?"

"Yes, Sir."

Luc ran his hand over her hair several more times almost as if he couldn't resist touching it. "You have beautiful hair."

Cassie smiled at him, her amber eyes glowing with happiness.

Luc gazed back at her, then leaned forward and slid his lips over hers. "You're getting twenty swats. Ten from me and ten from Logan. Do you understand?"

"Yes, Sir. Do you want me to say I'm sorry for the ice cream attack?"

Luc lifted a brow. "Are you sorry?"

"No, but it's the thought that counts, Sir."

Crinkles appeared around Luc's eyes and she grinned, pleased that she had made this stern man smile.

"Keep that thought in mind." He touched her hair one last time then moved to stand next to Logan and nodded at him. "You go first, Logan."

Logan began by running his hands over Cassie's body, beginning at her ankles then up the backs of her legs, and over her ass cheeks. He gave each of them a little squeeze and a pat, then slid his hands up to her lower back. He squeezed her waist and massaged her back through the thin material of her shirt. His fingers pressed into her back on either side of her spine and she shivered as he stroked up to her shoulders. She shivered again as the heat of his chest pressed against her. He gathered her hair into one hand and ran his hand down it then nibbled on the back of her neck. Goose bumps flared on her skin as he blew his breath over her neck then nipped her ear. He continued to nibble and kiss her neck while his hands ran over her sides and squeezed her hips. "You have the silkiest skin I've ever felt." Logan moved back down her body, touching her every step of the way. Cassie watched in the mirror as he squatted down and looked at her pussy.

"Sugar, you have a beautiful ass and your pussy makes me hungry." Logan walked his fingers down her crack then around her pussy, before he brushed his fingers over the outer edges of her swollen, wet labia.

He pressed on her clit and Cassie drew a deep breath into her lungs. He swirled his fingers over her clit and she gasped then wiggled, wanting more. Logan stood, smiled, and then swatted her ass. Once on each cheek.

Cassie squeaked with surprise then watched as Luc took Logan's place. He exactly copied Logan's words and actions, ending with a stinging swat to each ass cheek. "Oh, my god," she screamed. They were more diabolical than she had ever dreamt they would be.

Luc chuckled then glanced at Logan. "I like our new pet, bro."

Logan nodded. "I think she likes us, too, but she's getting two more for speaking without permission."

Luc nodded his agreement. "My turn."

Cassie watched in the mirror as Luc moved behind her, squatted down, then grasped her upper thighs with his hands and pushed them farther apart.

"You're right, Logan. This is one tasty-looking pussy."

Cassie held her breath and watched in the mirror as Luc leaned toward her. Her right leg blocked her view so she closed her eyes and focused her attention on the area between her legs. She trembled when Luc's warm breath flowed over her. *Yes, yes, yes, please touch me now.* Expecting him to kiss or lick her pussy, she whimpered with disappointment when Luc's lips slid down the inside of her left thigh. His hair brushed against the inside of her legs and tickled her pussy. She began moaning and rocking back and forth until Luc leaned back and swatted her, hard, once on each ass cheek. "Be still, Cassandra."

"Please, please, oh." She froze as he dipped his head and began kissing and nibbling on the silken flesh of her inner right thigh. She wiggled and he chuckled then swatted her again. His hands tightened on her thighs and pulled her back against his mouth. Luc kissed her pussy the same way he had kissed her mouth earlier. Starting out softly, he used his tongue to stroke over each side then slid it up and down her slit until she fluttered open for him. Cassie tightened her hands on the handholds and fought the urge to press back against him. If she moved, he would stop what he was doing and she absolutely didn't want him to stop. Breathing hard, her pulse pounding in her neck, she waited, then cried out as his tongue circled her clit before stroking up and down her slit again and then slipping into her. She lost the battle with herself and pushed back against his mouth. Luc stopped. Cassie opened her eyes and saw him grinning at her in the mirror before he swatted her ass twice on each side then rose to his feet.

Logan took his place and she whimpered.

"Please, please, Sir," she begged. Every nerve in her body was on high alert, wanting, needing the release Logan could give her.

Logan chuckled, grasped her thighs exactly the same way Luc had, and then he began kissing her left thigh.

"Damn you, damn y—"

"No cussing, pet." Logan swatted her twice on the back of each thigh where it curved into her butt.

Cassie cried out, her skin stinging.

Luc walked around the bench until he was directly in front of her. He crouched down until his eyes met hers. "There are rules to this game, pet. You broke one of them so now Logan has to start over."

Cassie protested, and Logan swatted her again, causing her eyes to tear and her vision of Luc to blur. She blinked, clearing them. Luc moved back to his position slightly behind her left hip. He crossed his arms over his chest and watched Logan touch her. The size of the bulge in the front of his jeans caught her attention, and she stared at it then glanced at his face and was surprised to see him watching her in the mirror. His eyes met hers, watching her closely as Logan tightened his hands on her thighs and began again. She moaned, licked her lips, then mouthed "oh my god" and the lines around Luc's eyes appeared again.

By the time Logan finished copying Luc's actions, Cassie was begging them to let her come. Both men chuckled and Logan ran his hands over her ass and her back, soothing her. Leaning over her, he whispered against her neck, "My turn, sugar," then laughed and nipped her earlobe when she whimpered.

Logan moved back, swatted her ass twice on each cheek, then crouched down and just stared at her pussy. Cassie watched him in the mirror and thought, oh, my, god, they have this down to a fine art. She whined when he slid his finger down her slit and up over her clit, circling it before strumming his fingers over it once and then again.

"Do you want to come, sugar?"

"Yes, yes, please, Sir."

He smiled then stroked his finger up and down her slit again. "Would you like me to finger you, sugar?"

"Yes, Logan, please." Cassie wiggled and felt the lips of her pussy flutter as a spasm of need tightened her belly and a stream of her juices trickled from her and ran down her slit. It coated her clit before making a little puddle beneath her. She blushed, knowing she was leaving a mark on the padded bench.

Logan smiled. "Too bad you marked no fingering on your limits, sugar," he said before running his fingers up and down her slit again and again, each time circling around her clit but never giving her the touch she needed.

Cassie gasped and moaned and wiggled. The need to come consumed her thoughts. With every fiber of her being she wished she was naked and being fucked by them until she couldn't move. It took her a moment to realize Logan had stopped touching her.

"Up you go, sugar," Logan said as he pulled her up then lifted her off the bench. "Knees, now," he said as he unbuttoned his jeans then pushed them to the floor and stepped out of them.

Cassie licked her lips before dropping to her knees in front of him. Logan was amazing clothed but naked he was magnificent. His cock rose from his well-groomed pubic area. It was beautifully thick and wonderfully long with a distinctly shaped mushroom-head that glistened with a drop of pre-cum. The sight of it made her wish she had highlighted the little box next to the words *"I want to be fucked"* and then drawn an entire circle of arrows around it.

"Open, sugar," Logan said as he stepped closer, his fist around his cock, stroking it. "Feel free to use your hands."

Cassie licked her lips, swallowed, and then told herself she could do this. She had read about sucking a man's cock, and she had seen it done many times so she knew what to do. She opened her mouth, and Logan rubbed the head against her lower lip, coating it with the drop of pre-cum. She licked her lips then his cock and opened her mouth wider as he pressed it between her lips. When he pulled back, she swept her tongue over the shaft, feeling each vein and bump along the shaft. She licked her lips again, wetting them before leaning forward and taking his cock into her mouth. She licked it, flicking her tongue over it and slowly taking more of the thick shaft into her mouth. When the head bumped the back of her throat, she swallowed and controlled her gag response as she lashed the length with her tongue.

Logan's hands slid into her hair and he held her still as he moaned and rocked his cock in and out of her mouth.

"That's so good, sugar."

Wanting to please him, Cassie sucked on him, hollowing her cheeks before humming then swallowing. Logan groaned and began fucking her mouth faster and a little deeper. She slid her hand to his balls and touched then with her fingertips, then gently cupped them and rolled them. She used one finger to stroke his perineum and Logan tightened his hands in her hair as she felt his balls draw up closer to his body.

"Swallow, pet," he demanded as his cock jerked, then his cum flooded her mouth in hot spurts.

Cassie swallowed and whipped her tongue from one side of his cock to the other as he groaned and shuddered. She held him in her mouth, reluctant to release him for another moment then licked and sucked on him as she let him go.

Logan lifted her to her feet and kissed her, his tongue swept into her mouth and tasted her. He swatted her ass one time, then lifted her and placed her back on the spanking bench. In the mirror, he smiled at her then looked at Luc. "Your turn."

Cassie trembled when Luc crouched down next to her, his eyes level with hers. Her lower lip trembled and tears blurred her vision. She wanted to come. *Right now.*

Luc lifted a tear from her cheek then licked his finger. "Do you want to come, Cassandra?"

"Yes, please, Sir."

Luc patted her on the back then stood up and ran his hands down her back as he moved behind her and crouched down. He stroked his finger up and down her slit. Once, then again. "Would you like me to finger you, sugar?"

"No, oh, no, no." Cassie whimpered, knowing what was coming next. Helplessly she wiggled and wished he would touch her clit.

"You don't?" Luc asked.

"Yes, yes, please, Sir, please." Cassie pressed back, opening her legs wider, offering herself to him.

"Too bad you marked no fingering on your limits." Luc ran his fingers up and down her slit again and again, each time circling around her clit but not touching it.

Cassie nodded her head in agreement and moaned. It took her a moment to realize Luc had stopped touching her.

"Up you go." Luc pulled her up then lifted her off the bench. "Knees, now." He unbuttoned his jeans then pushed them to the floor and stepped out of them.

Cassie glanced up at him then dropped to her knees. Luc was an exact match for Logan in height and build. Even his cock was thick and long, the head red and glistening with pre-cum, but he had an oddly shaped mark on his right hip bone. She reached out and traced it with her finger and tears filled her eyes when she realized it was in the shape of a small belt buckle. Without thinking she leaned forward and kissed it.

Luc threaded his fingers through her hair and tipped her head up until her eyes met his. "You're years too late to kiss it better." He used his thumbs to brush the tears from the corners of her eyes then gently tipped her head down.

She dropped back on her heels then licked her lips, wetting them in anticipation of what came next.

"Open, pet," Luc said as he stepped closer, his fist around his cock, stroking it.

Cassie opened her mouth and Luc slid the head against her lower lip, coating it with the drops of pre-cum. She hummed low in her throat then licked her lips and his cock before she opened her mouth wider and he pressed forward. Luc buried his hands in her hair and groaned, so she did it again before taking his cock into her mouth as deeply as she could. She hummed then swallowed around the head.

* * * *

Luc couldn't keep the groan of pleasure from rumbling from his throat. "That's good, pet. So good."

He tightened his hands in her hair and dropped his head back when she lashed his cock with her tongue then sucked on it. He wanted to pretend she was just another woman he and Logan played with but he had a strict policy about lying to himself. When she had kissed the scar on his hip he'd wanted to pick her up and let the scent and feel of her comfort him.

He shuddered then pushed his cock deeper into her mouth. She hummed and he felt the vibration along the length of his shaft. He looked down at her and her amber eyes trapped his as she swallowed and her throat tightened on the head of his cock. She slid her lips up and down his shaft. Her tongue licked and flicked over the head again and again.

"Cassandra." He rocked his hips, gently fucking her mouth, and another groan of pleasure escaped his lips. He felt the warning tingle of an impending orgasm and wanted to tell her to swallow but couldn't form the words. With his eyes still on hers he felt her tongue lash over him and a second later she swallowed and an intense explosion of pleasure slammed through him. "Cassandra."

She continued to suck on him and he shuddered as another spurt of cum shot from his cock. He shuddered again when she gently licked his cock before releasing him. A moment later she leaned forward and planted another tiny kiss on the mark on his hip.

He lifted her to her feet and kissed her once, then again as he ran his hands over her. He held her for a moment longer then gently swatted her ass one time before picking her up and placing her back on the spanking bench.

* * * *

Luc and Logan picked up their jeans and stepped into them. Cassie watched, puzzled, as they buttoned them then picked up their shirts and pulled them on.

Luc lifted her from the bench, set her on her feet, then hugged her and brushed his lips over hers. "Thank you. All is forgiven."

Logan moved up behind them and turned her around. He hugged her then brushed his lips over hers. "I'm proud of you, Cassie."

Cassie smiled. For the first time in a long time, standing between them with their arms around her, she felt happy and safe and like she belonged somewhere. Belonged to somebody. She tightened her arms around their waists. She could still taste them on her tongue. She sniffed Logan then Luc. They even smelled good. A combination of male flesh, cologne, sex, and her.

Logan picked her up and followed Luc to the door. Before she could protest, Logan carried her to her bedroom. Luc opened the door and Logan set her down.

Luc pinched her chin with his thumb and fingers and lifted her face until her eyes met his. "No masturbating."

Logan patted her on the bottom. "Not for twenty-four hours. Do you understand?"

"But, I didn't get to come, Logan."

"It's part of your punishment, Cassandra. So, no masturbating," Luc said, his voice firm.

"And, don't think we won't know because we will and then we'll double your punishment," Logan added.

Feeling uptight and jittery, Cassie glared at them. "You both got to come."

Logan grinned. "We know, sugar. You pleased us very much but this is for your own good. Now, be a good girl and go to bed."

"I think I hate both of you," Cassie said, her voice stunned.

Luc patted her on the top of her head. "You'll feel better in the morning, pet. Well, not in the morning but by this time tomorrow night."

Logan looked at him and chuckled. "Good one, bro. See, you do have a sense of humor."

"I wasn't trying to make a joke, Logan."

Cassie watched them walk off. In a temper, she slammed her door then leaned back against it. She was tempted to see if they really would know if she gave herself a little relief. Deciding they would, she stomped over to the bed and threw herself across it. *Bastards.*

She rolled onto her back and stared at the ceiling. It was probably better this way, she thought. She would have just embarrassed herself by running away if they had tried to fuck her. Sighing, she curled onto her side and hugged her knees to her chest. A few minutes later, she got up, locked the door, then grabbed her tote bag and carried it into the bathroom with her. She locked the bathroom door then found her father's gun and wrapped it in a towel and put it within reach while she showered. After drying off she dressed in loose black pants and a black T-shirt then placed a pair of soft-soled shoes next to the bed. She placed the gun on the bedside table then grasped her father's lethally sharp knife and slid her hand beneath her pillow.

A few minutes later, she realized she was crying. She never, ever cried. Tears wouldn't bring her dad back and they wouldn't wipe out the memory of being raped. She traced the nick on the handle of the knife with her finger. It had been made by a bullet that would have killed him if it hadn't hit the handle and ricocheted away from him. The knife had saved his life. When she held it she remembered him telling her that story and how much he had loved her. She should have loved him enough to keep the truth from him. If she had he would still be alive. She smothered her sobs in the pillow and cried herself to sleep.

Chapter Two

Two days later, Cassie knocked on the den door and waited until she heard a masculine voice give her permission to enter. She turned the knob then leaned in and looked around the room before committing herself to entering. Cade sat behind a desk with Addison perched on the corner. Her bare legs were crossed and one tiny foot swung back and forth as she smiled and waved hello. Cassie breathed a sigh of relief and stepped into the room as Jackson leaned around the edge of a large wingback chair and sent her a welcoming smile. Jenna got up from the matching chair, stepped over to him, and slid onto his lap.

"Have a seat, Cassie." Cade pointed to the chair Jenna had just vacated. "We were just talking about where Thor and I want to locate the new office building."

Cassie glanced around, relieved that Luc and Logan weren't present, and perched on the edge of the chair. She smiled at Cade then Addison and finally Jackson and Jenna. "Have you heard from Thor?"

"Yes. He said for you to e-mail him a list of the things you'll need and he'll bring them when he returns in a few days."

Cassie nodded and accepted that she wasn't getting away from the Ramseys any time soon. "So, you've decided to build the new office here at the ranch?"

"Yes. Somewhere between here and Club Mystique so we can combine the security of the ranch, the club, and the agency into one office," Jackson said.

"That's a good idea," Cassie said. "How many people are going to work at the new office and where are they going to live? Does Rendezvous have enough housing?"

Jackson laughed. "Told you, big brother. This is why Thor wanted Cassie to stay. She pays attention to the details."

Cade glanced at Jackson and nodded then grabbed Addison's foot and swiveled her around until she faced him. "I want you to make a list of contacts for Cassie." He handed her a notebook and a pen then turned back to Cassie. "I need you to keep us organized and on track. Set up a way to keep track of the building project from architect to builder to interior designer up to the move-in date. Once we decide on the personnel, I'll want you to hire a local real estate agent to help with housing." He glanced at Addison and she wrote something on the paper then smiled at him. "If there isn't enough housing in town then we'll build some housing out by the new office. There's plenty of land."

"It might be a better idea to go ahead and get that housing project started," Jackson said. "I'd put the housing on the paved road that goes to the back of Harry's Truck Stop on the interstate. That would put the staff close to the office and within three miles of the air field. It would also keep traffic off the main road from Rendezvous to the ranch and Club Mystique."

Jenna sat forward. "I think we should consider helping the new doctor in town build a better clinic between town and the ranch. After working with the contractors who are remodeling the old clinic I've decided it needs to be condemned." She looked at Cade. "You'd have a nice state-of-the-art medical clinic with a trauma surgeon turned family practitioner right on your doorstep. What could be better?"

"Not to mention an excellent emergency room nurse," Addison said, smiling at Jenna then looking at Cade. "You said you wanted to develop that land on this side of Rendezvous. Start with a new clinic and other businesses will follow."

"Good idea, angel." Jackson snuggled Jenna closer and kissed her forehead.

"It's a good idea." Cade sat back, a frown on his face. "Jenna, invite the new doctor and his wife to dinner in three weeks so we can discuss it with him. Cassie, I want you to contact Jacob Daniels. His company does commercial and residential construction. Thor and I agreed he's the best architect for this project and we trust him with the construction. Tell him I want to meet with him to discuss a new office building and a small housing development. I'll handle the details." He glared at Addison then hooked his arm around her waist and pulled her down onto his lap. "You will not speak to him, Addison. Do you understand?"

"Yes, Master."

Cassie looked down, avoiding Cade's eyes. She had not only been present the night Mark and Sherry Carlisle had taken Addison to Club Elysium, she had shown her around the club so she could see first-hand what the D/s lifestyle was about. She had also been present when Mark Carlisle had arranged for Jacob Daniels and Vincent Vitale to give Addison her first erotic spanking. Apparently Cade was still pissed off about that. Looking up, she saw Cade's eyes on her and knew he knew the part she had played that night. She blushed then paled, but quickly reminded herself that Cade had a reputation as a good Dom. If he was upset with her, he would have told her and given her a chance to earn his forgiveness.

"There's a small office next to this one," Cade said. "It was supposed to be Addison's but she's decided she prefers to invade mine so you can use it. You should find everything you need in there. The phone and computer systems are secure. If you need anything else, let me know."

"Okay, thank you, Cade." Cassie stood up, eager to escape as she headed for the door and freedom.

"Cassie?"

Turning back, she recognized the serious expression on Cade's face and lowered her eyes, knowing she wasn't going to like whatever he had to say. "Yes, Sir."

"Thor, Jackson, and I have respected your privacy. Luc and Logan won't. I wanted to make sure you realized that."

"There's nothing going on between us," she said.

Jackson laughed. "Baby girl, those two boys have a sweet tooth and you're pure sugar. Neither one of them is going to be able to stay away from you."

"I earned the punishment and that's over now." Cassie shrugged. "It won't happen again."

Cade snorted. "If that's the way you want to play this out then do that but never let it be said we didn't warn you."

Jackson smiled. "Remember Luc and Logan were Marines and served in the same capacity as your dad, Thor, and I. Don't ever underestimate them, Cassie. If they decide they want you, nothing will stop them."

"Then they'll be very frustrated. I have a safe word and I know when to use it." Seeing Jackson's dark brow fly up she quickly added, "Sir."

Addison jumped up from Cade's lap and hurried over to Cassie. "I'm going to show Cassie her new office."

"I'm going to help her." Jenna rose from Jackson's lap then bent down and gave him a little smacking kiss. She joined Addison and Cassie then urged them out of the room.

"Whew." Addison brushed her hand over her forehead. "That was a narrow escape."

"Men." Jenna laughed quietly. "I think Cade and Jackson are actually miffed that you don't want to play with Luc and Logan, Cassie."

Cassie nodded her head and smiled. "Like I've refused a play date with their lethal little toddlers." She giggled, then burst into laughter.

Addison giggled then got serious. "They are lethal. You have no idea."

"What do you mean by that?" Jenna asked.

"I gather information—I don't release it." Addison grabbed Cassie's hand. "Come on, let's go swimming. Cade and Jackson kept you busy all day yesterday, but I have two hours to swim before I'm banned from the pool until four."

"I'm supposed to call Jacob Daniels," Cassie said.

"You can do that later. Jacob's not going to make an appointment for today anyway. Come on, live a little." She pulled Cassie toward the stairs. "Jenna's going swimming with us. Aren't you Jenna?"

"I guess I am now that you've said I am. I'll meet you at the pool. I'm going to ask Jane to fix us a pitcher of tea."

"Okay." Addison climbed the stairs with Cassie on her heels. "Do you have a suit with you, Cassie? If not, I can loan you one."

"I didn't bring one but I've seen the suits you wear, so no thanks. I'll just wear a pair of shorts and a T-shirt."

Addison laughed. "I only wear those scandalous bikinis to get Cade's attention. I actually have several brand new one-piece racing suits. In fact, I have a dark aqua one that will look beautiful on you. You'll look like a peacock with your golden hair and eyes."

"I accept even though peacocks are males. The females are called peahens and they're plainer."

"Yes, so they can hide from the horny males," Addison said with a wink.

Cassie laughed and followed Addison through her bedroom and into her closet where she pulled out a bathing suit still in its wrapper.

"Thanks, Addison. I'll buy you a replacement."

"No need." Addison pulled the drawer open. "I have one in every color. I don't think I'll miss that one. Besides in a few months I won't be able to get into any of these." She ran her hand over her tummy then looked up and smiled at Cassie.

"I'm really happy for you and Cade, Addison. All your dreams are coming true. You got the man you love, a wedding in six days, and a baby on the way."

Addison nodded then her hand flew up to her mouth and she ran for the bathroom. Cassie grimaced and followed her, hoping she hadn't had strawberry ice cream and spinach for breakfast. She had just gathered Addison's hair and lifted it out of the way when she sensed a movement behind her. She whipped her head around, saw Cade, and breathed a sigh of relief. He gave her an odd searching glance then grabbed a washcloth and wet it.

"Baby, you okay?" he asked Addison.

"Y–yes," Addison said, then added, "No. I don't think I want any more ice cream and spinach."

Cade smiled, then helped her stand. Seeing the swimsuit Cassie held, he said, "I'll help Addison get changed then I'll bring her down to the pool."

"Okay." Cassie held the swimsuit against her belly, hiding behind it as she edged back away from him. "If you need anything I'll be in my room changing." She turned around but managed a small smile when she heard Cade ask Addison if Limo was making her sick. It was the funny name they had given their child since he or she had been conceived in the back of a limo after Addison had been returned to Cade by Juan Rios. Giggling to herself, she thought that must have been some ride home.

Deciding she better hurry, she rushed to her room, changed into the suit, and grabbed a long T-shirt that had once belonged to her father. She pulled it on over her head then smoothed it down her body. It fell nearly to her knees. The material was worn thin. The color was faded, the Marine Corp insignia nearly washed away, but she loved wearing it. Her father had always worn this shirt when he worked on his car. The car she still drove, a 1969 sports car that went too fast and used too much fuel. She'd been offered huge sums of money for that car but she knew she'd never part with it. Cassie gathered the shirt in her hands and held it to her nose. Sometimes she thought she could still smell the scent of the pipe tobacco her father had smoked.

After several moments, she heard laughter and wandered to the window and saw Addison and Jenna sitting at a table by the pool and knew she had lost more time again. The *zone outs* had begun happening more frequently and they seemed to be lasting for longer periods of time lately. After one, she would sometimes find herself with a sketchpad in hand while she drew bits and pieces of objects she couldn't identify or a word or phrase would stay with her and echo in her thoughts for days. She glanced out the window again and saw Jenna pouring three glasses of iced tea while Addison slathered on sunscreen. Cassie left her room and hurried down the stairs and out the backdoor. She waved back at Addison then pulled her T-shirt off and laid it on a chair before she jumped into the deep end of the pool. When she surfaced, she swam to the side and grasped the edge. "This feels really wonderful, Addison. I'm glad you suggested it."

Jenna stood up, grabbed two air mattresses, and walked down the steps into the water. When it was up to her waist, she floated one of the mattresses toward Cassie as she climbed onto the other one. "Addison just wanted to get you alone so she could ask you about the other night with Luc and Logan."

Addison laughed then dropped the bottle of sunscreen. She grabbed her own air mattress and joined them. "That's right. Information is power. So empower me, Cassie."

Cassie giggled and the three of them moved until they were lying on their bellies, floating and facing each other. "Well, I can tell you they definitely use all those silent signals to communicate with each other when they play."

"And—" Addison made a "go on" gesture.

"They're certainly, uh." Cassie blushed, then stammered, "A team. Very smooth and they really cooperate with each other. In fact, you could almost say it's like there's really only one of them."

Jenna laughed. "It sounds like the rumors we've heard are true, Addison."

Addison nodded then giggled. "We've heard they play this sort of copycat game. One of them does something and the other one has to copy it." Addison giggled again when she saw Cassie's blush.

Cassie sent a small splash toward Addison and Jenna. "It was wonderfully horrible. And very, very frustrating."

"Oh, no, don't say they wouldn't let you come." Addison looked scandalized. "That's just mean. I hate it when Cade does that."

"Cassie's going to learn to hate it, too," Logan said from the side of the pool where he, Luc, Cade, and Jackson stood listening to the three women.

Cassie squeaked a protest and flailed her arms. She fell off the air mattress and swallowed a mouthful of pool water. The wave she made rocked Jenna and Addison's mattresses, but they managed to slip off and find their balance before going under. Cassie surfaced, coughed and then wiped the water from her face as she glared at Luc and Logan.

"You shouldn't sneak up on us like that," Jenna said, trying to bluff her way through. "You nearly drowned poor Cassie."

Logan planted his hands on his hips and glared at Cassie. "Poor Cassie, my ass."

"Cassandra, get your ass up here, now." Luc held his hand out to her.

"Jenna, front and center." Jackson pointed to the tiles in front of him.

"Addison, I've just spent ten minutes on the phone with Doc Marshall and he says I can spank your ass as long as I'm careful. So, come here." Cade folded his arms across his chest.

The three women huddled together and moved into deeper water.

"You really shouldn't listen to other people's conversations, Cade," Addison said. "I never hear anything good about you."

Luc moved down the side of the pool until his shadow fell over Cassie. "Out, now, Cassandra."

"Why? I haven't done anything," Cassie said, her eyes flying to Luc's hands as he rested them on his wide leather belt.

"Were you gossiping about the other night with Addison and Jenna?" Logan moved to stand by Luc.

"She wasn't telling us anything we didn't already sort of know," Jenna said and Addison nodded in agreement.

"Cassie can speak for herself," Logan said. "Cassie, were you gossiping with Addison and Jenna?"

Cassie shook her head, her eyes locked on Luc's hands. "N–no," she said, beginning to panic at the thought of Luc using his belt on her. She covered her chest with her hand, feeling her heart racing as her throat tightened with fear.

"Cassandra, you just lied to us," Luc said, his voice flinty as he moved a hand to his belt buckle. "Don't make me come in there and get you."

Cassie shook her head even as she obeyed Luc's command. She wanted to trust them but she had run out of hope long ago. Heart racing, her breaths coming faster, she reached the side of the pool and looked up at Luc and Logan. She didn't know what she wanted to say to them. Before she could figure it out, Luc reached down, grabbed her wrists, and lifted her out of the water. Logan threw a towel over her head and began rubbing the water from her hair while Luc held her wrists, restraining her movements, and all hell broke loose.

Cassie screamed and struck out, her knee caught Luc on the inside of his left thigh as her fingernails gouged into his wrists. He released her and she swept her foot out and gave him a hard shove before she turned to face Logan. Behind her, Luc splashed into the pool as she kicked Logan in the stomach then grabbed him and shoved him toward the pool. He fell, knocking into Luc as he was hauling himself out and the two of them splashed down into the water together. Having fought, Cassie's flight instinct kicked in and she ran. Seconds later she disappeared around the corner of the house. Behind her Luc and Logan hauled themselves out of the pool and took off after her.

Heart pounding and panting with fear, Cassie ran across the ranch yard, leaving a trail of chaos behind her as she spooked several horses that were being groomed by the ranch hands. She ducked into the first open door she saw and ran down the stall-lined corridor. Realizing she had trapped herself, she stopped and looked around. Soft sobs left her mouth as she bent over and tried to catch her breath.

She could only see two ways to go. Straight ahead to the open door at the end of the corridor or into one of the vacant stalls. Blinded by tears, she stumbled toward the door and found an office. She stepped in then closed and locked the door behind her. Across the room she saw another door. Hoping it led to another exit, she opened it and found a small bathroom. Refusing to trap herself in the small space, she closed the door then moved to the window behind the desk. She opened it, and pushed on the screen. It popped loose and she climbed out then shut the window behind her before crouching down against the side of the building.

Cassie scrubbed the tears from her face then massaged her aching temples with her fingers. She felt trapped and scared and out of control but she wasn't sure why. She only knew that she had to get away. She crept to the corner of the building and peeked around it then took off for the house. She had to get to her room where she had left the tote bag that held her father's gun and knife. She entered the house through a side door then seeing that the coast was clear she took off for her room.

Once inside she pulled on a pair of jeans, a pullover shirt, and sandals then grabbed her tote, determined to make it to her car. She opened the door and found Luc and Logan on the other side. She screamed and tried to shut the door but her strength was nothing compared to Luc's, and she quickly lost the battle.

Backing away from the door, lost in a memory from the past, she screamed, "Go away, go away," while searching the bag for a weapon.

Luc and Logan froze, their eyes going to the bag in her hand.

"Cassandra, we're not going to hurt you," Luc said, his voice soft and calm.

"Go away," Cassie said, her voice cracking. She rubbed the tears from her eyes as tremors racked her body.

"Sugar, we want to help you," Logan said.

Cassie shook her head, then rubbed her forehead as images began to flash faster through her mind. The last image was her father's tombstone. Lips trembling, she backed away from them. "They'll know about you and you'll die, too." Another sob escaped her as she looked at Luc and Logan. She wanted them with everything in her but they would be safer away from her. She was going to get them killed the same way she had gotten her father killed. Her strength left her and she dropped to her knees. Not in submission but in defeat.

Luc pounced. He picked her up then sat down on the end of the bed with her on his lap. Her body shook so hard he could barely hold onto her. He held her tighter as Logan lifted her tote bag to the bed and dumped it out.

"Bro, what are you doing?" Luc asked as Cassie curled up on his lap, and tightened her arms around him, then buried her face in his neck and cried.

"I hate crying. I hate crying," she said.

"We know you do, pet." Luc nuzzled her neck.

Logan sorted through the weapons in the tote then read the labels on the two pill bottles he found and held them up. "Sleep medication and something for anxiety," he said as he opened Cassie's wallet and rifled through it then held up a card. "The doctor who prescribed the medication."

"You take her. I'll make the call," Luc said.

"No. You suck at talking to people." Logan pulled his cell phone from his wet jean pocket, frowned at it when he realized it was out of commission, then left the room.

Luc tightened his arms around Cassie and rocked her, all the while wondering how he had ended up with her, in tears and on his lap. He didn't do this kind of thing and he was completely out of his element. Wishing Logan would hurry up and return, he nuzzled his chin against the top of her head. "It's okay, pet. Logan will take care of you."

He didn't know if she heard him or not, but the crying seemed to be easing off. A few minutes later, after a couple sniffles and a few hiccups, he felt her body softening until she lay quietly in his arms, asleep. Feeling her shiver, he carefully laid her down and removed her damp clothes. Her feet had several small cuts and scrapes on them and he made a note to clean them and have the doctor check them out. Picking her up, he carried her to his room and gently laid her on his bed. He changed into dry clothes then decided Cassie would be scared if she woke up naked. He dressed her in one of his T-shirts, then smiled when he saw how it covered her to her knees. Standing by the bed, looking down at her, he thought, what the hell, and slid onto the bed and pulled her into his arms. He justified his actions to himself by deciding Logan would expect him to take care of her while he was busy calling her therapist.

A few minutes later Logan walked into the room, followed by Doc Roberts.

"How's she doing?" Logan asked.

"Sleeping." Luc stood up. "Wore herself out crying."

Doc Roberts moved to the side of the bed. After checking Cassie's pulse and heart rate, he used a small flashlight to examine her eyes then stepped back, rubbed his chin, and said, "Tell me again what the therapist said."

"I told her what had happened, and all she said was she couldn't discuss Cassie with me but that she needed to see her as soon as possible."

"I'll call her," Doc Roberts said. "From what you've told me, it sounds like something you did triggered a panic attack. It's best to let her sleep for a while."

"Her feet have some cuts and scrapes on them," Luc said.

Doc looked at Cassie's feet while Logan got a tub of water and several washcloths and a towel. After Doc cleaned the shallow cuts and put ointment on them. "They'll be okay." He walked toward the door to the hallway. "I'll be right back. I'm going to call Cassie's therapist."

Logan moved to the side of the bed, sat down, and held Cassie's hand. "What the hell happened?"

Luc shook out the cashmere throw that he kept at the end of his bed and covered Cassie with it before sitting down on her other side. He picked up Cassie's hand and ran his fingers over her wrist. "Limits. No restraints. I was holding her wrists."

"I put the towel over her head to dry her hair." Logan frowned. "She only plays in a club. Clubs have monitors. She feels safer there."

"No. She doesn't play there either."

"She played with Thompson."

Luc handed Logan his waterproof phone. "Call him."

After a short conversation, Logan handed the phone back to Luc. "Thompson said as soon as he put a cuff on her she freaked out on him. He calmed her down then talked to her about getting some counseling with a friend of his."

"Doctor Carson," Luc said, saying the name on the pill bottles and business card.

"Yes." Before Logan could say what was on his mind, Doc Roberts came back in the room.

"I can't disclose what Cassie told Doctor Carson other than that Cassie hasn't made any progress in her therapy sessions."

Luc glanced at Logan. A quick series of facial movements flew between them and then with a final nod they came to an agreement.

"One other thing I found interesting, though," Doc Roberts said. "Doctor Carson said two weeks ago someone broke into her office. She said she never would have known about the break-in but her assistant had been in a hurry the previous day and had stuck several files in the front of a drawer intending to file them the next day. When the assistant opened the file cabinet to get them they had been moved to another drawer—the one where Cassie's file is kept and her file was with them."

"They want to know what she's told the doctor," Logan said.

Luc tightened his hand around her wrist. "How do they know about Carson?"

"Maybe they're following her," Logan said. "She said 'they'll find out about you and you'll die, too' when we said we wanted to help her."

"So, maybe she knows someone is following her, but who died?" Luc asked.

"Her father, Ryan Edwards, when she was seventeen," Jackson said from the doorway.

"Tell us what you know," Luc said.

"Not much," Jackson said. "Just that while Ryan, Thor, and I were out of the country, something happened to her. She told her father and he called Thor in a rage. They arranged to meet at Club Elysium but on the way there Ryan stopped for gas and was killed in what the police decided was a robbery that turned into a homicide. A witness who was ex-military told Thor it was a professional hit. Two men. Well organized."

Luc lifted Cassie's wrist to his lips and kissed it. "Does Cassie know he was targeted?"

"Yes. We had to tell her. She was blaming herself for his death because she had driven his car and left the tank empty again."

"No, there's more to it than that. She's hiding something," Logan said. "She's afraid of something or somebody."

"Ryan was always very protective of Cassie after his wife left them when Cassie was three. At first we thought maybe some guy had done her dirty and he was upset about that. But over the years we've watched Cassie withdraw and we've been looking into what really happened that night."

"When Ryan was on a mission, who took care of Cassie?" Logan asked.

"Cassie lived with Ryan's sister, Velma."

"Where is she now?" Luc asked.

"Dead. Two months after Ryan died, Velma and Cassie were run off the road on their way home from shopping. Velma died. Cassie spent over two weeks in the hospital with a concussion."

"They wanted them both dead. Velma must have known whatever Cassie told her dad," Logan said.

"We've questioned Cassie but she says she doesn't remember. She was diagnosed with post-traumatic amnesia after the accident."

"Retrograde?" Doc Marshall asked.

"Yes. The doctor who treated her said she probably wouldn't ever regain the memories of those months."

"How many months does she say she can't remember?" Luc asked.

"She claims six months before the accident," Jackson said.

"So, something happened to her in the four months previous to her father's death," Logan said.

"We need to get Thor back here. Maybe he can force her to tell him the truth," Jackson said.

"Nobody's forcing Cassandra to do anything," Luc said. "Unless it's me and Logan." He sent Logan a series of silent gestures then stood up and left the room.

"Where's he going?" Jackson asked.

"He has computer things to do." Logan lifted Cassie to his lap and cuddled her up close to his chest then settled back against the headboard. "Doc, tell me about this amnesia."

"Post-traumatic amnesia? Its most often brought on by a head injury, like Cassie's concussion. Retrograde means memory loss that can go back months or even decades before the injury occurred. Some people will recover the memories, but the more severe the injury the less likely it is that they will." Doc looked at Jackson. "You said she was in the hospital for over two weeks. That would indicate a fairly severe head trauma."

Luc walked back into the room, frowned when he saw that Logan was holding Cassie, and took her out of his arms. "My turn," he said, before he sat down on the edge of the bed with her on his lap. "The hospital Cassie was in after the wreck had a problem with their computer system a couple weeks after Cassie was discharged. Their medical records office was hacked."

"For eight years she's made them believe she couldn't remember what happened but now that she's seeing a therapist she's got them worried she might be remembering. They'll come after her again," Logan said.

"They already have," Luc said. "She was attacked outside her apartment a week ago. A passerby called 9-1-1. The police report states they couldn't find the victim but the description matches Cassie." He tightened his arms around her and nuzzled her neck before he looked at Logan. "I'll help you protect her until we catch these fuckers."

Logan smiled and Luc glared at him. "Protection only. No playing. No contract."

"Speak for yourself," Logan said. "I'm playing with her every chance she'll let me. You can join us or not."

Luc frowned. "Not."

Logan smiled again. "Fine with me. I won't have to share."

"Thank god." Cassie reached up and rubbed her temple. "The two of you together give me a headache."

Luc looked down at her and the lines appeared around his eyes. "That's not what we make ache, Cassandra."

Logan leaned forward and pushed Luc's head out of the way, putting his own face directly above Cassie's. "Hi, sugar. Feeling better?"

Nodding, Cassie lowered her eyes. There was no way she could get away with speaking a lie so she kept quiet, hoping they would let it go. She looked around and realized she wasn't in her own room anymore. This room had to belong to one of the twins as it was definitely a man's room with charcoal-gray walls and taupe-and-medium-blue accents. The bed was a four poster but the square posts and the headboard were padded leather. She could see discreetly placed hooks in a decorative edging along the frame of the canopy above her. She ran her hands over the throw she was wrapped in and smiled with pleasure at its luxurious feel.

"Cassandra, we need words," Luc said.

She glanced at Luc then quickly returned her gaze to Logan. "I feel better now, Sir." She was saved from further questioning when her tummy growled.

Logan laughed and gave her an upside-down kiss. "Let's get you dressed and fed."

Cassie managed to give him a little smile before Luc pushed him away. "You put her in the shower. I'll get her things."

"I can use the shower in my room." She needed some time away from them to build up her defenses.

"No. From now on you stay with one of us," Luc said.

"Why?"

"We'll discuss that after lunch, Cassandra."

"There's nothing to discuss."

"Then Logan will talk and you'll listen." Luc stood up then tried to give her to Logan.

Logan ignored him. "You've got her. I'll go get her things." Before Luc could stop him he walked away.

Luc frowned then gave in and carried her into the en suite bathroom. He hit the button that turned on the overhead rainfall showerhead then set her on her feet. When he grabbed the hem of the T-shirt she wore, she grabbed his wrists and tried to keep him from pulling it up.

"Luc, stop. I can undress by myself."

"What's your safeword?"

"Red."

"Use it or let go."

Cassie thought about the situation for a moment but didn't move her hands. "I don't know what to do," she said, her voice broken.

"Trust Logan. He'll never do anything to harm you."

"What about you, Sir? Are you going to hurt me?"

Luc slid his finger beneath her chin and lifted her face to his. "Don't try playing your games with me, Cassandra. I'm immune. Now, let go."

Cassie held on for a moment longer then dropped her hands to her sides. It wouldn't do any good to proclaim her innocence. Luc had already decided the kind of woman he thought she was so she'd let him go on believing that. Besides, what did it matter? She wasn't staying here much longer no matter what Thor said. In fact, it might be better if she took that job offer in Houston. That would get her away from Thor, the Ramseys, and possibly the people who were after her.

Luc stripped the T-shirt over her head then backed her into the shower stall until she was beneath the warm spray.

She stood there, head down, for several moments while the warm water ran over her. When she raised her head, she saw Luc and Logan standing at the entrance to the shower, watching her. She paused, waiting for the fear and panic to take over, then breathed a sigh of relief when it didn't. Cheeks pink, she washed herself then rinsed off and moved toward the entrance and reached for the towel Luc held. He pulled it away then gestured for her to step forward. She did and he used the towel to dry her.

Logan handed her another towel, then said, "Dry your hair, sugar."

Cassie ran the towel over her hair then stood still while Logan combed the tangles from it and smoothed it down her back. Smiling, she saw the pile of clothes Logan had brought for her and reached for them.

Luc grabbed her hand and shook his head. "Logan will dress you."

Cassie froze for a moment then nodded and waited to see what he would do.

Logan shook out a short, peach-colored sundress. "Arms up," he said. Cassie raised her arms and Logan pulled the dress over her head, pulled her hair out of the collar, and then smoothed the skirt down her body. He straightened the straps over her shoulders then turned her to face the mirror and held his hand out for the blow dryer Luc held. Luc ignored him then combed through Cassie's hair while he moved the warm blast of air from the blow dryer over the silken strands. He combed through it one last time until it lay in a burnished golden river down her back to her waist. "Beautiful," he said then kissed her. "Time to feed you."

"Shoes." Logan knelt down and slipped a pair of beaded sandals on Cassie's feet. He touched the soft pink polish on her big toe then lifted her dress and looked at her pussy. "Bro, they're the same pink."

Cassie groaned with embarrassment and shoved her dress down. "You two are really good at dressing a girl. You've had a lot of practice apparently."

"We're better at removing a girl's clothes." Luc hugged her until she squeaked, then led her past Logan. He bumped shoulders with Logan before leading her out of the room and down the stairs to the dining room. The three of them entered the room, and Luc and Logan pulled her to a stop between them. Cade and Jackson sat at either end of the table. Addison and Jenna were on one side and their younger brother, Zane, sat across from them. Luc led Cassie around the table, stopped behind Zane and waited. Zane grumbled then got up and moved to the chair between Addison and Jenna. Luc seated Cassie in the middle chair then he sat down on her left while Logan took the chair to her right.

Cassie caught Addison watching her. Addison smiled then winked at her, and Cassie thought, *Oh hell, what's she up to now?* She shook her head at Addison then caught Jenna hiding her laughter behind her hand.

Jane pushed a cart loaded with covered dishes into the room and began setting them on the table. She looked around, shook her head, then quickly set the last dish on the table and pushed the cart back to the kitchen.

Luc and Logan loaded food onto their plates and Cassie's then passed the dishes around the table. When everyone was served and had begun eating, Addison said, "Jenna and I are going to the spa at Club Mystique this afternoon, Cassie. We'd like you to join us."

"What time?" Logan asked.

"Our appointments begin at two-thirty but we were going to go to town and shop first," Addison said.

Cassie could feel her fear growing at just the thought of going to town and being out in the open. "I need to stay here and make some calls."

"You only have to make one call and you can do that in the morning," Jackson said.

"Logan wants to talk to me after lunch," Cassie said.

"We'll talk this evening after dinner, sugar."

"I don't want to go," Cassie said. *It's not safe.*

Logan leaned over and she leaned back in the chair and tried to keep some distance between them. He nuzzled her neck then said, "Sugar, you can go to Club Mystique with me and Luc where we'll definitely end up playing our version of spa day, or you can go shopping then to the spa with Addison and Jenna. Either way, your body, including your sweet little pussy, is going to be smooth as silk by bedtime."

Blushing, Cassie swallowed then said, "I'll go with Addison and Jenna."

Logan smiled then said, "Rosy Red Love."

"What?" Cassie asked.

"Nail polish," Logan said, lifting her hand and looking at her nicely shaped nails. "You have beautiful hands, sugar."

"Thank you, Logan," Cassie said, smiling. "I'll remember the color you suggested."

Luc snorted then sighed. "He wasn't making a suggestion. He's telling you what polish he wants on your nails. Do you understand?"

"Yes, Sir," Cassie said, confused and wondering why Luc would care either way as he had already made it clear he didn't want anything to do with her.

Luc looked at his watch then Cassie's plate. "You haven't eaten your vegetables."

"I'm full, Sir."

"If we're going to have time to shop we need to leave in a few minutes," Addison said.

Cade stood and pulled Addison's chair back then helped her to her feet. "Be good and no gossiping."

"Yes, Master," Addison said, lowering her bright blue eyes.

Jenna snorted, then laughed when Jackson pulled her from her chair and swatted her bottom. "That goes for you, too, angel."

"Sir, yes, Sir," Jenna said, then smiled. "I will do my best to not listen to any idle chatter at the spa."

"Damn," Cade said. "That spa is probably the biggest hotbed of rumors in Texas." He pulled Addison into his arms and whispered something that made her laugh before he released her.

"I need to get my tote bag," Cassie said. "I'll meet you on the front porch."

"You don't need your purse, Cassie. We have accounts at all the businesses in town," Logan said.

Cassie leaned down and brushed an imagery spot from her skirt, letting her hair hide her frown. If Logan thought she was going to let him or Luc pay for anything for her, including the spa, he was nuts. She wasn't one of the women who chased after them as if they were some sort of exotic animal she wanted to own. "I pay my own way or I don't go."

"Again, not a suggestion, Cassandra," Luc said.

Jenna and Addison stepped back then froze, focusing on the situation going on in front of them. "Damn, I wish we had some popcorn," Jenna said and Addison nodded.

"I said I pay my own way or I don't go, Sir."

Logan stepped between Cassie and Luc. "It's no big deal, sugar. Whatever you want we're happy to provide it for you, aren't we, Luc?" Logan smiled at her encouragingly and ignored Luc's deepening frown.

Cassandra turned and had made it up two steps when Luc stopped her.

"Logan and I are driving you to town," Luc said. "You don't need your tote."

"I need to change my shoes."

Logan pointed to her feet. "I like those sandals."

"We're shopping, Logan, for hours. I need shoes like Addison and Jenna are wearing."

Addison nodded and pointed to her own comfortable trainers.

Jenna stepped forward. "We don't want you to have to follow us around and then hang around waiting for us while we're at the spa, Luc. We can drive ourselves."

"We don't mind," Logan said, looking up at Cassie. "Hurry up, sugar. We'll wait for you here."

Luc leaned back, and softly banged his head against the wall as Cassie disappeared at the top of the stairs. He tipped his head back, and growled. "Logan, at lunch you didn't even notice Cassandra hadn't eaten and just now you let her manipulate you into getting her own way."

"She's fragile right now," Logan said.

"Yeah, and everybody's been tiptoeing around her and look where that's gotten them—nowhere," Luc said. "You've got to get tough before she ends up dead."

"I'll talk to her this evening and maybe she'll tell me what's making her so unhappy," Logan said, smiling. "I'm sure she just needs some tender, loving care."

Luc growled, then banged his head against the wall again.

"Is Cassie in danger?" Addison asked.

"You don't need to worry, Addison. I have it under control," Logan said.

"No, you don't," Luc said, "and, yes, Cassie is in danger and so are you and Jenna. All three of you need to be on your guard and stick close to home or make sure one of us is with you if you leave the ranch."

Jackson and Cade had been going toward the den when Jackson stopped, said something to Cade, then moved to Jenna. "I think I'll tag along today. There's some things I need to get in town."

"I think the talk with Cassie needs to be done now," Luc said, "and the trip to town needs to be cancelled."

Cassie heard the last part of Luc's statement as she came down the stairs and breathed a silent sigh of relief until she saw the disappointment on Addison's and Jenna's faces.

"What's going on?" Cassie asked as she stopped on the bottom step and leaned against the newel post.

Luc took her arm. "We're going to have a little talk." He glanced at Cade, and Cade opened the den door and waved his hand, indicating they would talk there.

"Why?" Cassie asked. "What's going on?"

"Let's get comfortable and then I'll talk and you'll listen." Luc led her into the den and seated her in the middle of the couch. He pointed to Addison and Jenna, indicating they should sit on either side of Cassie. Cade sat behind his desk while Logan and Jackson took the two chairs across the desk from him, and swiveled them around so they could see the three women.

"Bro, you never do the talking," Logan said. "Maybe I should do it."

Luc sent him a silent message then scooted an ottoman over with his foot until it was directly in front of Cassie. He sat down then reached out and took her hands. He gently chafed her hands. "Cassandra, look at me."

Cassie shook her head, then felt Luc squeeze her hands, encouraging her to be brave. She raised her amber eyes to his face.

"I'm going to tell you what Logan and I have figured out and I just want you to listen. Okay?"

"Do we have to?" Cassie asked, her voice soft and shaking with nerves.

"Yes, we do." He rubbed his thumbs on her wrists. "First, I want you to know that we're all here to help you." When she tried to jerk her hands out of his, he tightened his hands and held onto her. "When you were seventeen, two, maybe three, men broke into the home you shared with your aunt Velma and they took you."

Cassie shook her head as panic flared inside her and her trembling increased.

"They held you for at least two days. They kept you blindfolded and tied up but they talked in front of you. You know their voices. Am I right, so far?"

Cassie nodded, then shook her head, her face pale. Her eyes were stark and glazed with tears.

"What did I say wrong, Cassandra?" Luc asked.

"Sometimes they drugged me and then they would remove the blindfold."

"Is that when they raped you?"

Cassie nodded as silent tears began sliding down her cheeks.

"How many were there, sugar?"

Cassie looked into Luc's hazel eyes. It was the first time he had called her by anything other than her name and she could see that he was madder than hell about what those men had done to her. She cleared her throat, swallowed, and then whispered, "Four. The fourth one was in charge. He had a whip. He—" She was shaking so hard she couldn't go on.

Luc lifted her from the couch and set her on his lap. He held her and ran his hand over her lower back where there were three scars that only a whip could have made. "He used the whip on your back."

Cassie nodded. "He raped me." Grimacing with pain, she rubbed her temples. "I don't remember all of it. Only parts."

Luc nuzzled her neck then kissed her cheek. "How did you get away, sugar?"

"Two of the other men wanted to kill me but the third one argued with them. When they left the house, he put me in the trunk of a car and took me home. He dumped me in the back yard. I crawled to the door and my Aunt Velma heard me banging on it."

"She had reported you missing but the police said you were a runaway. When you were returned, she called them and said you had returned and the police case was closed."

"Yes."

"Damn," Jackson said. "We never thought to check the juvenile runaway reports."

"Why didn't she take you to the hospital?" Luc asked Cassie.

"The man who took me home said they would kill me and anyone I told. The hospital would have called the police. Velma was a nurse so she took care of me."

"When your dad got home you told him."

"They killed him." She started sobbing. "It's my fault they killed my dad. They'll kill you, too."

Luc tightened his arms around her, sheltering her as her tears ran down his neck. He kissed her cheek and cupped the back of her head with his hand. He looked up as Logan crouched down next to them and wrapped his arms around Cassie.

"Nobody's going to kill us, sugar," Logan said.

Next to them Jackson sat down and pulled a crying Jenna into his arms as Cade slid Addison onto his lap and dried her tears.

Luc rocked Cassie as he held her. The entire time he and Logan sent each other silent messages. Jackson nudged Logan's shoulder then handed him a handful of tissues. Logan gently dried Cassie's cheeks even as more tears fell.

"Tell me about the car wreck, Cassie," Luc said.

Cassie shook her head. "I don't remember the wreck. There's other things I don't remember. I remember my dad's funeral."

Luc heard the truth in her voice. "Is that how you decided to lie about remembering being abducted?"

"Sort of. The neurosurgeon knew the marks on my back were made by a whip. He asked me about them. He said while I was under the anesthesia I talked a lot about what happened. He told me what to say about the amnesia and he made sure several people heard him talking about it at the nurse's station. I think that's why they've left me alone all these years."

"But, then you went to see Dr. Carson and two men attacked you outside your apartment?"

Cassie looked surprised then nodded. "They had on masks. They called me a bitch and said they were going to kill me. I know it wasn't the same men from eight years ago because I didn't recognize their voices." She waited for a moment while Logan stroked a tissue over her cheek. "I think I heard the voice of one of the men from eight years ago in the hallway outside of my office several weeks ago. By the time I worked up the nerve to open my door and look into the hallway he was gone."

The sound of Thor cursing startled her when it came from the phone on Cade's desk and then he asked, "Is that why you started locking your office door, baby girl?"

Cassie stiffened on Luc's lap.

Luc patted her back. "It's okay, sugar. Thor's not mad at you. He's as worried about you as the rest of us. You're not alone anymore, Cassie."

"I'm afraid they're going to hurt you. All of you." Cassie looked around and tears began falling again.

Luc laughed, but it wasn't a joyful sound. "Sugar, you don't ever have to worry about them ever again."

Thor said, "I'll be at the ranch by this evening. I'm bringing Ben Harrington and Mac Malone with me as well as Marisol. She and I will stay at the hotel at Club Mystique but I want Ben and Mac to stay at the ranch with Cassie."

"We have plenty of room," Addison said. "You and Marisol are welcome to stay, too, Thor."

"Thanks, Addison, but we'll stay at the club," Thor said.

"Okay, but I expect you and Marisol to have dinner with us this evening."

"That's one invitation I'll accept, especially if Jane is making apple pie."

"I'll make sure she does."

Cade placed a finger beneath Addison's chin and tipped her face up to his. "We're going to have a talk, baby."

"Why? What did I do?" Addison asked.

Cade hugged her then said, "Later." He looked at Cassie and asked, "When you were taken home, were you still blindfolded and tied up?"

Cassie leaned her head against Luc's chest and he tipped his head down as Logan leaned closer and comforted her. "Yes. He took the blindfold and duct tape off of me just before he dropped me over the fence at Velma's house. It was dark and I couldn't see him but I felt a scar on his neck. It was V shaped and right here," she said, touching the side of Luc's neck where it met his shoulder.

"Sugar, was he really tall and sort of lean?" Logan asked.

Cassie nodded. "Really tall. He barely had to lift me to get me over the fence."

Logan cursed then stood up, took a couple steps, and cursed again. "That fucker Tyson. If he wasn't already dead, I'd rip his heart out and feed it to him."

Cassie whimpered and her face lost what little color it had as she swayed. Luc tightened his arms then wrapped his hand around the back of her neck. "Sugar, you doing okay?"

Cassie trembled then leaned against him. "Did they kill him because he freed me?"

Luc kissed her temple then looked at Jackson. "Give me that blanket, Jackson."

Jackson pulled the cover from the back of the couch and handed it to Luc. He took it and wrapped it around Cassie. "Better?"

Cassie huddled into Luc and asked, "Can we stop now? I want to stop now."

Luc surrounded her with his arms and rubbed his cheek over the top of her head. "Soon, sugar."

"Who the hell is Tyson?" Thor asked.

"Leroy Tyson was a mercenary. When I knew him he worked for a guy named Larry Taylor," Logan said. "Neither one of them was around very long before they were caught doing some illegal shit in South America. Last I heard Leroy Tyson was hiding out from the law."

"What kind of illegal shit?" Cade asked.

"You name it, he and Taylor did it. Mostly drugs and artifacts but there were rumors about other stuff." Logan sent a warning glance toward Cade and Jackson.

A rumbling sound came from the phone then Thor said, "I understand, Logan. Cassie?"

"Yes, Thor."

"After dinner tonight we're going to have a talk."

"No," Logan said. "Cassie belongs to me and Luc. We're going to take care of this."

"You've both been out of the game too long," Thor said. "I'm handling this."

Logan laughed. "You do that. In the meantime Luc and I will go hunting."

Luc almost smiled when Thor cursed and Cade glared at him and Logan.

"How long?" Cade asked.

"We never stopped," Luc said quietly. Cassie relaxed in his arms as the stress of the past hour caught up to her. He pulled her closer to his chest as she fell asleep. "If they needed a special job done, they'd call us. We'd decide if we went or not."

"Contractors," Cade said.

"Specialists," Logan answered. "We only took jobs that we believed would make a difference."

"How?" Jackson asked. "Luc doesn't even carry a gun."

Logan smiled and lines appeared beside Luc's eyes.

"Shit," Jackson said. "I heard rumors about a shooter who had broken my record. You?"

Luc gave one nod. "Inherited it from dad."

"Logan?" Jackson asked.

"As good as you," Logan said. "But, mostly I was Luc's spotter."

"Partner," Luc said.

"Well, isn't that nice," Thor said, his voice ringing with sarcasm. "We could have used you two jokers in Columbia last month."

"We went hunting for three days while you were out of the country," Logan said, then laughed.

Luc stood up and carried Cassie toward the door. "I'm putting Cassandra to bed for a nap then Logan and I have things to do."

"Wait a minute," Thor said. "I still have a couple questions. Why did they target Cassie, and how did you know what happened to her?"

"We worked on a similar case nine years ago," Logan said.

"No more questions," Luc said as Logan opened the door to the hallway. "You can talk to her later with us present."

Chapter Three

That evening at dinner, Cassie sat between Luc and Logan again with Zane on Luc's left. Marisol sat directly across from her with Thor on her left and Mac and Ben on her right. Cade and Addison shared the head of the table while Jackson and Jenna sat at the foot of the table.

Cassie smiled at Marisol then blocked Luc when he tried to place several more spears of grilled asparagus on her plate. "Da, uh, dang it, Luc. I said I didn't want any more."

Addison laughed. "Since when do you say 'dang,' Cassie? We don't mind if you say a cuss word every now and then. No need to change the way you talk for our benefit."

"Well, uh, thank you, Addison." Cassie had been around Addison long enough to know that the gleam in her eyes meant she was up to something. A second later, she saw Addison smile and knew that dinner was about to get a lot more interesting.

"You know, Marisol, I have a wonderful idea," Addison said, her smile widening as she turned to Marisol. "Jenna was going to stay at my house but now she's living here with Jackson. So, then I thought I would ask Cassie if she wanted to live there while she helps Cade, but now it looks like she'll be sticking close to Luc and Logan. So, the house is empty. Would you like to stay there?"

"Yes, thank you, Addison," Marisol said.

"What are you up to?" Thor asked, his voice suspicious, his eyes narrowed and locked on Addison.

"I'm not up to anything," Addison said.

"You're always up to something," Logan said.

"Cade should do something," Luc said as he snuck another couple bites of his steak onto Cassie's plate.

"I will as soon as I figure out what she's doing." Cade tightened his arm around Addison's waist and looked down at her, his black brows drawn down over narrowed green eyes.

Addison smiled innocently. "I'm just trying to help, Master."

"By the time you figure out what she's up to it will be too late," Zane said. "Addison's fast." He sent a sympathetic grimace to Jackson. "Sorry, bro."

Jackson chuckled and nuzzled Jenna's neck. "No need to look so concerned, Zane. I'm happy and you will be, too, when it's your turn. It only hurts for a moment." He *oomphed* then laughed when Jenna gave him a little fist to the belly.

Addison smiled at Cassie then narrowed her eyes at Zane. "Now that you've ruined my evil, secret plans, I'll have to seek revenge, Zane." She rubbed a hand over her expanding waist. "I'm feeling very, very creative."

Zane groaned. "Cade, do something."

Cade laughed. "I can't spank her. Every time I bend her over she barfs."

Luc chuckled. "Thanks for drawing her attention away from us, Zane. For a moment there I thought we were doomed." Next to him, Cassie glared at him and picked up the salt shaker.

"Me, too," Thor told them with a relieved sigh. Then he quoted, "'The only really happy folk are married women and single men.'"

Cade, Ben, and Mac froze then looked at each other to see who was going to try to guess who Thor was quoting. Ben and Mac shook their heads. Cade sighed, got out his wallet, pulled a twenty from it, then said, "Oscar Wilde."

Thor laughed and shook his head then caught the twenty Cade threw at him. "Mencken," he said. "That makes a thousand dollars in the donation jar. I'll have Dania take it to the youth center on Monday."

Addison laughed then saw Marisol's puzzled look. "Thor is a big fan of quotes. He says one and the guys try to guess who he's quoting. When they're wrong, they have to put twenty dollars in a jar. When there's a thousand dollars in the jar, they donate it to the local youth center."

Marisol smiled. "A good cause." She looked at Thor. "Perhaps you are redeemable after all, *Señor*."

"No, he's not," Ben said, "but what about us? You didn't say you had plans for us, Addison." He pointed to himself then to Mac.

"Oh, I have really special plans for both of you." Addison smiled. "When you're ready."

"What do you mean? When we're ready?" Ben's voice sounded relieved but still slightly offended.

"You're both still sowing your wild oats so you're not good marriage material yet."

"Thank God." Mac's voice sounded like the voice of a man who'd just dodged a bullet, as he collapsed back in his chair with relief.

Thor laughed. I'm still sewing wild oats, too. Yup, I'm just a farmer at heart. A *lifetime* farmer."

Addison smiled a secret smile then winked at Thor before glancing at Marisol Rios, who sat next to him, her lips moving as she mumbled something in Spanish.

Thor glared at Addison then looked at Cade. "Make Addison stop, Ramsey. Now."

Cassie dumped a handful of salt on Luc's mashed potatoes while he and everyone else was looking in Thor's direction. She glanced at Jenna, and realized she had seen her quick sleight of hand and was hiding her laughter.

"So, Marisol, is that a yes to my offer?" Addison asked. "I can get the key for you if you like?"

"Yes," Marisol said. "*Señor* Larkin is busy. I do not want to be—how do you say—guest that stinks like fishes?"

Cassie sent Marisol a laughing grin. She had visited with Marisol before dinner and she knew she spoke perfect English thanks to a British mother and an Oxford education.

Thor said, "You mean, 'Guests and fish go bad after three days.'"

"*Sí*. So you, too, feel this?" Marisol said. "I go."

Addison smiled and said, "Wonderful. I'll get the key for you after dinner."

"You are not moving into Addison's house, Marisol," Thor said.

Marisol took a sip of wine then set her glass down. "My father gives you his greatest treasure but you have no use for me. You go every night to do this farming so I go to Addison's house."

Thor smiled. "You can't protect yourself. I can."

"No. You think I stink. I call the drug peoples to protect me."

"The DEA," Cassie said helpfully as Luc lifted a large forkful of potatoes to his mouth. He chewed once, then again, before his face scrunched up and he lifted his napkin to his mouth and spit the potatoes out. He grabbed his glass of water and gulped it as his eyes shot to her then to the salt shaker by her plate then back to her. She smiled sweetly.

Across from her, Marisol stood up and grabbed Thor's plate just as he lifted a piece of steak to his mouth. She stacked his plate on top of hers then reached for Ben's plate, which he protected by grabbing it and turning his back to her.

"What the hell do you think you're doing, Marisol?" Thor asked. "I'm eating that."

"Helping Jane," Marisol said. "In Columbia I help the"—Marisol looked at Cassie—"what do you call the place where many women live and work?"

"A convent?" Cassie asked innocently, knowing Marisol really spent her time rescuing young women from brothels.

Marisol smothered a laugh then said, "*Sí*, a convent." Looking pious she asked, "There is one in your village?

"Convent? What the hell are you talking about, Marisol?" Thor reached for his plate but Marisol twisted away from him. "There's no way in hell you're a nun—not with that face and body."

"What would you know? You move me to your house then ignore me," Marisol said.

"I'm working on the flash drive you gave me. It's encoded or something."

"*Estúpido*," Marisol said, her hands busy doing a lot of the talking for her. "That is a diversion for the traitor in your agency. I am the gift my father sent to you."

"What fucking traitor?" Thor asked.

"You're a gift?" Mac turned to Thor. "If you don't want her can I have her?"

"Piss off, Malone," Thor said. "She's not going anywhere."

"Do you see what happens when you don't keep a tight rein on Addison? Everything goes to hell," Zane said.

"You've all told me to loosen the reins." Cade relaxed back in his chair. "So I did."

"That's right and I'm only trying to help. This way Thor can spend more time farm—uh, working," Addison leaned back against Cade and he slid his hands over her belly, "and Marisol can spend her days in prayer."

"*Sí*," Marisol agreed, folding her hands and looking up while mumbling something in Spanish that sounded suspiciously like a request for bad things to happen to Thor's manhood.

Addison, Cassie, and Jenna giggled while the men shifted nervously. Thor growled and jerked Marisol back into her chair. "Stop that. Most of us speak Spanish."

While Thor tried to get his plate back from Marisol, Cade stood up with Addison in his arms. "I'm taking this bad girl upstairs for a very stern talking to," he told them with a chuckle. At the door he turned back and looked at Logan and Luc with Cassie sitting snugly between them. "You two won't be able to keep Cassie close without playing with her. You need to get Zane to draw up a contract for you." His eyes flicked by Thor as he turned to leave the room. "Thor, good luck with the nun." Chuckling, he snuggled Addison closer and left the chaos behind.

Addison tightened her arms around Cade's shoulders as he carried her up the stairs to their room. After kicking the door shut, he dropped her onto their bed then stood over her. Addison sat up, leaned back on her arms, and smiled at him. "Our plan went a lot better than I thought it would, Master."

Smiling, Cade shrugged out of his shirt. "You owe me big time, brat. Strip and get that ass in the air now."

* * * *

Cassie sat on the leather couch in Cade's den with Luc and Logan on either side of her. Zane watched them from Cade's leather desk chair as he rocked back and forth. "I've given each of you a copy of a standard D/s contract. I want you to read through it and tell me what parts you want to keep and what you want to change. We can at least get a rough draft worked out tonight."

Cassie dropped the pages onto the coffee table. "I can't do this."

Luc picked up the papers and handed them back to her. "Yes, you can, sugar."

"Before we go any further, we need to know how much experience you've had with this lifestyle," Logan said.

Blushing, Cassie lowered her eyes then leaned back. "I know the rules but I've never really played with anyone except you and Luc."

Zane looked exasperated. "What is it with you people? Haven't any of you ever had a long-term relationship before?" He sat back with a disgusted look on his face. "First, I had to negotiate a new contract for Addison because Cade is such a control freak he can barely stand to let her out of his sight. Now, the three of you are sitting here like deer caught in a hunter's headlights."

"I don't see you signing a contract," Logan said. "Besides we know exactly what we want."

"Well, then, start talking." Leaning forward with his chin in his hands, Zane looked at Logan. "Give me a list of five to ten rules you want Cassie to follow."

Logan nodded, then turned toward Cassie. "First, you will not go anywhere without me or Luc with you."

Cassie began to roll her eyes then stopped herself. "Okay, I agree, but what's that got to do with this contract?"

"Sir," Luc said.

Seeing her open her mouth to protest, Logan said, "Unless you don't respect us enough to address us properly. In which case this stops now."

Shaking her head, Cassie knew she didn't want the negotiations to end. She just hoped she could get through this process without running away. "No, I respect both of you, Sir."

"Good, and we can put anything in the contract we want as long as you agree to it," Logan said. "You will call us Sir when we're at the club or with people in the lifestyle. When we're with strangers or people who aren't in the lifestyle, you will use our names but still speak with respect. Do you understand?"

"Yes, Sir."

Logan chuckled. "You can also use our names when you're begging one of us to let you come."

Luc chuckled then said, "When we are home alone you will call me Luc unless we're playing and it doesn't matter what room we're in at the time. If we're playing you will call us Sir. Do you understand?"

"Yes, Sir." Cassie looked at Logan, waiting to see if he would tell her to call him by his name. He smiled at her but not in a good way.

"Everyone thinks I'm easygoing, but sugar, you need to know right up front, Luc and I have very little tolerance for bratty behavior. That's why we run the club." He ran his hand down her hair, smoothing it. "Luc and I like that you can tell us apart so at home you can call me Logan as long as we're not playing. Do you understand?"

"Yes, Sir."

"Eyes on us at all times. Do you understand?"

"Not down, Sir?" she asked, surprised.

Shaking his head, Luc repeated, "On me or Logan. We like your eyes, sugar. We like them even better when they're on us."

"Yes, Sir." A little smile curved her lips.

Logan wrapped his arms around her waist and pulled her back against him. He angled his body in the corner of the couch, one leg resting against the back of the couch, the other stretched out on the floor with her between them. She rested back against him, feeling safe in his arms.

"No talking in public unless one of us asks you a direct question. If you have something to say then ask permission. We like your voice so we'll always say yes unless there's a reason we want you to remain quiet. Do you understand?"

"Yes, Sir."

Logan nibbled on her neck then kissed the soft spot beneath her ear. "Dresses or skirts unless you're going riding. No panties ever. Do you understand?" Logan asked.

"I really like beautiful lingerie, Sir. It's my addiction."

Logan tightened his arms then kissed her neck while his eyes met Luc's and a silent message passed between them. "We'll make sure you get the chance to model your lingerie for us. Okay?"

Nodding, Cassie glanced over her shoulder and gave him a little smile. "Okay, Sir."

"No lying. No fighting. Absolutely no screaming at us. Understand?" Luc asked.

"Yes. I agree with that. I don't like to be yelled at either, Sir," Cassie said as Luc picked up her foot, removed her shoe, and began massaging her instep. He grinned when she moaned with pleasure and wiggled her toes. She smiled when he touched her brightly polished toenails then glanced at her.

"You have a problem you come to one of us. Do you understand?" Luc asked.

"Yes, Sir. I've been on my own for a long time. I never realized what a relief it would be to have someone willing to help me." Seeing the pleasure on Luc's face she smiled and knew she had made the right decision. In the morning, she would try to explain to them the flashes of memory she had been having recently as well as the things she had remembered.

"Excellent, sugar," Luc said.

Logan stroked his finger over her lips. "No more cussing, sugar, or Luc and I will turn your ass red. Understand?"

"Yes, Sir, but I have a little bit of a potty mouth. I blame Thor and Jackson."

"But, sugar, they're not in charge of your mouth." Luc squeezed her foot. "We are and we say no cussing."

Realizing he hadn't asked her a question, she kept quiet then smiled at him as Logan drew her back against him.

"Okay, now, tell us what you need from us." Seeing her puzzled look, Luc added, "Take your time and think about it, and sugar, you can speak freely."

Cassie looked past Luc to the shelves loaded with books and small objects, some looking like things a child would pick up and give to their mother. Her lips curved in a gentle smile. She wanted to get a closer look at those shelves. She looked back at Luc as she snuggled against Logan. "I want the same things you want. No lying, no fighting, honesty, trust, and respect, and I would like us to only be with each other for the time we're together please, Sirs."

Logan kissed her neck. "We can give you all those things, sugar."

"What about Linda?" Cassie asked.

"She's signed a contract with someone else in Dallas," Logan said. "You, me and Luc—we belong to each other now."

Cassie knew Luc felt the shiver of arousal that raced through her when Logan said that. For some women, having two men was only a fantasy, but for others like her, it was something more. Something they didn't just dream about but something they yearned for, needed.

Logan lifted Cassie's hand to his mouth and ran her fingers over his lips. "I promise we will never do anything you don't want."

Luc lifted her foot and kissed her slender ankle. "We will never do anything that will not give you pleasure"—he looked up at her—"eventually."

Cassie licked her lips as Luc and Logan seduced her senses with their touches and kisses and suggestive glances. "Promise me you won't get mad if I get scared."

Cassie waited, watching as Luc and Logan held one of their silent conversations. Apparently they came to an agreement of some kind because Logan tightened his arms around her as Luc squeezed her ankle.

"For the next two weeks your safewords are red for stop, yellow for slow down, and green for okay. After two weeks we'll talk about changing it. Do you understand, sugar?" Logan asked.

Cassie gulped, then swallowed, fear and elation filling her. She wanted this but she was scared. "Are you sure, Sirs?"

Luc pulled her onto his lap and she wiggled around until she was comfortable, and then rested her head on his shoulder. She felt his hard cock pressing into her hip and wondered if he and Logan would fuck her tonight.

Luc combed his fingers through the long strands of Cassie's silky hair. "We're sure."

"If you get scared we will slow down and talk about what is scaring you. We will never hurt you. Do you understand?" Logan asked.

Cassie forced herself to look at them. "I'm not sure I'll ever be able to tolerate being restrained or blindfolded. I don't want you to be disappointed, Sirs." She twisted her hands together then fisted them.

Luc slipped his finger into her fisted hand and slowly straightened each finger then planted a kiss in the center of her palm. He did the same to her other hand. "For now, no restraints but eventually we're going to push you on that, sugar." He tugged her head back and gave her a little smacking kiss on the lips. "You'll always have your safewords to use. What else?"

"I don't want to be shared with anyone else. Ever. Please, Sirs?"

"Sugar, you just made Luc and me the two happiest men in Texas." Logan chuckled. "We're going to enjoy showing you off knowing only we get to touch you."

Cassie smiled then brought up the last thing she felt she needed. Space. "I think it would be best if I moved into the hotel at the club. It's secure."

Luc and Logan looked at each other, one brow raised, then Luc lowered his brow and Logan squeezed her hand and asked, "Why don't you want to stay with us, Cassie?"

"I'm going to be working with Cade during the day but playing with you at night. It would just feel strange to be living in a house with all of you, too."

"You mean Cade, Jackson, and Zane?" Logan asked.

"Yes, Sir."

Logan chuckled. "That's an easy fix, sugar. We'll just go to our house."

"You have a house?" she asked, surprised as one had never been mentioned, and she knew they lived in the ranch house.

"Sure. Luc and I built a house a couple miles from Club Mystique. We just don't stay there because it's easier to stay here," Logan said.

"Cade's housekeeper Jane cooks," Luc said as he slid her onto Logan's lap then pulled his cell phone from his pocket and read a text.

Cassie laughed. "Well, that's very practical of you."

"Katherine cooked for us," Luc said, then glanced at her before looking away again.

"She made peanut butter chocolate chip cookies," Logan said.

"I have a recipe for those. They're my favorite," Cassie said.

Luc glanced at Logan. A dark brow flicked up then down, and Logan said, "We'll move to our house tonight and you can make them."

"Won't you have to open the house?" she asked. Then, seeing their puzzled looks she said, "You know, get it ready to be lived in?"

"We have a housekeeper," Luc said.

"Her name is Isabella and she's really hot but she doesn't cook," Logan said. "Or do windows."

"She's a Marine," Luc said.

"She said she wasn't cooking for any sorry bastards," Logan said.

"Like you and Luc?" Cassie asked then realized what she had implied when Luc looked at her, a black brow raised, eyes narrowed. "Sorry, I meant Isabella's a Marine like you and Logan and she doesn't want to cook for any more soldiers."

"Not soldiers, Marines," Logan said. "She's meaner, though. She made us build her a house of her own because she said we were sick bastards for spanking bad little subs and then fucking them together."

Cassie burst into gales of laughter. Leaning against Logan she wiped her eyes and said, "I can hardly wait to meet her."

"She'll try to take you away from us," Luc said as he finished sending a text and put his phone away while sending Logan another unspoken message.

"Yeah, Isabella says if anyone's getting their ass slapped it isn't going to be a woman on her watch," Logan said. "She just doesn't understand the whole D/s dynamic."

"She's needs a good spanking," Luc added.

"Don't go there, bro. If you even tried she'd beat the shit out of me with the broom again thinking I was you," Logan said.

Luc's eyes crinkled and Cassie laughed again. There was a story behind that look.

"We want to fuck you," Luc said, the extreme calmness of his voice giving away how important her answer was to him.

"Luc and I both had checkups yesterday. We're clean," Logan said. "Are you on the pill?"

"The shot, and I just had an annual physical three months ago. I haven't been with anyone."

"When was the last time you were with someone?" Luc asked.

Cassie looked down, then looked at Luc, forcing herself to meet his eyes. "Eight years ago."

Logan ran his hands up and down her arms then said, "Luc and I are honored that you trust us not to harm you, sugar. We'll never betray that trust."

Cassie tried but failed to keep the tears from her eyes as her lower lip quivered. She closed her eyes and felt a tear slide down her cheek as another pair of arms surrounded her. Two hard chests pressed against her, one against her back the other against her breasts. She slid her arms around Luc's lean waist and buried her head against his neck. Luc nudged her face up, used a tissue to dry her cheeks, and then held it to her nose. "Blow."

She reached for the tissue but dropped her hand when he gave her a narrow-eyed warning glare. She let him have his way then leaned back. "I'm not a baby, Luc."

"Sure you are. You're our sugar baby." He brushed his lips over her mouth.

"We want to play with you, spank you, tease you, and make you scream with pleasure when we fuck you," Logan said.

"Yes, I *want* that, too, Sir, but I'm not sure I can give that to you. What if I can't?"

Logan smiled. "We'll take it one day at a time, sugar. You're going to be okay. Luc and I are proud of how well you've taken care of yourself and protected the people who care about you. From now on, though, we're in charge of doing that for you. Do you understand?"

"Yes, Logan."

"Good, sugar. Now, come on and I'll help you pack," Logan said.

"I'll call Isabella," Luc said.

"Won't do any good." Logan glanced at his watch. "By now she has a drink in her hand and she's watching her shows."

Concerned, Cassie asked, "Isabella drinks?"

"Yeah, a scotch every night. She says we drove her to it," Logan said, "but I think she drank before she met us. We're not allowed at her house."

"She smokes cigars," Luc said.

"Cigars?" Cassie asked, surprised.

"Yeah. They smell like horse manure," Logan said. "She was stinking up our house so we built her house a mile away."

"Downwind," Luc said.

Zane spoke up from his position behind Cade's desk. "All right, I have enough to get something on paper for you."

Cassie blushed then laughed. "Sorry, Zane. I guess we forgot you were still taking notes."

Zane smiled. "That's okay, Cassie." Now, I want to read this back to you and make sure you agree with it."

"Okay, thank you, Zane," Cassie said.

Zane listed the rules and what each of them expected from the three-month contract.

"Yes, that's what I want," Cassie said as Luc and Logan nodded in agreement.

"Okay, then, I'll fax the contract to the club in a couple days."

"Great." Logan stood and pulled Cassie up next to him. "I'm going to help Cassie get her things."

"I want to see the lingerie," Luc said.

"Luc likes lingerie," Logan said.

"No, I don't. I like girls in lingerie. There's a difference."

And, here we go again with the bickering, Cassie thought as she smiled at Zane then hurried to catch up to Luc and Logan.

They got in her way while she packed but Luc included the lingerie.

* * * *

Cassie looked around curiously and realized Luc and Logan's house looked like a replica of a huge antebellum house. Soft lights glowed on a broad porch that stretched across the front of the home with an ornate balcony above it. She followed Luc and Logan up two steps and across the porch. They each carried part of her luggage, leaving her free to look around.

Luc turned the knob, dipped his head down, and slid his lips over hers before pushing the door open and nudging her forward. As she passed Logan, he leaned down and kissed her then nuzzled her neck. Cassie smiled and stepped into the large foyer. A pair of paneled doors to her left led into a formal dining room while a twin set of doors to her right led into a formal living room. A large curving staircase was directly in front of her with a hall on each side leading to the back of the house. The entry was empty other than a large round table with a floral arrangement on it and two armless upholstered chairs, one on each side of the hallway against the wall. Behind her she heard Luc and Logan chuckle and then the sound of her luggage hitting the floor.

"Cassandra, strip," Luc said.

Cassie spun around then stepped back. The Dominating Duo was back. Hiding her smile, she untied the bow on the side of her aqua wrap dress then undid the single button that held it together on the inside and shrugged it from her shoulders. She let it fall to the floor behind her.

Luc drew in a deep breath. "Damn, sugar. You look amazing." He walked around her, sweeping his fingers over her golden skin and seeing goose bumps rise on her skin. "Where did you find this?" he asked as he touched the cup of her bra that was a light pink lacy flower with satiny green vines as straps.

"I made it, Luc," she told him. "It's my hobby."

"Some hobby," Logan said, kneeling down to get a closer look at her thong. Another lacy flower covered her bare mound and he could see her satiny skin through it. He ran his finger under one of the vine-shaped straps that circled her hips then leaned around her and traced the vine that disappeared between her ass cheeks. He chuckled when she shivered with arousal. "I'm beginning to see your fascination with lingerie, Luc."

"Not lingerie. Girls in lingerie," Luc said absently as he traced his finger over the pink nipple that stuck through the opening in the cup of the bra. He flicked his finger over it and watched as it hardened then he pinched it between two fingers.

Cassie squeaked with pain then sucked in a shallow breath and leaned into Luc's hand. He tightened his fingers then bent down and surrounded her nipple with his lips. Cassie slid her fingers into his hair and he tightened his arms around her waist, and pulled her to him until their pelvises were pressed together. As he bent her back over his arm, Cassie was distracted by the wonderful feelings rushing through her as Luc sucked and nibbled on her nipple while pinching the other one. He lifted his head, his eyes staring into hers as he unhooked the front closure then pushed the bra from her shoulders. Without stopping, he slid his hands down her body and pushed her thong from her hips. She stepped out of them when he tapped her right hip.

"Knees, sugar," Logan said. "I'm going to show you how we want you to greet us."

Logan moved behind her as Luc stepped back, his eyes blazing greener than she had ever seen them. She lowered herself to her knees, but kept her eyes focused on his.

"Knees spread wide so we can see our pussy," Logan said. "Good, sugar. Now, hands resting on your thighs, palms up, eyes down." Logan walked around her, adjusted her shoulders back so her breasts were lifted, then slid a finger beneath her chin and tipped her head up. He smoothed his hand over her hair. "Perfect, sugar."

"Beautiful," Luc said.

"When we enter, you will wait until we tell you to look at us and only then will you raise your eyes. Do you understand?"

"Yes, Sirs," Cassie said, her gaze on their boots.

"Excellent. Now, look at us," Logan said.

Cassie slowly raised her eyes upward and knew she would never grow tired of looking at them. They stood in front of her, legs spread apart, arms crossed over their chests. Their jeans were old and faded and the T-shirts they wore were tight and clung to their bodies like a second skin. Two identical faces looked down at her, eyes blazing with arousal, cheeks and chins dark with a five o'clock shadow. Their hair was blue-black and shaggy as if they couldn't be bothered to take the time to get it cut.

"Good. Now, tell us about last night," Luc said.

"Um, what about it?" she asked even though she knew they wanted to know how she'd relieved the aching arousal they'd forced her to endure for twenty-four hours.

"Cassandra," Luc said, his voice uncompromising with a hint of warning, "have you forgotten the rules?"

She shivered and started talking. "No, Luc."

When Luc cocked a brow at her, she licked her lips, pressed them together for a moment, and then said, "Sir. No, Sir. Um, well, I took a shower and, you know?" She shrugged.

"This is going to take a while," Logan said as he moved to his right, grabbed the chair, then pulled it to a position a few feet in front of Cassie with the back facing toward her. He straddled it, laid his crossed arms on the back, and rested his chin on them. Luc moved his chair next to Logan then copied his posture.

"Cassandra, look at me," Luc said.

Cassie met Luc's eyes, glanced at Logan, then looked back at Luc.

"You're a beautiful, sexy woman and you can do this," Luc said. "Now, you were in the shower and—" He waved his hand at her, indicating she should continue.

Cassie licked her lips then swallowed. "I washed my hair and conditioned it and then I used the vanilla and lavender gel I like. It smells really wonderful and it's really creamy. I like the way it feels on my skin," she said, then glanced at Logan again. Having two hot guys totally focused on her and every word she said was surprisingly *arousing.* Getting into the spirit of this scene, because that was what this was, she corrected her posture and softened her voice. "I smoothed it all over, especially over my breasts and my nipples. I brushed the sides of my breasts with my fingertips because that always makes my nipples really hard. I did that over and over, really softly, and then I started pinching them. Sort of softly at first but then harder, because I like that, too. It really arouses me." She swallowed, took a deep breath, and licked her lips again. Luc's eyes tracked over every wet centimeter. She took another deep breath and smelled her own arousal and wondered if they could smell it, too.

"Do that," Logan said, his voice raspy.

"What?" she asked. "Uh, Sir."

"Touch your breasts," Logan said.

"Now, Cassandra," Luc said, his voice a definite command.

Cassie's eyes flew to Luc and he held her gaze as she slid her hands to her breasts and cupped them. His eyes dropped to her hands and she swore she could feel the heat of his gaze warming her breasts. She gave them a little squeeze then drifted her fingertips over the sides of her breasts and felt her nipples harden. She pinched each nipple and moaned. "Then, I ran my hands down my belly to my pussy, like this." She stroked her hands down until she reached her bare mound. "I like to touch myself, all over." Panting, heart pounding, she rose up onto her knees, her body arched back, as she slid her hands between her legs. She moaned and let her head fall back as she stroked her fingers over her clit.

She heard Luc shift, then Logan, and she knew they were adjusting their cocks in their jeans. She opened her eyes and watched them watching her pleasure herself and admitted she could be a total exhibitionist for them.

"Did you finger yourself?"

Breathless, on the verge of an orgasm, it took her a moment to form words. "Yes, Logan."

"Do that," Luc said.

Cassie blinked, fluttered her lashes down, and then slid one finger into her pussy.

"Only one finger?" Logan sounded disappointed.

"No, two."

"Use two," Luc said.

"Did you use both hands?" Logan asked.

"Yes."

"Show us," Luc said.

Cassie used two fingers to stretch the lips of her pussy open as she stroked her middle finger over her clit and fingered herself with two fingers of her other hand. Panting, moaning, she arched her body and pumped her hips against her hands on the verge of an orgasm.

"Stop, Cassandra," Luc said.

Lost in the wonderful sensations rushing through her body, she moaned and continued to touch herself, just a couple strokes away from an orgasm.

"Cassandra, stop now," Logan said.

She froze, her eyes flying open and ping-ponging between Luc and Logan. Thinking fast on her knees she asked, "But, don't you want to see me come?" she asked, while thinking please, please, please, say yes.

"Yes, we do," Logan said.

Thank god.

"Later," Luc said.

For a moment she wondered what they would do if she ignored them and gave herself those last few strokes, then seeing the expressions on their faces, she slowly drew her hands away from her pussy. She lowered her body then rested her hands on her knees, palms up, fingers wet with her juices.

Luc and Logan stood then lifted her to her feet. Cassie watched in awe as they each took a hand and licked her fingers clean.

"Good girl." Luc brushed his lips over hers before deepening the kiss. "You've pleased me."

"You're as sweet as sugar." Logan pulled her into his arms and brushed his lips over hers then deepened the kiss. When he raised his head, he smiled at her, then said, "Tell us what rules you just broke, sugar."

Cassie reviewed the rules then said, "Forgetting to address you properly?"

"Yes, that's two swats," Logan said. "What else?"

"For speaking without permission?"

"Yes. That's two more." Luc stroked his hand down her hair then nuzzled her neck. "Bend over the table and spread your legs, Cassandra."

Cassie hesitated then took the few steps required to reach the table. It was an act of trust on her part and she realized it. She slowly widened her stance then bent over and rested her arms on the table. She laid her cheek on the cool surface, but kept her eyes on Luc. He moved up behind her then swatted her on the ass twice. Then Logan swatted her twice. Together they rubbed and squeezed her ass.

"Your ass is such a pretty shade of pink, sugar." Luc lifted her into his arms. "Shower, then cookies."

"You want me to bake cookies tonight?"

"We'll help." Logan followed them up the stairs and down the hallway to a set of double doors at the end of the hall. Luc kicked them open and carried her across the threshold.

"Wow!" Cassie looked around as Luc set her on her feet. The room was huge and probably took up the entire back of the house. To her right was a large sitting area and to her left the biggest bed she had ever seen. It was a replica of the four-poster canopy bed in Luc's room at the ranch, but bigger. A lot bigger! The wall across from her was almost entirely made of windows draped in what looked like silk in a taupe color. The walls were charcoal-gray with panels trimmed in white. Each paneled area held a large colorful landscape. The carpet was a soft silvery gray, trimmed in a wide black-and-white band. The accent color was a soft, faded blue that somehow blended in and stood out at the same time. The color scheme was exactly the same as Luc's room at the ranch house and she'd bet anything that Logan's room there was the same.

"Do you like it, sugar?" Logan asked.

"It's beautiful." Cassie walked over to one of the large chairs in front of the fireplace and ran her hand over the off-white-and-black-patterned fabric.

"I'll go get Cassie's bags," Logan said.

She turned as Logan left the room and Luc took her hand and led her toward a door to the left of the bed. It opened into a luxurious bathroom that was bigger than the living room in her apartment. Luc opened a panel by the shower, pushed a button, and hot water began to rain down from the ceiling as well as from several wall spouts. He crowded her back into the shower then watched the water run down her body as he unbuttoned his shirt and shrugged it from his broad shoulders. After tossing it toward the laundry basket, he unbuckled his belt and pulled it loose then tossed it on the counter. Cassie licked her lips in anticipation as she watched him unbutton his jeans then lower the zipper. She hummed an approval then grinned when she saw he went commando and he sent her a wink. Luc kicked his boots off then dropped his jeans. They fell to the floor but she didn't see them land as her focus was on his cock.

"You like what you see, sugar?"

"Yes, Luc."

He stepped in beside her and poured some shampoo into his hand then smoothed it through her hair. He backed her under one of the sprayers and rinsed the shampoo from her hair then slicked some conditioner through the golden strands. "You have beautiful hair."

Cassie stepped closer and leaned against him as he smoothed bath gel down her back and over her bottom. He rubbed circles on her butt cheeks then stooped down and washed her legs, making sure to run his hands between her legs and nudge them apart. "You have a beautiful cunt, sugar. All pink and bare just the way I like it." He leaned forward and blew his breath over her pussy then held onto her hips and used his tongue to part her swollen lips. Cassie gasped when he found her clit and wiggled the tip of his tongue over it. "Oh, Luc, that feels so good." Cassie moaned, then slid her legs farther apart as she combed her fingers through his hair. "I didn't know—oh, oh, so good."

Luc slid a finger into her and she stiffened and tried to pull away.

"Cassandra, am I hurting you?"

Cassie shook her head then answered, "No. I just, uh,—haven't let anyone touch me like this. Ever."

"If you want me to stop you're going to have to tell me to stop. Do you want me to stop?"

Cassie thought about it for a moment, wiggled, then said, "I want to try please, Luc." Her answer must have pleased him as he rubbed his hands up and down her legs then kissed her on the top of each thigh.

"Good girl. Keep your eyes open and on me," he said as he slid his finger back into her. He continued to suck on her clit then slowly added a second finger.

Cassie wiggled as he gently pulled them out then slid them back in, going a little deeper.

"You're so tight, sugar, but so responsive. Logan and I are going to make sure you love being fucked by us."

Cassie felt herself tighten and contract around his fingers. She shivered then tightened her fingers in his hair as the beginning of an orgasm flared in her lower belly.

"Come for me, sugar," Luc said, then sucked her clit into his mouth and gently bit down on it.

"Yes, oh, yes. Luc, Luc." Cassie screamed and the sound of her voice echoed off the shower walls. She held onto him as she shuddered and the orgasm slammed through her. Her legs gave out on her.

Luc caught her then pulled her up and held her against him until she was steady on her feet.

Cassie leaned against him and enjoyed the feeling of his arms around her as the warm water rained down on them. She rubbed her tummy against his hard cock and he tightened his arms around her until she squeaked. She opened her eyes and saw Logan watching them from the entrance to the shower. Luc clenched his hand in her hair, then pulled her head back and ran his lips over hers before sliding his tongue along the seam of her lips. Cassie opened for him and he danced his tongue over hers before he sucked it into his mouth and played with it. He nipped her bottom lip then raised his head and looked down at her.

"Logan's waiting for you, sugar." He swatted her bottom then pushed her toward Logan.

Logan wrapped her in a fluffy towel then carried her to the vanity and set her on it. Before she could catch her breath, he pushed her legs apart and lowered his mouth to her pussy. She groaned and leaned back against the mirror behind her. There was no denying these two Doms and really, why should she when they were giving her so much pleasure? Accepting that she wanted them, she spread her legs wider and slid her hands into Logan's hair, and kept her eyes on him. "Logan, oh, Logan, please, please." For a moment, she wondered if she should be ashamed of begging but quickly dismissed the idea. Luc tightened his hands on the inside of her thighs and held them farther apart and the sensation of being controlled by him washed over her. "Please, Logan, please."

Logan slid one, and then two fingers into her slick channel and twisted them. He sucked her clit into his mouth and held it captive between his teeth as he rapidly strummed his tongue over it. Relentlessly he drove her toward an explosive orgasm.

Cassie cried out when Luc clenched his fist in her hair and slammed his lips down onto hers and pumped his tongue into her mouth in a fucking motion. She grabbed his shoulders and held on as a huge wave of pleasure began in her belly and slammed through her body. She screamed her pleasure into Luc's mouth.

Logan licked Cassie's pussy a couple more times, then kissed her pussy, stood up, and shoved Luc out of the way. He kissed her mouth then hugged her to his chest and lowered her to the floor. "Now that we've had dessert, it's time to bake cookies."

Cassie blushed then realized she was standing naked in a bathroom with one naked man and one clothed man. She blinked and felt her face pale as black dots swam before her eyes.

Logan didn't reach for her. Instead he said, "Cassie, look at me. You're safe here with me and Luc. Take a deep breath, hold it for three seconds, and then let it out, slowly."

Cassie nodded and struggled to slow her breathing. She drew in a deep breath while she kept her eyes on Logan.

Logan waited until he saw her exhale then said, "Again, sugar."

Cassie took several more breaths then stepped forward and slid her arms around Logan's waist. "I'm sorry, Logan."

"You don't have anything to be sorry for, Cassandra." Luc shook out a large, dark blue T-shirt and held it out to Logan.

Logan took it and pulled it over Cassie's head then helped her get her arms through the armholes.

Luc's lips actually curved up at the corners. "You look cute but sleepy. We'll do the cookies tomorrow. Let me dry your hair then its bedtime."

Logan sat down on the edge of the bathtub and pulled Cassie onto his lap while Luc ran the warm air over her hair. After a few minutes, they apparently came to a decision of some kind because Luc put the dryer away, Logan picked Cassie up and carried her to the bedroom.

He placed her in the center of the huge bed before undressing and walking back into the bathroom. He passed Luc coming out.

"I locked up and turned on the security system when I was getting Cassie's bags," Logan said.

Luc nodded then walked over to the bed, naked, and slid under the covers on Cassie's left side. He pulled her into his arms. She scooted up until her head rested on his chest then slid one of her slender legs between his.

Logan came back into the room and slid into the bed on Cassie's right. He scooted up behind her and spooned her then said, "Lights. Out," and the room went dark.

"That's awesome," Cassie said.

"Luc's put a lot of technology in the house and the club," Logan said. "We'll program your voice into the system tomorrow."

"Okay." Cassie sighed then wiggled until she was comfortable. "Thank you, Luc. Thank you, Logan."

"For what, sugar?" Luc asked.

"For today."

"We'll always be here for you, sugar," Logan said.

Luc combed his fingers through Cassie's still damp hair, soothing her with his touch. "Go to sleep, Cassandra."

Cassie smiled at the gruffness of Luc's voice then closed her eyes and let herself relax into sleep. For the first time in years, she felt safe and fell asleep quickly.

"I'm going to kill them," Luc said into the darkness of the room.

"I'll help you," Logan said.

Chapter Four

Cassie became aware of three things as she woke. She was surrounded by warmth. She could hear the sound of breathing on either side of her and there were two very large hands on her belly, skin to skin. Her first instinct was to panic until she opened her eyes and the soft morning light revealed Luc on her left and Logan on her right. A little grin curved her lips. They even inhaled and exhaled at the same time and she wondered if there was anything the two of them didn't do together.

She took advantage of the opportunity to get a long, hard look at the two of them. Most people appeared softer or younger when they were asleep, but not these two. They were just as powerful asleep as they were fully awake and aware and she wondered how quickly they could move when they were threatened. Logan always seemed to have a quick smile and an even quicker hug while Luc could sit deceptively still and yet be aware of everything going on around him. His smile was non-existent and the only way she knew he was amused was by the depth of the lines by his eyes.

Comfortable, but completely awake, she stayed where she was for another couple minutes until she couldn't put off getting up any longer. Climbing over one of them was sure to wake them. Her best escape route was either up or down. She chose down and slid her hands beneath their hands and held them up as she slid to the bottom of the bed and then onto the floor. A silent sigh of relief left her lips as she tiptoed to the bathroom and quietly closed the door.

When she came out, they were still sleeping so she went hunting for the kitchen with the intention of getting the coffee brewing. On her way downstairs, she peeked into the other rooms. There were six large bedrooms with bathrooms upstairs. Downstairs she followed the hall through the house. She took note of the formal living room and dining room, a theater room and den, a sunroom at the back of the house, and then finally the kitchen.

She stopped in the door and stared at her idea of the perfect kitchen. The appliances were stainless steel. The range had eight burners with a grill down the center. The wall next to it held two large ovens and at least one of them was convection. The fridges were commercial with glass fronts that made her drool with envy. There were enough granite counters to host a marathon cooking session. A large central island sat in the center of the room, surrounded by backless stools. The large double sinks were situated in the center of the outer wall and the large windows above them let in a flood of natural light. She opened a door at the other side of the room and found a large well-stocked pantry, and grabbed the ingredients for peanut butter chocolate chip cookies and carried them to the island.

Twenty minutes later the first baking sheet of dough was in the oven. Cassie was at the bar with her first cup of coffee when the backdoor opened. A few seconds later the sounds of the alarm system being turned off reached her and then a slender woman with short, curly hair and doe-like brown eyes entered the kitchen.

"Who are you?" the lady asked.

"Are you Isabella?" Cassie smiled when she saw the aqua streaks in the woman's light brown hair.

"I asked you first?"

"I'm Cassie," she said. "Luc and Logan's, uh, guest."

Isabella laughed, and Cassie smiled again. Count on Luc and Logan to have an outspoken housekeeper with aqua hair and a joyful-sounding laugh.

When Isabella stopped laughing she pointed at Cassie's chest. "I recognize that T-shirt. You're no guest. How's your butt?"

Cassie blushed and Isabella laughed again. "There's never a dull moment around those two boys." Then she sniffed the air and asked, "What's that smell?"

"Cookies."

Isabella poured herself a cup of coffee and sat down across from Cassie. "They've already got you cooking for them. Must be serious."

"I'm in a little bit of trouble and they're protecting me. That's all." Cassie shrugged. "I like to cook."

"Your reason for being here doesn't matter to me. I hate to cook. My advice to you is don't give those two charmers their way all the time. They're spoiled enough. Try to shake them up every now and then."

"It's just temporary. A few months at most."

Isabella laughed again then put her finger to her lips and winked as the sound of running feet came from the direction of the stairway. Her expression changed from friendly to disgruntled. "It just isn't right. A young girl like you being exposed to those two lechers. I think you should move in with me," she said just as Luc and Logan rushed into the room and slid to a stop next to the breakfast bar.

Luc growled and grabbed Cassie. "Ours. Hands off." He glared at Isabella.

"Yeah," Logan said. "Hands off." He ran his hand down Cassie's hair. "Don't listen to her, sugar. She needs a spanking."

"I'd like to see the man brave enough to try," Isabella winked at Cassie as she got up. "I have things to do. Call me when breakfast is ready."

Cassie giggled as Isabella left the room. A second later the oven timer went off. "Luc, put me down, please. I need to get the cookies out of the oven."

Luc set her down then patted her on the bottom as he and Logan slid onto the stools around the island. They watched as she took the pan of cookies from the oven and set it on a cooling rack before sliding the second prepared pan into the oven.

Luc reached over and grabbed a hot cookie from the plate. He tossed it back and forth between his hands to cool it as Cassie set two cups of coffee in front of them along with the cream and sugar. She slid two cookies onto a plate for Logan and one cookie onto a plate for Luc then moved the rest of them to a platter.

"What do you two want for breakfast?"

"Cookies," Luc and Logan said.

Cassie grabbed the platter of cookies and moved it farther away, then opened the fridge and gathered the ingredients for southwestern omelets. "Who usually does the cooking?" she asked, curious since the kitchen was so well stocked.

"Isabella has a lady named Doris who helps her clean and she cooks for her unless she's pissed off at her. Doris won't cook for us, though," Logan said.

Cassie's brows flew up and she laughed. "Is she ex-military, too?"

"No," Luc said. "Just misguided."

"By Isabella," Logan said. "They started a society. It's called 'Southern Women Against Terrible Spankers.'"

"S.W.A.T.S.?" Cassie asked then laughed until tears covered her cheeks. "I love it. I'm joining just so I can attend one of their meetings. How many members do they have?"

"Two," Luc said then stood up and moved around the island. He pulled her up against him and looked down at her. "When I woke up this morning, I expected to see you, not Logan. New rule—don't go anywhere without one of us means anywhere, inside or outside. Do you understand?"

Cassie nodded then said, "Yes, Luc."

"Good." He patted her ass. "Now give me another cookie."

"Nutrition first," Cassie said, then added, "Logan, put those back." She turned and caught Logan with two cookies in his hand.

"Damn, how do women do that?" Logan asked.

"It's a secret only women are allowed to know." Cassie wiggled out of Luc's arms and reached for a cutting board. "Southwestern omelets and toast okay?"

Logan put one cookie back, bit into the second one and grinned at Luc's scowl. Cassie sighed, picked up a cookie, handed it to Luc, and then said, "I'll have breakfast ready in just a minute." The buzzer went off and she removed the pan from the oven.

Luc retrieved the milk and orange juice from the fridge and set them on the table while Logan set the table with silverware. A few minutes later Isabella wandered into the room and sat down at the table.

"Smells good," Isabella said.

Cassie smiled and buttered the last piece of toast then grabbed the platter of omelets and set it on the table before sitting down. Luc and Logan sat on either side of her. Luc poured the milk while Logan poured the juice.

"I don't drink milk," Cassie said, wrinkling her nose at the small glass of milk Luc set by her plate.

"You need calcium," Luc said. "Do you like chocolate or strawberry?"

"Chocolate, of course," Cassie said.

Luc disappeared into the pantry then returned with a bottle of chocolate mix. He squirted some into her glass then stirred it.

"Thank you, Luc," Cassie said.

"You can thank me properly tonight," Luc said.

"We're taking you with us to Club Mystique after breakfast," Logan said. "Addison, Jenna, and Marisol are going to meet you at the spa."

"What time? I'll need to clean up the kitchen and shower and get dressed."

"You cook, I'll clean," Isabella said.

Cassie smiled at her. "Thank you, Isabella."

"You're welcome," Isabella said. "By the way I want to talk to you about joining my society."

"No," Luc and Logan said, together.

Cassie smiled and shrugged. "Sorry, Isabella."

"That's okay. You'll come to your senses eventually."

"No, she won't," Logan said and Cassie laughed, realizing she had laughed more in the last few days than she had in the previous eight years.

"Time to get showered and dressed, sugar," Luc said. "Logan and I have to be at the club by nine."

Cassie took his hand and he twirled her around and swatted her bottom then urged her toward the door. Logan dropped his fork, stood up, and followed them.

As soon as they entered the bedroom, Luc tugged Cassie to a stop then stripped the T-shirt over her head. "Bend over the bed, sugar."

Cassie lowered her eyes then stepped back. "Permission to speak, please, Sir."

"Permission granted," Luc said.

"Did I do something wrong, Sir?"

Logan chuckled. "No, sugar. Luc and I just want to put our mark on you before you go to the spa."

Cassie moved to the side of the bed. She looked at them then spread her legs and slowly bent over. She went up on tiptoes and stuck her bottom up and out. "Like this, Sirs?" She gave them a little tantalizing wiggle.

Luc moved behind her, and ran his hands over her ass, then gave each cheek a squeeze. "Yes, sugar, just like that." He chafed his hands over her one more time then swatted her left cheek. Logan moved to her right side and swatted her right cheek. They went back and forth, one after the other, until her butt was stinging and she was wiggling to get away and yet pressing back into their hands.

Luc bent over and ran his lips over her butt cheeks. "You have the sweetest ass I've ever seen, sugar. It's a beautiful rosy pink now. Beautiful." He dropped another kiss on her bottom before he stepped back. "I'll be hard and thinking about your ass all day."

Logan leaned over, kissed the back of her neck, and chafed her ass with his hands. He laughed when she squeaked. "You have the prettiest ass, sugar. So plump and soft." He kissed her neck then bumped his hard cock against her hip and smiled before he led her into the bathroom. Working together they had her showered and dried off in less time than it took her to decide which gel scent she wanted to use. Luc pulled a sundress from the closet and dropped it over her head and buttoned it as Logan stood by with her sandals. Once she was dressed they stood back and examined her then Luc stepped behind her and braided her hair. Logan handed him a leather thong to tie the end and then they grunted their approval.

"The club has good security so you'll be safe in the spa. When your appointments are over, we'll come and get you. Don't go with anyone else unless it's one of our brothers or Thor," Logan said.

"What about Mac or Ben?" Cassie asked, then waited while they came to a decision.

"Ben and Mac but nobody else from Thor's agency. Do you understand?"

"Yes, Luc."

Luc almost smiled at her. "Excellent. Tomorrow night we're going to Club Mystique. It's always crowded on Friday night."

"Luc and I want to show you off, sugar. We're planning an erotic spanking scene. Do you think you can handle that?"

"No restraints?" Cassie asked.

"No restraints," Luc said, a little frown in his eyes.

Won't people think that's odd?" Cassie asked, biting her lip.

"Don't worry about what people think, sugar. We don't," Logan said.

Cassie smiled. Of course, the Dominating Duo wouldn't care what anyone else thought.

"Do you like to role play, Cassie?" Luc asked.

"I don't know. I've never actually done it but I've fantasized about it."

"Then, we'll have fun finding out," Logan said, "but Friday night we're just going to do an erotic spanking scene and you'll have your safewords to use if you get scared."

Cassie smiled. "Thank you, Sirs."

"We're going to spank your beautiful ass, finger your pretty little cunt, and have you suck our cocks, sugar," Luc said. "Today, Logan and I want you to think about the scene we've planned. If there's anything you want to add, or think you wouldn't like we expect you to discuss it with us this evening. Understand?"

Cassie smiled. "Yes, Luc."

"We want to use a vibrator on your sweet little pussy and taste your sweet cream. Do you agree?" Logan asked.

Cassie nodded. "Yes, Logan."

"One last question," Luc said. "Where do you stand on anal sex?"

Cassie remembered the two days the men had held her and shivered, then paled. "I don't think I'd like it."

Luc moved over to her, grasped her braid at her nape, and then tipped her head back. "Are you afraid we'll hurt you or are you opposed to anal sex?"

Cassie looked into his eyes and could see his concern for her. "I'm afraid it will hurt."

Luc kissed her once, then again. "Thank you for being honest, Cassandra."

Logan pulled her into his arms then brushed his lips over hers. "We won't play with your ass at the club for now. We will eventually touch you there but only here at the house. We'll take it slow and easy until you're ready."

"What if I'm never ready for that?" Cassie looked away, worried that she would disappoint them.

"Then, sugar, there's a lot of other things you'll love," Logan said.

Luc frowned and sent Logan their signal for "wuss" then turned Cassie toward him. "Sugar, once we start playing with your ass you're going to love it so much you're going to be begging us to fuck it."

Just the thought of having Luc and Logan inside her at the same time made her ache with need. It was something she had always wanted even though she was no longer sure she could handle the experience. Logan moved up behind her and pressed his chest against her back. They surrounded her with their arms and she signed with pleasure. "I promise I'll try."

Luc kissed the tip of her nose. "That's my brave girl."

Logan kissed the back of her neck. "Let's go. The sooner we take care of business the sooner we can get back home and take care of you, sugar."

* * * *

Cassie groaned with pleasure as the masseuse worked on the muscles of her shoulders. From the other side of the curtain, she heard Marisol say something in Spanish and the masseuse answered back in Spanish then laughed.

So far the four of them had been given manicures, pedicures, and the inevitable waxing. Cassie giggled as she remembered the curses from Jenna during her treatment. She opened her eyes and admired the rosy red color on her fingernails before she dropped her head back into the headrest of the massage table and looked down. An image of herself was reflected back to her in the conveniently placed mirror.

She stared at herself as she thought about Luc and Logan. They would keep her safe until they found out what she had done, and then they would hate her. A tear fell onto the mirror followed by several more. The pool they formed distorted her image just as her faulty memory hid the truth of the past from her. All she knew was one moment she had been a happy teenager with a father she adored and the next she had been a terrified, and enraged, young woman standing beside her father's grave.

Would Luc and Logan forgive her if she told them how she had gotten involved with the drug gang? Would it be better to tell them or keep her secrets and hope they never found out? She bit her lip and admitted to herself that when they learned the truth she wouldn't be able to bear the hatred and contempt she would see in their eyes. She also knew she would endanger them if she stayed without telling them everything she had remembered. She shouldn't stay but she didn't want to go.

Lost in her thoughts, she was startled when the masseuse covered her with a warm blanket then left the room. She pulled in a deep breath and decided there was no time like the present to leave. She sat up then smothered her gasp of surprise when she saw Addison, Jenna, and Marisol lined up against the wall, watching her.

Addison smiled. "Hi, Cassie. Feeling better now?"

Oh, shit they know something's up. She decided to try to bluff her way out of what looked like an intervention of some kind. "Hi, Addison. Everybody done? Time to go?"

"Not yet," Jenna said. "We wanted to talk to you about yesterday."

"Oh." Cassie looked down. "What about it?"

"You fell asleep before the end of the meeting," Addison said. "You missed Thor asking why you were targeted by those men."

Cassie bit her lip. "I, uh—"

"Cassie, we all have secrets and we want you to know your secret is safe with us," Addison said. "For instance, I know a lot of things that I haven't gotten around to telling Cade yet and I don't intend to tell him until he asks me about them."

"And, I speak exceptional English but Thor doesn't know and I don't intend to tell him until I'm ready to do so," Marisol said. "I was in his office yesterday and I heard the conversation between you and Luc. Thor intends to find out why you were targeted."

"And, well, I don't have a secret yet, but someday I will and when I do Addison, Marisol, and you will help me keep it," Jenna said.

Cassie gave a little laugh then tears glazed her eyes. "It's not that simple. If Luc and Logan knew my secret they would hate me. You would hate me."

Addison grabbed Cassie's hand and squeezed it. "We are your friends, Cassie. Your best friends. No matter what we will always love and protect you just as you will always love and protect us."

A sob escaped Cassie's lips and suddenly she was crying, her shoulders jerking with the intensity of her grief. Addison, Marisol, and Jenna huddled around her.

The masseuse pulled the curtain back, took one look, and said, "There's a private lounge at the end of the corridor. I'll bring you a pitcher of ice water and a tray of snacks."

Addison tugged on Cassie's hand and the four of them moved to the lounge and made themselves comfortable. As soon as the promised tray had been delivered, Jenna leaned forward and said, "Okay, talk."

Cassie shook her head.

Marisol bumped Jenna aside then took Cassie's hand. "Cassie, my father is a very bad man. He is the head of a drug cartel and he has done many bad things but he is my father and I love him and he loves me and my sister, Valentina. I tell you this so you know that all of us have things in our past that are not good. Things we had no control over. Do you have something like this?"

Cassie glanced at Marisol, then at Addison and Jenna. "I can't tell you because it wouldn't be fair to you. If I did and you kept it from Cade and Jackson, it would be like you were lying to them."

"That's true," Jenna said. "Jackson would be really pissed off."

Addison bit her lip, nodded, then grinned and said, "Jenna and I will leave the room and you can tell Marisol."

"Yes, I have no obligation to tell the farmer what I know," Marisol said, then laughed.

Addison and Jenna hugged Cassie then left the room.

Marisol sat down next to Cassie and held her hand. "Now, tell me this sorrow."

Cassie tried to smile but couldn't. "When I was seventeen, a girl named Julia Wilson moved into my neighborhood with her parents, Don and Linda Wilson. I didn't know her very well but we began going places together. She had an older boyfriend named Jimmy but everyone called him Ice. I didn't know why until later."

"He was involved with drugs?"

"Yes and he would have Julia take packages to his friends."

"Drugs?" Marisol asked.

Cassie nodded. "When I found out what was in the packages, I tried to talk Julia into going to the police. I didn't realize she knew all along that she was delivering drugs."

"That's when they abducted you," Marisol said.

Cassie nodded. "Yes, but I've only recently begun remembering a lot of this. It's hard to sort out what I've always remembered and what I've only recently remembered. Does that make sense?"

"Yes," Marisol said. "What happened to Julia?"

"I don't know. I think she and her family moved away while I was healing. I never saw her again after I was taken."

"You need to write down everything you can remember about her and Jimmy and his friend. Her parents, too. Name, age, birthday if you know it, her address, phone number, what kind of car she drove," Marisol said. "Maybe we can find a sketch artist to draw them."

"I already have a file on each person I remember. I've also done drawings of them." Then seeing Marisol's questioning glance, she said, "Before my father was killed I wanted to go to art school. After I was taken I decided to do something in law enforcement instead."

"Thor was going to talk to you about this tonight but he has been called back to Dallas. He said he probably wouldn't be back until the day of the wedding. Do you have the sketches and information with you?"

"Yes. I keep one copy with me at all times. It's a good thing I do because the backup copy was stolen from my apartment a couple weeks ago." Cassie began to cry again. "I don't want to tell Luc and Logan. I'm afraid they won't believe me, but if I keep this from them it's the same thing as lying to them. I thought I could stay here but I can't without putting everyone in danger. That's why I've decided I have to leave."

"No, you can't leave. I know the kind of people who are hunting for you. They are killers, Cassie," Marisol said.

"This will change everything," Cassie said. "Luc and Logan won't trust me now. Nobody will."

"Addison, Jenna and I will trust you," Marisol said. "Have you signed a contract with Luc and Logan?"

Cassie shook her head, her newly conditioned and trimmed hair fell over her shoulders and caught the light in the room. "We negotiated one but haven't signed it yet."

"Then you must tell them before you sign the contract and let Thor listen. Perhaps you can do this with Thor on the phone again, but your first obligation is to Luc and Logan. You were a young girl when this happened to you and you must remember you were a victim of evil men." Marisol gave her a searching look. "Do you want to stay with Luc and Logan, Cassie?"

Cassie nodded. "More than I ever thought possible. They're the only men I've wanted to be with since I was seventeen."

Marisol smiled. "You have been brave for a long time, Cassie, but now it is time to fight for your men."

* * * *

Cassie examined herself in the mirror, then smiled. She loved the dress Luc had picked out for her. It had a high waist with cap sleeves. It reminded her of a Victorian gown, except the material was so sheer it didn't conceal anything. The hem ended less than an inch below her butt cheeks and her nipples, which were already hard in anticipation of the coming evening, pushed against the bodice. The white lace tops of her thigh-high hose were several inches below the hem of her skirt.

Behind her Addison whistled then giggled and Jenna joined in.

"Wow," Jenna said, walking around Cassie. "Did Logan and Luc give you that outfit?"

Cassie nodded. "I never realized I have so many curves."

"Yum," Jenna said. "If I was gay I'd totally do you."

"Me, too," Addison said, then smiled, and stepped back and stared at Cassie and Jenna as a gleam appeared in her eyes.

"Ah, oh," Jenna said. "Addison's thinking up a scheme and you and I are going to be a part of it, Cassie."

"Is that bad?" Cassie asked.

"Yes, always," Jenna said.

"No," Addison said. "I was just thinking Cade's birthday is coming up in November. A couple weeks ago I caught him and Jackson watching the single subs doing an all-girls shower scene. Cade and Jackson really enjoyed watching it."

"No," Jenna said then looked at Cassie. "Say no, Cassie."

"Uh, no?" Cassie said.

"Yes," Addison said. "It would be fun. The three of us could do a shower scene for Cade, Jackson, Logan and Luc. They would love it." She smiled again. "Really love it."

"Buy him a tie," Jenna said.

"He already has a huge collection of ties," Addison said.

"Wait," Cassie said. "I might be interested in doing this."

"Traitor," Jenna said.

Cassie laughed. "I have a lot of catching up to do." She looked at Addison. "What would we have to do?"

"Well, not as much as they did but we could get in the shower together and use the sponges to wash each other, maybe touch each other's breasts. Things like that."

"Oh, god," Jenna said. "Jackson would totally love that."

"I think Luc and Logan would, too," Cassie said.

Addison clapped her hands together like a child with a secret. "Then, it's a deal. I'll make all the plans."

Jenna groaned then kicked off her shoes and placed them in her locker. She adjusted her hand-embroidered, dark blue corset. Ready?"

"Not yet." Addison pulled a piece of paper out of her locker. Jenna recognized it and snorted. Addison gave her a shushing motion then said, "Cassie, I have something for you. When I was having trouble with Cade—"

"You're still having trouble with Cade," Jenna said, and Addison gave her another shushing motion.

"As I was saying—when I was having trouble with Cade, my friend Maggie Lamont gave me this brochure. It really helped me and I want you to have a copy because I think it will help you, too."

Cassie took the brochure and her brows went up as she read the title. "Why are you giving me a brochure about training horses? I don't even know how to ride, Addison."

"Open it," Addison said.

Cassie read part of it, then gasped and giggled and turned it over in her hands. "I don't understand. Someone's gone through it and marked out the word 'horse' and replaced it with the word 'Dom' and then they marked out the word 'human' and replaced it with the word 'sub.'"

"It helps you figure out how to deal with your Doms," Addison said. "I think you should use this rule tonight." Addison pointed to a rule on the brochure.

"'Let your Dom know you appreciate him by giving him a treat,'" Cassie read out loud. "Like what? Cookies? They really like cookies."

Addison and Jenna giggled. "No, not that kind of treat," Addison said. "A BDSM treat."

"You're afraid of restraints, right?" Jenna asked.

Cassie nodded.

"But, we have some breakaway restraints for you," Jenna said holding up several pairs of black bands. "If you panic you just tug on them really hard and they come apart."

"Do you think you could do something like that?" Addison asked. "We could put them on you now and you can see how easily they come apart."

"I don't know." Cassie took one of the bands from Jenna and examined it. She snapped it between her hands and it broke. "They're really just for show?"

"Yes, and we would be there to protect you." Jenna said.

"The entire time?"

"Yes, from start to finish," Addison said.

Cassie took the bands and examined them to make sure they were all the same. "Is that something Luc and Logan always do? Restrain their sub?"

"Absolutely," Addison said, "especially Luc. He really gets off on it and it makes him really hard." She held out her hands about eight inches apart and grinned.

"Ewww, Addison," Jenna said.

"Hey, I'm only human," Addison said.

"You're a voyeur," Jenna said.

"Look who's talking," Addison said. "I've seen you watching, too."

Cassie laughed then said, "How can I say no when I have you two watching my back?"

"We'll be watching more than your back," Addison said, grinning.

Cassie rolled the bands into tight coils then closed her hands around them. "Then, all I can say is I'll try. Okay?"

"Just the fact that you're willing to try will make them happy," Jenna said and Addison nodded.

"Okay, let's go before I change my mind." Cassie pulled in a deep breath and tightened her hands on the bands. She led the way out of the women's locker room and into the main room of the club. She had been in this room several times over the years but every time she entered it she felt as if she was stepping back in time. The modernized décor of an old west saloon never failed to please her. The artist in her imagined the Doms at the tables as fierce adventurers, some outlaws and some lawmen, while the ladies in the room were dance hall girls and ladies of the night. "We should get the subs together and teach them the cancan."

"That would be so amazing," Addison said.

"And fun," Jenna said as Jackson slid his arms around her.

"Excellent idea, sugar," Luc said as he and Logan stepped up behind Cassie.

"This way, pet." Logan took her hand and led her across the dimly lit room to a well-lit, raised area in the center of the long wall. Logan lifted her to the stage then he and Luc stepped up behind her.

Cassie moved several steps away, turned, then gracefully went to her knees. She slid them far apart then placed her fisted hands on the top of her thighs. She kept her eyes down as she waited for Luc or Logan to tell her to look up at them. Around her she heard the soft sound of people moving closer to the stage. She straightened her shoulders and licked her lips nervously and swallowed. She used her peripheral vision, expecting to see a spanking bench on the stage. Instead she saw what looked like a miniature version of parallel bars. They were connected with a narrow center beam and the entire thing was padded in red leather with chrome eyebolts where restraints could be secured.

Luc and Logan drew her attention back to them when they moved to stand in front of her.

"Cassandra, look at us," Luc said.

Cassie met Luc's eyes, then glanced at Logan and her stomach tightened as more moisture gathered between her legs. Two pairs of lust-filled eyes stared down at her. She met them for a moment then let her eyes drift down. They were dressed in open black leather vests, faded blue jeans, and cowboy boots. The jeans hung low on their hips, revealing every bronze inch of their washboard abs. Saliva filled her mouth and she licked her lips then swallowed as she raised her eyes to their faces. She let her hunger for them show on her face.

"Pet, look at me," Logan said.

Cassie obeyed Logan's command.

"You know better than to fist your hands."

Cassie raised her hands and opened them, palms up, revealing the two restraints she held.

Logan gave her a wide smile while deep lines fanned out around Luc's eyes. They each reached for a restraint. Logan secured the inch-wide black band on her right wrist while Luc secured the one he held on her left wrist then together they lifted her to her feet.

Luc curved his arm around her waist, lifting her as he grasped her hair at her nape and pulled her head back. His mouth crashed down onto hers, his tongue pushed between her lips, demanding entrance. She opened to him, tangling her tongue with his as she felt Logan press his chest against her back, his heat warming her. Logan's hands cupped her breasts. His fingers strummed over her nipples then pinched them. She hummed with pleasure and Luc nipped her bottom lip. His tongue made one final sweep of her mouth before he sucked her bottom lip into his mouth, gave it another little nip, and then released her. His eyes blazed with arousal as he lowered her to her feet.

Logan spun her around and his mouth covered hers, his tongue sweeping over her lips then stroking between them before pressing into her mouth. Luc's hands cupped her shoulders then slid down her arms to her wrists. His fingers traced over the restraints as he kissed her until she felt faint. She wiggled when she felt Luc's erection press against her ass as he bit her neck. Logan sucked her bottom lip into his mouth then placed several small kisses on her lips before releasing her. He smiled down at her then his smile disappeared, his demeanor changed, and Cassie fought the need to lower her eyes.

"Good girl," Logan said. "Keep your eyes on us at all times."

Luc turned her to him then led her over to a chair. "Place your foot on the seat and remove your stockings. Slowly." He stepped back to stand beside Logan.

Cassie remembered what they had said about how much pleasure it would give them to show her off while knowing only they could touch her. A small smiled curved her lips as she gracefully set her right leg on the chair and slowly bent over. She felt her dress ride up and knew the people watching could see everything. She glanced at Luc and Logan and knew from the expressions on their faces that they knew it too.

She pinched the top of her hose then rolled it down her leg and bent farther forward until she pulled it over her toes then dropped it to the floor. She lowered her leg and did the same with her left stocking then turned to face Luc and Logan and waited for their next instruction.

"Come here," Luc said.

Cassie moved to him and Logan moved behind her and pulled her dress over her head then handed it to her. "Fold it then place it on the stool and return to me." She followed his directions then returned to him. He smoothed his hand down her back. "Feet apart, hands behind your head and fingers interlaced, pet."

Cassie followed his command and waited as Luc and Logan shrugged out of their vests then walked around her. Their hands roamed over her body until she couldn't keep track of whose hand was touching her and where. Fingers slid between her legs and stroked into her. She watched as Logan licked his fingers then kissed her and she tasted herself on his lips. When he raised his head, Luc took his place and kissed her, giving her another taste.

Luc ended the kiss then hooked his arm around her waist and guided her to the contraption. "Logan had this made for you. Step up here"—he pointed out two raised places for her feet to go—"then bend over and rest your torso on the central beam."

Cassie followed his instructions. She adjusted her feet until she felt comfortable then leaned forward. The padded central beam was wider where her tummy rested and narrower between her breasts. She wiggled into position, then grasped the handholds and relaxed. Even though she was a lot shorter than Luc and Logan, this put her at the right height for them to be able to fuck her or for her to be able to suck their cocks.

Luc and Logan each took hold of one of her wrists and secured it.

"Give these a little tug," Luc said.

Cassie tugged on them and for a moment she wanted to panic but then Luc ran his hands down her arms again and touched the bands on her wrists. His eyes met hers and she could see how the sight of her in restraints affected him.

Logan gathered her hair and placed it over her right shoulder. "Okay, sugar?"

"Yes, Sir."

They walked around her, testing to make sure her weight was evenly distributed on the padded surface and her feet wouldn't slip off the footrests. Luc circled around then crouched down in front of her. "Look at me, sugar. Logan is going to give you ten swats and you're going to suck my cock. Keep your eyes on me."

Cassie smiled at him and nodded. A second later she felt Logan's hands stroking over her ass then down her legs to her ankles and back up. His hands closed on either side of her waist, squeezed, then moved up her back to her shoulders. He bent over and nuzzled her neck then nipped her ear. "Brace yourself, sugar."

In front of her Luc kicked off his boots then unbuttoned and unzipped his jeans. He stepped out of them, tossed them aside and turned back to her. Pre-cum covered the head of his cock and she licked her lips as he took his cock in hand, stroked it a couple times, then swiped the head over her lips. She licked her lips and opened her mouth. He pressed forward and she took as much of his cock into her mouth as she could. She relaxed her jaw and he slid in deeper as she felt Logan rub his hands over her ass cheeks again then swat her left cheek.

Cassie gasped, and tears filled her eyes as a muffled cry left her mouth. Before she could take a breath, another swat landed on her right ass cheek. Logan rubbed her ass again and the sting changed to warmth and zinged to her clit. She wiggled as moisture leaked from her pussy and ran over her clit, tickling it. Logan's fingers slid over her labia then between them. He spread the moisture around then circled her clit. She wiggled and he swatted her ass again then repeated the same stroking between her legs. She pressed back into each swat and moaned with pleasure as she tried to concentrate on pleasuring Luc.

She whipped her tongue around his cock, sucking and hollowing her cheeks as he fucked into her mouth. When he bumped the back of her throat she struggled to control her gag reflex and he pulled back.

"Breath through your nose, sugar," Luc said.

She relaxed her jaw and took him as deeply as she could as she stroked him with her tongue, sucked on him, then swallowed. He moaned and she felt his body freeze. He pulled his cock from her mouth, then surprised her by dropping to his knees in front of her. He grasped her hair and kissed her, hard. He stared into her eyes. "Good girl." He stood up and moved away his cock still rock hard.

Logan took his place. "Look at me, sugar."

Cassie looked up but her attention got caught on Logan's hands as he unbuttoned then unzipped his jeans and shoved them down. He had already removed his boots and his feet were bare and for some reason she found the sight arousing. He stepped out of the jeans and kicked them to the side. She examined his body from his feet to his cock, licked her lips, and then raised her eyes to his face.

"Open your mouth, sugar."

Cassie licked her lips again then opened her mouth as Logan pressed the head of his cock to her mouth. She licked the drop of pre-cum then stiffened her tongue and slid it through the slit at the top.

She wiggled her tongue and felt him jerk then heard him moan. She would have smiled if her lips hadn't been stretched so tightly around his cock.

"Eyes on me, sugar."

Cassie focused on him as he slid deeper into her mouth. She slicked her tongue over his cock from side to side as he fucked her mouth in shallow thrusts.

"Luc is going to spank you. He's not going to be easy on you. If you bite me, I'll use a crop on your ass."

Cassie shivered, with fear and arousal, as she sucked on Logan's cock and felt Luc's hands sliding over her ass. He slid his hands over her butt cheeks then between her legs. One finger and then two pressed into her. He circled her clit then stroked his slick fingers over her anus, once and then again. She wiggled and tried to move her legs farther apart, offering herself to him.

She heard a rusty chuckle from behind her and Logan's eyes flew up in surprise, then back down to her. She watched him as she wiggled again and pressed her ass back toward Luc.

"That's it, sugar. Give Luc what he needs," Logan said.

Luc pressed on her anus again and she felt his finger slide into her a short distance. She caught her breath, moaned, and pressed back again. Inside her head she was screaming, "Yes, yes, oh, my god, yes."

Luc's finger slid away and she heard a whooshing sound and then fire struck her ass. She screamed around Logan's cock. The burn lit up the nerves in her ass cheek then struck her clit so hard she shook. He landed another swat and she shook again. Logan thrust into her mouth and she hummed a moan of pleasure on the head of his cock as Luc swatted her a couple more times. The harder he swatted her the harder she sucked on Logan's cock and the more aroused she became.

Luc stroked his hands over her ass then down her legs. She felt his breath on her pussy a split second before his tongue swept over one side of her pussy then the other then down the center, then wiggled its way into her. She screamed around Logan's cock as Luc ate at her pussy the same way he had eaten at her mouth earlier, devouring her, tasting her. Aroused more than she had ever thought possible, she sucked harder on Logan's cock then swallowed on the head and he groaned.

"Sugar, you are really good at this." Logan threaded his fingers into her hair and gripped her head as he smiled.

Luc continued swatting her. She tried to keep count but gave up at eight and concentrated on pleasuring Logan. She flicked her tongue over and around his cock then swallowed on the head, once then again.

Luc moved up behind her and she felt his cock press into the crack of her ass as he leaned over her and the heat of his chest warmed her back. He nuzzled her neck, his breath hot. "Sugar, my cock is so hard. I want to fuck you." He nuzzled her neck again. "Are you going to let me?"

Cassie released Logan's cock but kept her eyes on him as she made her decision. "Yes, oh, yes, please, Luc."

"Slow and easy, sugar." Luc kissed her neck, then sucked on it and left a mark behind. "If you get scared use your safeword."

"Look at me, sugar," Logan said. "Don't come until I give you permission." He pressed his cock into her mouth again.

Cassie tried to concentrate on pleasing Logan but couldn't help letting her focus slide to what Luc was doing to her. She pursed her lips around Logan's cock then flicked her tongue over him. She slid her lips until only his cockhead was in her mouth, then slid back down, taking him as deep as she could. Behind her she felt Luc rub the head of his cock against her pussy before he pressed into her. She froze, her breath beginning to catch in her throat as she tried to fight off the fear building in her chest.

Logan tightened his fingers in her hair. "Sugar, eyes on me." He drew his cock from between her lips. "Where are you, Cassie?"

Cassie took several deep breaths, and pushed her fear away. "With you and Luc, Sir."

"Yes, you're safe with me and Luc." Logan smiled into her eyes. "Ready?"

"Yes, Sir."

Logan nodded to Luc then touched the tip of his cock to Cassie's lips. She opened for him and he let her work at getting his cock into her mouth again. He saw her eyes widen and looked up in time to see Luc burrow into her then pull out and press back in again as he tightened his hands on her hips. Luc rocked against her, then opened his eyes and for the first time in years Logan saw the brother he had known as a child. "I've got you covered, bro."

Luc acknowledged him with a single nod of his head then slowly fucked Cassandra in long, deep thrusts. He felt her tighten around him and he knew she was close to an orgasm. He reached beneath her and slicked his fingers over her clit. "Come now, Cassandra." He watched her shudder then heard her muffled wails of pleasure before he dropped his head back and continued a slow, deep slide into her.

Cassie felt another explosive orgasm building and wasn't sure she could survive it. Luc was so deep inside her. Each deep thrust increased her need to come again. Logan pushed his cock to the back of her throat and she swallowed on it and moaned with the building pleasure. She tightened her hands on the handholds and pressed back toward Luc. He responded by beginning a pounding rhythm. Cassie wailed with pleasure and swallowed hard, tightening her throat around Logan's cock.

He groaned then tightened his hands in her hair and said, "Now. Come now, sugar."

The orgasm ripped through her, shaking her body as she screamed and felt Logan's cum fill her mouth. She swallowed as quickly as she could as she shuddered with pleasure. The muscles of her pussy fluttered around Luc's cock as he came and she felt him flood her with his hot semen. She held Logan captive for a moment then released him and dropped her head, exhausted. Luc reached beneath her and pinched her clit.

"Come now, Cassandra." Luc's voice demanded obedience as he slid a finger into her ass.

Cassie screamed his name as her clit exploded with pleasure that went on and on.

Logan and Luc stroked her back then Luc leaned over her, kissed her nape, and said, "Such a brave girl."

Logan removed the restraints while Luc covered her with a soft blanket then picked her up and carried her off the stage. Logan grabbed their clothes and followed closely behind them. Luc dropped onto the couch and cuddled her on his lap while Logan pulled on his jeans, vest and boots then took Cassie from Luc and held her while Luc dressed.

Luc dropped down next to them and handed Logan an open bottle of water before he pulled Cassie's feet onto his lap. "How's she doing?"

Logan smiled then looked down at Cassie's still face. "Dozing."

Luc lounged back in the corner of the couch with his legs stretched out and his ankles crossed. He laid his head back and closed his eyes. A moment later, he reached over and took Cassie out of Logan's arms. He turned her until she faced Logan, then smoothed her hair with his hand. "Are her feet cold?"

Logan reached over, felt her toes, and then tucked the blanket around her feet. He took a sip of water then leaned back in his corner of the couch and laughed. Luc sent him a questioning look and he said, "I just realized this is the first time I've ever done a scene in the club and not been aware of the crowd watching us."

Luc looked out into the main room. Several people watched them, and he caught others looking away. He looked down at Cassie then back at Logan. "Let's go home."

"It's early yet."

"I'm taking Cassandra home." Luc stood up. "You can come or not."

"No, I'm coming." Logan capped the water bottle then rose. "I'll tell Hank he's in charge."

"I'll meet you at your truck." Luc carried Cassie to the private entrance he and his brothers used and strode to Logan's truck.

Cassie stirred in his arms and looked up at him. "What's going on?"

"We're going home."

"Okay." She snuggled against him then buried her head against his neck. She sniffed him then licked him, once, then again.

"Baby, you keep that up and I'm going to fuck you again."

"Okay," Cassie breathed against his neck.

The word had barely left her lips before the blanket was on the ground and he had her shoved up against the side of the truck. He unbuttoned his jeans and shoved them down just far enough to expose his dick before he pulled her legs around his waist and thrust into her. He lowered his forehead to her shoulder and froze. "God, baby, you feel so good." He grasped the back of her neck and devoured her mouth as he thrust into her. After several deep strokes he tugged her head back and stared into her eyes as he made sure each stroke slid over her G-spot.

"Oh, my god, Luc—"

"Come now, Cassandra."

The walls of her pussy rippled and pulsed around him. He pushed in deep and held back his own orgasm for another moment before he gave in and let the pleasure slam through him. Cassie smiled at him as she caught her breath and he kissed her then turned his head and looked at Logan.

"Really, bro, you couldn't wait for me?" Logan asked, before he got into the truck and slammed the door.

Luc rested his head on Cassie's shoulder then threw his head back and laughed before he set her on the hood of the truck while he fastened his pants. Still grinning, he picked up the blanket, shook it out, and wrapped it around her before picking her up and climbing into the truck.

Logan glanced at them, opened his door, and walked around the truck and opened Luc's door. "Give her to me. It's my turn to hold her. You drive."

Luc handed Cassie over then got behind the wheel while Logan arranged Cassie on his lap.

Logan uncapped a water bottle then held it to Cassie's lips. Cassie took a sip, then smiled. "That's good."

"Did greedy old Luc hurt your pussy, sugar?"

Cassie choked, then coughed. "Logan!"

"Did he?"

Luc caught Cassie's attention. "He really wants to know if you're okay because he wants to fuck you."

Cassie giggled then dropped the sheet and said, "Okay." She turned on Logan's lap, straddled his legs, then reached for his jeans, but stopped and looked into his eyes. "May I, Sir?"

"Yes, sugar."

Cassie unbuttoned his jeans then slowly lowered his zipper. Logan lifted up and pushed them down until his cock was exposed.

"Damn, sugar. It's been years since I've done this in a truck," Logan said.

Cassie stroked his cock then squeezed the mushroom-shaped head. "I've never done it in a truck." She leaned forward and kissed him.

Logan scooted down in the seat then lifted her and let her own weight impale her. Cassie threw her head back and a long, drawn out moan of pleasure hummed from her lips. "Oh, Logan. You feel so good inside me."

Logan groaned. "Damn, baby, I love a dirty talking woman."

Cassie smiled. "Oh, Logan, your cock is so big and it feels so huge. I just want you and Luc to fuck me all the time."

Luc groaned and Logan laughed then held Cassie by the waist and pumped up into her. "Get us home, Luc."

Luc backed the truck away from the building then took off down the drive, slowed at the end, and turned toward their house. Less than three minutes later he pulled the truck to a stop, left the keys in the ignition, and jumped from the truck. By the time he got around it, Logan had Cassie out of the truck and pushed up against the side as he thrust into her.

Cassie pumped her hips against Logan then threw her head back and wailed her pleasure to the stars. A moment later, Logan came and shouted her name as he collapsed against her.

"Squashing me," she gasped then wiggled as she tried to get her breath.

Logan managed to turn until his back was against the side of the truck. "Take her, bro."

Luc wrapped the blanket around Cassie then walked toward the house. Logan followed behind them then laughed when Cassie wrapped her arms around Luc and giggled. "I feel so good."

Luc kissed her nose, then stepped into the house. "Are you hungry, Cassie?"

"I don't know," she said. "Maybe."

Logan activated the alarm. "I'll grab some stuff from the fridge and bring it up. She needs to drink some water, too."

"I'll get her showered and in bed."

"I'll let you," Cassie said, then giggled again and laid her head on Luc's shoulder. By the time he reached the top of the stairs, she was asleep.

Chapter Five

Cassie stretched, then opened her eyes and smiled. She was in Luc and Logan's bedroom. She scooted up in the bed and looked around, then felt the sheets on either side of her. They were cold and she wondered how long they had been awake. She glanced at the clock on the bedside table and threw back the covers when she saw that is was after nine.

Gathering clothes, she hurried into the bathroom, showered, dried her hair, then dressed and hurried down the stairs and rushed into the kitchen. It was empty but the coffee was still on. She got herself a cup, added cream and sugar, then went hunting for Luc and Logan. She wandered toward their study, heard voices, and pushed the door open and stepped inside.

Luc and Logan sat at their desks across from each other, while Cade, Jackson, Ben, and Mac sat on the four chairs in the large area between the desks. Thor stood at the window with his back to the room. He turned at her entrance, glanced at her, then turned back to the window.

"Logan?" she asked, suddenly scared. "What's happened?" When he didn't answer, she turned to Luc. "Luc?"

Thor turned around. "Sit down, Cassandra."

Cassie sat down on the chair in front of Luc's desk then set her coffee down before she looked at him again. Luc's eyes were cold and hard, and she knew in her heart he and Logan had somehow found out the truth.

Luc swiveled his chair to the side until he was facing Thor. "Let's get this over with so you can get her the hell out of here."

"I can explain," Cassie said.

"We'd have a hard time believing anything you have to say at this point," Logan said. "It's hard to know when a liar is telling the truth."

"We agreed I would handle this," Thor said to Luc and Logan before he turned back to Cassie. "I received a DVD in the mail at my office yesterday. I've shown it to the Ramseys." The TV came on and the DVD began playing. It showed a seventeen-year-old version of her standing at a kitchen counter with a man whose back was to the camera. She was talking to him, laughing, while he tried to open the box she had just set down on his counter. He finally managed to tear the box open and several small plastic bags filled with what looked like a white powder fell out of it.

Thor paused the player and Cassie bit her lip and fought back the tears that wanted to fall. Before she could say anything he asked her, "Do you know the man in the recording, Cassandra?"

She nodded. "His name is Mike. I never knew his last name." She didn't realize that by admitting she knew him she had just sealed her fate as far as Luc and Logan were concerned.

"Was he one of the men who abducted you?" Thor asked,

"No," she said, so scared she was shaking. "They were older. Mike was in his early twenties, like Jimmy."

"Who is Jimmy?" Thor asked.

"He was Julia's boyfriend," Cassie said, scooting forward until she was perched on the edge of the chair. She glanced at Luc then Logan, then back at Thor. "I know this looks bad but I was going to tell Luc and Logan today. I swear."

"You didn't answer my question, Cassandra," Thor said. "Who are these people? Julia and Jimmy?"

"Julia moved into my neighborhood while you and my dad and Jackson were deployed. We became friends. Jimmy was her boyfriend, but they called him Ice."

"Of course, they did," Luc said. "As in crystal meth."

"I didn't know that," Cassie said, defending herself. "Sometimes he would have Julia deliver packages to his friends and I would be with her. One night she said she'd hurt her ankle and she asked me to take the package to Mike for her. That's when that film"—she nodded toward the TV—"was made. Jimmy made it. He threatened us. He said if we didn't deliver packages for him he would send the tape to the police."

"So, he had a film of Julia delivering packages, too?" Thor asked.

"Yes—no, I don't know. That's what I thought then," Cassie said, realizing with every word she said she was just making matters worse. "Please, just let me tell you what happened. What I remember about what happened. Please?"

"So, you started delivering packages for Jimmy because he blackmailed you into working for him?" Logan asked, ignoring her request.

"No, of course not. I tried to talk Julia into going to the police."

"But, somehow you just never managed to contact the police," Luc said.

"I didn't have a chance to do that because later that night the men broke into Velma's house and took me." Cassie rubbed her temples and grimaced with pain. "They told me Julia had told them I wanted to go to the police."

Logan laughed, an ugly sound. "You just have an explanation for everything. Let's see if you can explain this." He nodded to Thor and Thor turned the DVD player on again.

An older version of Julia popped up on the screen. She was sitting at a table across from two men in suits, one older and one younger. The older man said, "Ms. Wilson, I'm Special Agent Johnson and this is my partner Special Agent Lake. We're with the FBI and we want to talk to you about a girl you may have known in Fort Worth—Cassandra Edwards."

On the film Julia started crying but nodded her head. "I knew her."

Agent Johnson asked Julia, "Did Cassandra Edwards introduce you to Jimmy Martin and Mike Smith?"

"Yes. She lived in the neighborhood my family moved into when we moved from Chicago. I didn't know her very well."

"How long did you know her before she introduced you to Jimmy Martin and Mike Smith?"

"Only about three weeks," Julia said, wiping the tears from her face then accepting the tissue Agent Lake offered her. "About a week later I went with her when she delivered a package to her boyfriend. She called him Tyson. I think that was his last name. I don't know his first name. He was a lot older than me and I was afraid of him."

Cassie jumped up. "No, no, that isn't true. She's lying." She turned to Thor. "She's lying, Thor. I wouldn't have done that. You know I wouldn't have deliberately gotten involved with anything like that."

The video went on. Cassie stood stunned as Julia described what had happened eight years ago, but she twisted the facts and made Cassie appear to be the villain. On the screen Julia told the agents that she had been tricked into delivering drugs for Cassie, Tyson, and Mike.

"How did they trick you?" Agent Johnson asked.

"One night Cassie said she had hurt her ankle and she asked me to take a package to Mike. I did and while I was in his apartment he opened the box and some small, plastic bags filled with something white fell out of it. I knew what was in the packages because my dad works for the DEA and he'd talked to me about drugs. I was really scared and I got out of there. Tyson and Cassie had recorded the whole thing and they showed me the tape. They threatened to send the video to the police if I didn't deliver other things for them."

"What kind of things?" Agent Lake asked.

"I don't know. Just small boxes. One night they drove me to a park and had me leave a package in the branches of a tree by the lake. That was the night they did this." On the film Julia pulled up her shirt and showed the two agents a scar on her side. "Tyson said he didn't trust me and then he stabbed me. Cassie was there and she laughed when he threw me in the ditch and left me for dead. She said 'good riddance to cheap crap' before they drove off. I'll never forget the sound of her voice saying that." On the film Julia's crying increased until she was sobbing.

"Oh, my, god," Cassie said, falling back into the chair. That phrase had been her father's go-to statement whenever he had worked on anything that he considered below standards. But how had Julia known that? "I don't understand? I never told her my dad said that." Tears glazed her eyes as she looked at the faces of the men in the room. "Thor?"

"You have to tell me the truth now, Cassandra. You know too much and these men are hunting you. They want to kill you and I can't protect you if you don't tell me the truth."

"But, that's the lie." Cassie stood and pointed at the TV. "Everything Julia said is a lie. All those things she said I did were the things she did."

"Dammit, Cassandra, do you think I don't want to believe you?" Thor paced from one side of the room to the other then stopped in front of her. "Julia's father, Don Wilson, works for the DEA. He'd been transferred to Texas from Chicago. He and his family had to be transferred again when you got Julia involved with you and your boyfriend." Thor turned away, ran his hands over his face, then turned back to her. "Your dad was my best friend. He died because of your involvement with these people, Cassandra. You owe him, and us, the truth. I'll try to protect you as much as I can."

She couldn't believe Thor wouldn't even give her the chance to explain what had happened. She looked at Luc then at Logan. Both of them had their chairs turned away from her and she knew they had already decided she was guilty. She backed away from them, moving closer to the door. "You're wrong. You're all wrong. I'm leaving."

Logan rose to stop her but Luc stopped him. "Let her go, Logan."

"She can't just walk away from this," Logan said.

"Cassandra, you can't leave," Thor said, his voice full of sorrow but determined. "One way or the other we're getting the truth out of you. Once we've made sure these guys can't get to you I'm turning you over to the police."

Cassie ran out into the hallway, stopped, then looked around. She didn't know what to do, where to go. She sank to the bottom step of the stairway and bent over her knees as silent tears slid down her cheeks. In the study the men continued to argue. She got up and ran outside then remembered she didn't have her tote with her and decided to hell with it. She ran over to the car and knelt down by the front tire and felt around the wheel well until she found the small magnetic box she kept there with a spare key in it. She grabbed the key, dropped the box to the ground, and unlocked the car door. When she tried to start the engine nothing happened. She tried again then again. She got out and raised the hood. The battery was gone.

"Looking for something, pet?" Luc asked from behind her.

Cassie spun around, saw Luc and Logan, and glared at them. "I'm leaving."

"Go back into the house," Logan said.

"You can't make me stay here. I trusted you. You said you would protect me but you've betrayed me."

"You have five seconds to get back in the house," Luc said.

"Or what? You think you're going to make me?" Cassie moved into a fighting stance that her father had taught her.

Logan sighed and Luc smiled and she shivered with fear. *Oh, my god, I'm going to die.*

"I've got this." Luc moved forward. "Two choices—go into the house or I'll take you there."

"Stop smiling," Cassie said. "You're scaring me."

"Don't hurt her," Logan said, stepping forward to intercept Luc.

Luc cursed and turned his head to look at Logan and Cassie struck. She got in one solid punch before Luc had her on the ground, her arms behind her back. One large hand held her wrists while the other shielded her cheek from the rough surface of the drive.

"Nice try, pet," Luc said. "Ready to give up?"

"Fuck you, Luc."

Luc leaned over her, his fingers tightening around her wrists, as he clenched his hand on the hair at her nape. "No, thanks, pet, just the thought of touching you again after I know you let those thugs fuck you makes me sick."

Before Cassie could say anything, Luc jerked her up from the ground and forcibly marched her toward the house. Cassie struggled and tried to get away from him. "I didn't mean fuck you like I was going to fuck you—I meant fuck off."

Luc ignored her. "Until you tell us what we want to know—"

"And, you're locked up behind bars where you belong," Logan said.

"We're not letting you out of our sight," Luc said.

"I'm not going to prison and you're going to be sorry for being a bunch of dumbasses." She saw Thor, Jackson, and Cade standing on the porch, listening to them. As Luc pulled her past Thor, she dug her heels into the porch and forced him to stop. She looked into Thor's eyes. "They're going to come after all of you now. You have to be careful."

Luc marched her into the house and up the stairway to a door at the back of the house. He opened it, revealing another set of stairs that led to the third floor. Cassie froze as the memory of a similar set of stairs flashed through her mind and she fought to get away. "No, no." She strained her arms and kicked out at Luc.

He picked her up and tossed her over his shoulder then took the steps two at a time with Logan a couple steps behind them. She heard one of them key in a code on an electronic panel and then the sound of a door latch clicking open and more images flashed through her mind.

"Welcome to your new home, pet," Luc said as lowered her to a bed then grabbed her ankle and locked a wide cuff around it.

Cassie jerked away from him and scrambled across the bed. Before she could slide off the bed and run Luc held her down and Logan attached a chain to the cuff. They moved back and stared at her. Cassie backed away from them, her body shuddering as she shook her head in denial then bent down and clawed at the restraint. "You promised," she screamed, "you promised."

"You'll have enough length on the chain to get to the bathroom," Luc said as pulled the chain loose from the hooks it hung from at the corners of the bed. Logan went into the bathroom and a moment later he came out with something wrapped in a large towel.

Luc emptied the two tables on either side of the bed then he and Logan placed the items in large cabinet in the corner and locked it. Then without another word or look the two of them left the room. A second later she heard the door lock.

Cassie looked around the room. Other than the bed there was a St. Andrew's cross, a bench with many, many places where restraints could be attached, a doctor's padded examination table with stirrups, and the large cabinet. The wall across from the bed was mirrored from floor to ceiling and two chairs and a table sat in front of it. She watched herself in the mirror as she backed up, sat down on the bed, and wrapped her hands around the post. Her heart pounded with fear and the pulse in her neck was going crazy. She swallowed then tried to take a deep breath but her chest was too tight and all she could manage was another shallow breath and then another.

A few minutes later she heard the door open and Luc and Logan entered the room. Luc carried a tray with several covered dishes on it. He set it on the table then pulled it and one of the chairs close enough to the bed that she could reach it. Logan tossed a pile of her clothes and her cosmetic bag on the bed, followed by a sketchpad and her box of art equipment.

Luc walked over to her. "Open your mouth."

"Why?"

Luc held up a small white pill. "Wouldn't want you to go into withdrawal, pet."

She looked at the pill, tempted to open her mouth and take it. She pressed her lips together and shook her head. "I only take the pills when I need to, Luc. I don't need one right now."

"Fine," Luc said. "When you decide you need one let us know."

Logan reached out to touch her then drew his hand back. "The remote on the bedside table operates the TV. You're going to stay in this room until you tell us the truth about Tyson and Mike and your involvement with them."

Cassie watched them leave then she sat down on the chair and curled into a ball. She buried her head against the wingback of the chair and closed her eyes. She should have trusted her instincts and left days ago. They hadn't even given her a chance to explain and they hated her now.

* * * *

A week later the sounds of her own screams woke her. Cassie sat up and covered her pounding heart with her hand then reached over and turned on the lamp. She searched the room as her breath shuddered in and out of her chest. When her breathing calmed, she got up and began to draw the object she had seen in her nightmare. After drawing as much as she could remember, she tried to figure out what it was but couldn't identify it. She slid the sketchpad between the arm of the chair and the seat cushion, then yawned and fell asleep.

Hours later, the sound of the door opening woke her. She opened her eyes, than sat up and stretched her arms over her head. The T-shirt slid up her legs to the top of her thighs.

"Sorry, pet, I'm immune," Luc said as he set a tray of food on the table next to her.

"What?" Cassie asked, her voice husky from sleep.

"Stretching and showing a little skin doesn't do a thing for me."

"I wasn't trying to seduce you, Luc."

Luc shook his head. "Huh-uh, pet, in this room you call me, Sir."

Cassie stood up and the T-shirt fell to her knees. She tossed her hair over her shoulders, looked Luc straight in the eyes, and said, "Sir," in a flat voice.

Luc narrowed his eyes at her then swept them down her body. "Is that my shirt?"

"Yes. It was in the pile of clothes Logan brought me."

"Give it to me."

"What?" Cassie took a step back. "It's the only thing I have to sleep in."

"I said give it to me." Luc held out his hand.

Cassie looked around, saw her thin pink robe on the end of the bed and reached for it. She turned to go into the bathroom and Luc stopped her.

"No. Take it off and bring it to me. Now."

"Why are you doing this?"

"Why are you pretending to be a victim when we both know you're not?"

Cassie whipped the shirt over her head and threw it at him, then shrugged into her robe. "Happy now?"

Luc slung the shirt over his shoulder then walked out of the room. Before he closed the door he told her Logan would bring her lunch.

"Wonderful," Cassie said, "I'll make sure I'm naked. Maybe I can seduce him instead." She smiled when she saw Luc's frown. Her smile disappeared when he smiled.

"Don't bother, pet. We spent a few hours at the club last night after Cade and Addison's wedding. Logan's as worn out as I am today."

Cassie looked down, then turned her back to him. When she heard the door close behind her, she dropped into the chair, pulled her feet up, and curled her arms around her knees. She had given them a week to come to their senses but now it was time to leave. Marisol had said she had a cousin, Vincent Vitale, who'd been a cop in Chicago. He might be able to find out more about Julia's family and why her father had been transferred to Texas.

She rested her chin on her knees as she made plans to leave. She had a third spare key hidden on the car but she doubted the battery had been replaced. She couldn't take the time to find it so she would have to run, literally. She would have to use all the skills her father had taught her about tracking if she was going to get away from Luc and Logan. She wasn't worried about getting out of the room. They had made the mistake of installing a large exhaust fan in the bathroom ceiling. All she had to do was use the small tool kit hidden in the bottom of her art supply box to pick the lock on the cuff around her ankle and then remove the fan. Once in the attic she could use the access door to move into the third floor hallway and from there it was a piece of cake to get out of the house.

Now to decide whether to keep moving or find a place to stay and lay low. Her dad had taught her to keep a backpack packed and ready to go at all times. Hers was hidden in the trunk of her car and held several weapons, high-energy foods, a pre-paid phone and cash as well as some basic hiking and camping equipment. Two hours north was a large lake and camping area. She could go there but she might not be able to recharge her phone which meant she needed a place that gave her access to electricity. She also needed access to food, she thought, as her stomach growled and she decided it was time to eat. She had until midnight to complete her plans.

While she ate, she opened her sketchpad and began adding a line here and another line there until the object she had drawn in the early morning hours began to take on a recognizable shape. Every now and then she added shading or a curve to the drawing. She held it up and decided it looked like an anchor with some sort of design on it. She turned it and looked at it from several angles. She wasn't sure what it was but the sight of it made her want to cower in a corner and scream.

She stood up and shoved her hands in the pockets of her robe and paced back and forth as far as the chain would let her.

Frustrated, and angry, she went into the bathroom and turned on the shower then shrugged the robe off and let it drop to the floor. She stepped into the shower and stood beneath the spray. Images of the object she had drawn began flashing through her mind. At first it was just a blur of color, then it took on the shape of an anchor, then an anchor with two initials on it.

Cassie dropped to her knees, banging them hard against the tile floor as she grabbed her head and screamed, then screamed again. In her mind she saw the mark, a tattoo, on the back of a large hand. Her face had pressed against it as the man had held her down and raped her. She curled forward, and rocked back and forth, comforting herself as the water grew cold. Minutes or hours later, she shivered then forced herself to shut off the freezing cold water. She wrapped a towel around herself then ran into the bedroom and grabbed the sketchpad. A few minutes later the door opened and Logan entered with a tray of food. He set it down and picked up the breakfast tray then started to leave.

"You could stay and talk to me, Logan."

He turned to look at her. "Are you ready to tell the truth?"

"I've already told you the truth. You just won't believe me."

"Because we have proof you're lying. Every trail we've followed leads straight back to you. Tell the truth, and Thor will make sure you get a reduced sentence."

"But I'm not guilty, Logan. I've been set up."

Logan smiled. "That's what they all say, pet." He walked over to the door. "Last chance. Thor's coming up to talk to you tomorrow and then he's notifying the feds. They'll be coming to arrest you."

"I've remembered something, Logan." Cassie tore the drawing of the tattoo out of the sketchpad and held it out to him. "This is a tattoo one of them had on the back of his hand."

Logan took it and glanced at it. "Leroy Tyson's tattoo. Those are his initials."

"No. He never did that to me." Reluctant to talk about the details, Cassie knew she would have to if she was going to convince Logan. She looked away and swallowed, then said, "That one." She nodded at the paper in Logan's hand and blinked her eyes trying to clear the tears away. "He would put his hand down on the bed next to my face when he—" She swallowed again, then said, "I could see his hand."

"I don't know what you're trying to pull here but I know this tattoo. It was on the back of Tyson's right hand."

"Then why did I draw it on his left hand, Logan?"

"Because you were flying high on the drugs you had taken, pet."

Before she could tell him she had never willingly taken drugs, he wadded up the paper and threw it on the table then walked away from her. She heard the door lock engage as she reached for the paper, smoothed it out and stared at it for a few moments. She placed it back in her sketchpad and laid it on the table.

After eating, she took a nap then got up and exercised. Finally she turned on the TV and caught up with the news and that was when she remembered Addison's house was empty. She knew the codes to the security system because she had used it as a safe house when she'd helped the Ramseys investigate the local chief of police. Satisfied with her plan she settled back and waited.

That evening Luc came to retrieve her dinner tray then left before she could say anything to him. She let him go then got the tool kit out. Thirty seconds later the lock on the cuff clicked open. She dropped it on the floor then went into the bathroom and climbed up on the counter. She removed the four screws that held the chrome frame in place, then she removed the screws on the inside that held the unit in place and shoved it up into the attic.

Cassie climbed down then closed the door to the bathroom before she went back into the bedroom and picked up the cuff and wrapped it around her ankle again. She didn't lock it.

At midnight, she removed the cuff, stretched, then went into the bathroom and looked up at the opening. The attic appeared to be pitch dark and she wished she had taken the time earlier to climb up there and take a look around.

Shrugging, knowing there was no hope for it now, she stood on tiptoe and reached up and grasped the wood frame. Her fingers barely curved over the top and she knew she would get only one chance to do this. If she fell, Luc and Logan might hear the thump she would make when she hit the floor and they would come to investigate. She pulled herself up, then adjusted her hands and with a soft grunt lifted herself into the attic.

There was just enough light coming in through the dormer windows that she could see where she was going. She went over to the pull-up attic stairs, said a prayer that they wouldn't squeak, then lowered them and breathed a sigh of relief when they went down without a sound. She climbed down them into the storage area of the third floor then pushed them back up into place.

Cassie held her breath as she tiptoed down the stairs then disarmed the alarm system and slipped outside. Almost free, she thought to herself, as she stuck to the shadows and worked her way over to her car. She slid under the car and searched for the hidden magnetic box. When she found it, she smiled then crawled to the back of the car, opened the trunk and lifted the carpet that hid the spare tire compartment. After removing the spare backpack she placed the towel in the trunk, along with the sketch of the tattoo. The trunk snapped shut with a soft click. The last thing she did was put the key back in the magnetic box and stick it to the top of the trunk.

Once she was far enough away that Luc and Logan wouldn't hear her footsteps she broke into a run, heading north for three miles. Ahead of her lay a road that led to Rendezvous and Addison's house if she went east or to the main highway if she went west. She figured she had about twelve miles to run but she knew she could make it. She'd run farther distances in the past. She blanked her mind and concentrated on her footsteps. She set a steady pace until she hit the intersection, then she stopped and rested for a moment. She hid her backpack in the weeds by the side of the road then ran west toward the truck stop.

Every now and then she let her foot slip off the shoulder of the road the way a tired runner would, but she was deliberately leaving a false trail for Luc and Logan to follow. When she reached the back of the truck stop, she hid in the shadows until the coast was clear then she turned around and ran back toward the intersection where she had left her backpack.

If she had looked back at the truck stop she would have seen three men glance her way then hurry toward a car in the overflow parking lot at the back of the truck stop. She also would have seen a large man step out of the shadows and take them down. In less than twenty seconds the three men were tied up and loaded into the back of a windowless van. Another, smaller shadow jumped out of the van then ran toward the men's car. A moment later the car led the way out of the parking lot with the van following behind it.

* * * *

The sun was lighting up the eastern sky when Cassie reached Addison's house. She found the spare key Addison hid in a fake rock in the flower bed then opened the back door and changed the security system to the correct setting. She moved to the spare room and threw her backpack into the closet. In the bathroom, she splashed water on her face then cupped her hands and took several sips. Breathing a sigh of relief that she had made it, she got her gun out of her bag, checked to make sure it was loaded, then sat down in the chair by the window. A small line of light struck her in the eyes where the curtain didn't quite close. She adjusted it then sat back and stared at the pattern on the drapes.

Gradually the room lightened as the sun rose. The longer she sat there the angrier she became. They really hadn't given her a chance to explain and they had believed everything Julia had said on the recording. She got up, and got the pre-paid phone from her backpack, and then went into the kitchen. She got the phone out of its casing and plugged it in then put on a pot of coffee. There wasn't much food left in the cupboards but there was enough to get by for a few days.

She drank a cup of coffee then ate some cereal straight from the box. After another cup of coffee, she made a list of the things she needed to do and people who might be able to help her. When the list was complete, she took the phone back to the spare room and plugged it in so it could finish charging. The clock said nine. By now they knew she was gone and they would be tracking her. She would wait a day or two before she called Marisol.

* * * *

Luc moved along the side of the road and carefully swept the ground for a sign that Cassandra had gone this way. He and Logan had been looking for over an hour and he was beginning to wonder if she had been picked up by the men hunting her. He and Logan had been too rough on her and she had sent them an "in your face" gesture by escaping. The fact that she could have left at any time but had stayed to give them a chance to come to their senses weighed heavily on his mind. The longer he looked for her the more he felt like an unfeeling bastard who didn't deserve a woman like her.

He blinked his eyes to clear the dust from them then went to one knee and signaled Logan. Feeling relieved, he pointed to the ground. Cassie's foot had slipped off the shoulder of the paved road and left an impression in the soft dirt. Logan crouched down next to him and examined the print.

"She was tiring by the time she got this far." Luc looked toward the west.

"Think she was going to Harry's Truck Stop to hitch a ride?"

Luc nodded. "If she got in one of those trucks there's no telling where she is by now."

"Or, if she's in trouble."

The wind gusted and blew several black strands into Luc's eyes. He brushed them away then looked west again. "We have to find her."

"If they were watching for her she may not have made it to the truck stop."

"She would have fought them. We haven't found any signs of a fight."

"Yet." Logan stood up.

Luc nodded then followed the edge of the road as Logan went back to his side and kept pace with him. Luc found another print, signaled Logan, then kept going. The closer they got to the truck stop the less sign they found until Logan drew Luc's attention and crouched down to examine the track he had found. Luc joined him.

"She crossed the road here," Logan said.

Luc looked at the truck stop that was located about fifty yards away. "Maybe someone at the station or café saw her."

The two of them increased their pace until they reached the doors of the truck stop. Luc pointed to a large car parked at the end of the building. "Harry's car is here. Let's talk to him and see if any of his employees saw her or anything unusual last night."

As soon as they entered the truck stop, multiple pairs of eyes turned toward them. Luc ignored the attention they were drawing and moved to the counter where a young blonde girl sat winding a long strand of blonde hair around her finger as she read a celebrity magazine. He leaned down, read the nametag pinned to the front of her shirt, then stood up and said, "Hi, Cherry."

The little blonde shrieked then jumped off the stool and covered her heart. "You scared me," she said, her southern accent as heavy as the eyeliner she wore.

"Sorry about that," Luc said. "Could you let Harry know Luc and Logan Ramsey are here to see him?"

Cherry's eyes widened as she looked from him to Logan then back to him. She smiled and stuck out her chest.

Logan chuckled then said, "Baby, you're too young. Be a good girl and call Harry for us."

Cherry blushed then reached for the phone. A few seconds later she said, "He said he'd meet you in the café."

Logan smiled at her then he and Luc made their way into the café. They slid into a corner booth with walls behind them and a clear view of the room in front of them. They had just ordered coffee when Harry came puffing up, grabbed a chair, and pulled it over to the table and flopped down.

"My doctor says if I don't lose some weight I'm going to die but hell it's hard to diet when I own a restaurant," Harry said.

Luc grinned. He'd known Harry all his life and the guy was the same weight now that he'd been twenty years ago.

The waitress brought over three cups of coffee along with a large slice of lemon meringue pie that she set down in front of Harry. Luc grabbed the pie. "Harry, you should listen to your doctor," he said before he took a large bite.

Harry's belly shook as he laughed. "So, what can I do for you two cowboys?"

"We're looking for a young woman," Luc said.

"You and me both, buddy," Harry said with another laugh.

"This one sort of belongs to us," Logan said. "Petite with long, golden-blonde hair. She may have been here sometime between midnight and seven this morning."

"I have surveillance cameras everywhere," Harry said. "You're welcome to look at the video."

Luc took another bite of pie and quickly swallowed it. "Anybody working now who was here during those hours?"

"My cook works midnight to one."

"Can you get him out here?" Logan asked.

Harry laughed. "Best place to find him this time of day is out back, smoking one of his stinking cigars. Come on, I'll take you back there, that is, if you're done eating my pie?"

Luc took the last bite then washed it down with a sip of coffee. "Good pie, Harry, but not as good as Jane's."

"Well, hell boy, nobody's pie is as good as Jane's but no matter how much I offer her she won't come work for me." Harry got up and led the way through the kitchen and out the back door.

A large man wearing a pristine white apron sat on a wooden crate smoking. When the screen door slammed he turned his head. The right side of his face was covered with scars. He lazily took a drag from the cigar and puffed out several smoke rings. "Harry," the cook said, his voice a deep, painful rasp.

"Nate, these guys would like to talk to you for a minute." Harry pointed at Luc and Logan.

"I'm on my break."

Luc stepped forward. "Last night did you see a woman on foot coming from the south?"

"Why do you want to know?" Nate asked.

Logan put a hand on Luc's shoulder. "She's in trouble. Some bad guys are hunting for her."

"How do I know you aren't the bad guys?" Nate asked.

Harry stepped forward. "I've known Luc and Logan Ramsey since they were boys. They're Marines."

Nate laughed, then looked toward the parking lot. "So, you're Isabella's two perverts?" He laughed again.

"You know Isabella?" Luc asked.

Nate nodded then puffed out a cloud of smoke that smelled like horse manure. "I saw your little gal. Around two, maybe a little earlier. She ran up to the intersection, stepped off the shoulder into the dirt then jumped back onto the shoulder and ran back to the south."

"Are you sure?" Luc waved his hand in front of him, clearing the wall of smoke.

"Yeah." Nate almost smiled before he took another puff.

"Was she alone?" Logan asked. "Anybody following her?"

"She was alone." Nate stood up, his eyes level with Luc and Logan's. "Looked like she knew what she was doing so I didn't offer to help her." He laughed again. "She's damn good at laying a false trail. Good runner. Wasn't even winded."

Luc and Logan thanked Nate and Harry and then they took off. Luc glanced back and saw Nate watching them. "That is one tough-looking bastard."

Logan glanced back then grunted. "I'd hate to meet him in a dark alley." He sent Nate a last look then caught up with Luc. "Where do you think she was going?"

"I'm not sure but she's somewhere west of the intersection and she couldn't have gotten too far. We've had people out looking for her since seven. She's got to be holed up somewhere."

"We need to call the police department and see if anyone has reported a stolen vehicle," Logan said.

"Damn. If she's stolen a car I'm going to use a paddle on her ass when we find her."

Logan used his cell phone to make the call while Luc checked in with Thor.

"No stolen cars reported."

"Thor said he had ten guys watching the roads for her. No sign of her."

Once they reached the intersection they continued on south.

"She has to be hiding out on the ranch somewhere. You take that side of the road and I'll take this side," Logan said.

An hour later Luc stopped and knelt down. "Here, Logan." He pointed to a small mark on the ground. "Looks like she stumbled."

Logan looked at the mark, then surveyed the area around them. "Only thing out here is trees and the river."

Luc pulled a bottle of water from his pack and took a sip. "Don't forget Addison, Jenna, and Marisol. I think she'll try to contact one of them."

"Then we need to make sure when she does we're listening in." Logan moved farther down the road. "Let's see if we can find where she left the road. I'll move into the field a few yards and you stay on the shoulder. If we don't find anything on this side then we'll search the other side."

Six hours later, dusty and tired, the two of them walked down their driveway. When they reached Cassie's car, they stopped and leaned against it.

"Damn, I'm tired," Luc said.

Logan pulled a bottle of water out of his own pack and squirted a stream into this mouth. "This is a hell of a car." He tapped the top then leaned down and looked through the window.

Luc frowned. "It's too fast for her."

"I think that's the whole point of a car like this." Logan admired it as he walked around it. "She and her dad rebuilt this car. That's how she knows so much about it."

"He taught her a lot of things I'd just as soon she didn't know."

Logan chuckled. "At least she's never boring." The sound of his voice faded as he rounded the trunk. "Luc?"

"Yeah?" he asked, taking another sip of water.

"Cassie left us a message."

Luc hurried to Logan's side and saw the metal key case. He opened it and shook the key out into the palm of his hand then used it to open the truck.

"That's the sketch she drew of the tattoo on the back of Tyson's hand." Logan picked it up.

"No, it's not. That's the tattoo on the back of Larry Taylor's left hand. He and Tyson had the same initials."

"Oh, shit," Logan said. "Cassie showed me that drawing yesterday and I told her I knew it was the tattoo on Tyson's hand. She swore it wasn't because he had never—" Logan cursed. "I think he's the reason she's afraid of anal sex. Dammit, I should have listened to her."

Luc grasped his shoulder. "What'd she say, Logan?"

"She said the guy with this tattoo would put his hand down on the mattress when he raped her and she could see the tattoo."

"That's why they're hunting her. They know she's starting to remember more details and she'll be able to identify them. We've got to find her."

"We will," Logan said.

"We need to search her things then we'll talk to our brothers and Thor."

Chapter Six

Cassie waited until after nine the next evening before she called Marisol.

After one ring Marisol answered. "Cassie?"

"Yes. It's me."

"Everyone is hunting for you."

"The police?" Cassie asked.

"No. Luc and Logan, their brothers, and Thor and his guys."

Cassie quickly told Marisol everything that had happened and that her memory was coming back. The more she talked the more Marisol cursed in Spanish. "Where are you, Cassie?"

"Do you promise not to tell anyone? Not even Addison or Jenna?"

"Listen to me. You're not safe. Thor and the Ramseys are not the only people hunting for you."

"I know that but I don't trust them anymore. They betrayed me, Marisol." Cassie grabbed a pen and pad of paper. "You said your cousin might be able to help me."

"Cassie, you've got to call Luc and Logan. They're going out of their minds worrying about you. Let them protect you."

"No. I don't trust them now."

After a pause, Marisol said, "Promise me you'll call Vincent and tell him everything you just told me."

"I promise." Cassie wrote down the number Marisol gave her. "Don't worry about me. I'll be okay. I have a car now and I need to get going."

"Cassie, did you steal a car?"

"No, I'm borrowing a friend's beige tank. I've got to go now."

"Wait, don't hang up yet. They found your case. The one with your sketches and all the informa—"

Cassie heard Marisol yelling at someone then Thor came on the line. "Cassandra, tell me where you are right now."

Cassie took a deep breath then hung up. A few minutes later she called Marisol's cousin Vincent Vitale. After introducing herself, she told him a short version of what had happened and then she asked him to help her prove her innocence.

"I still have a lot of contacts in Chicago," Vincent said. "I'll see what I can find out about Julia."

"While you're at it, check into her father, Don Wilson. I think he was dirty and that's how Julia got involved with the drug gangs."

"Damn," Vincent said. "Are you sure?"

"My godfather, Thor Larkin, said Julia's dad works for the DEA. He said they had to be transferred from Chicago to Dallas but there was just something about them I didn't trust. At first they appeared to be the perfect family but they never asked Julia where she'd been or what she'd been doing."

"You think it was because they already knew?"

"Yes."

"Cassie, I know Thor Larkin—why haven't you gone to him with all this?"

"He thinks I'm guilty. I tried to tell him the truth but he wouldn't listen."

"From what you've told me all of the evidence points to you, hon," Vincent said.

"My point exactly—it's too easy. I'd have to be a complete idiot to leave that much evidence leading right back to me."

Vincent cursed. "You're right. I'm going to help you. Can I contact you at this number?"

"Yes, but I've stayed here as long as I can. I'm leaving tonight."

"No. Cassie, stay where you are."

"I can't do that. Eventually they're going to realize I'm close by and this is the first place they'll look. I'll call you when I find another place to stay," Cassie said then hung up. She got her backpack then grabbed the car keys from the hook where Addison kept them. After unlocking the car she threw her things on the front floorboard then started the engine, and used the remote to open the garage door. She backed out and a movement in the rearview mirror caught her attention. Luc's large black truck pulled up behind her.

The truck doors opened and Luc and Logan stepped out and walked toward her. She locked the car doors and kept the engine running. One of them tapped on her window. For a moment she ignored them then rolled her window down an inch. "Move your truck."

"Get out of the car, sugar," Logan said.

"Move your truck."

"Cassie, I want you to get out of the car right now," Luc said.

"No. I'm leaving."

Luc banged on the window. "You have five seconds to open this door."

"Or, what? You'll accuse me of some other crime I didn't commit? You said the sight of me made you sick." She wiped the tears from her face, pissed off at herself for crying.

Lights flashed over them and Cassie saw Thor pull in behind Luc. He, Jackson, and Cade got out and walked over to the car. She heard Luc and Logan talking to them then Cade pulled something from his pocket and a second later her door flew open.

"Get out of the car, Cassandra," Thor said.

"Go to hell."

A growl rumbled from Luc's throat. "Cassandra, you know the rules."

"Fuck the rules, Luc. You and Logan can fuck off. You betrayed me."

Logan shouldered Luc out of the way then bent down until he was on eye level with her. "There are men hunting you, sugar."

"I'd rather take my chances staying one step ahead of them. They just want to kill me, but you're destroying my hope." Cassie gripped the steering wheel then put her head down on the back of her hands and sobbed.

"Dammit." Luc tried to pull her out of the car but she wouldn't, or couldn't, let go of the steering wheel. Logan reached in and uncurled her fingers then Luc lifted her out and carried her toward Logan's truck.

Jackson glanced into the car. "I'll get her things and put Addison's car back in the garage."

"We'll see you at the ranch," Logan said before he followed Luc and climbed into the truck.

Cassie sat on the back seat with her hands fisted on her lap and her head down. Her hair hung down on either side of her face, hiding her expression, and the only light in the truck came from the lights of the dashboard. She stared at her hands and tried to figure out how she felt about Luc and Logan now. They had turned on her and she wondered if she would have done the same thing if she had been in their place. The answer came quickly. She would have believed them because she had been falling in love with them from the moment she had met them. But, they didn't love her. She was their temporary sub, or at least that's what they wanted her to be, but they'd never gotten around to signing the contract. Now they never would.

By the time they arrived at the ranch house, she had decided she would answer their questions, and then she would depend on Vincent Vitale to help her. As soon as Logan parked the truck and Luc climbed out, she slid out behind him. She ignored the hand he held out to her and walked around him and up the sidewalk to the porch then into the house.

Addison, Jenna, and Marisol came out of the living room and surrounded her.

"Cassie, we've been so worried about you. Are you okay?" Addison asked.

"Yes, of course." Cassie forced a smile to her lips. "Sorry I missed your wedding, Addison, but I was tied up."

Addison smiled. "I understand."

"Have you eaten?" Jenna asked. "I could get you something.

"No, thanks. I just need to talk to Thor and then I'm going home."

"To Luc and Logan's?" Addison asked as Luc and Logan entered the house followed by Cade, Jackson, and Thor.

Cassie shook her head. "No, to my home in Dallas."

"Sugar, you can't go there," Logan said.

Cassie walked away. "I guess we'll probably talk in the den. Isn't that where the interrogations take place?" Behind her, she heard Luc curse and she smiled. Maybe it was time to turn the table on them.

Cassie sat down and folded her hands in her lap. Once Thor and the Ramseys were seated she looked up and waited for the questioning to begin.

Thor smiled at her. "Cassandra, first I want to apologize to you. We were wrong and we didn't give you a chance to explain."

Before he could say anything more, Cassie said, "Apology accepted. Thank you."

Thor cleared his throat, then picked up her case and opened it. He held up her sketches of Julia, Jimmy, Mike, and several other people. "You drew these?"

"Yes."

"They're very good," Thor said.

Cassie decided she would use their own rules against them—don't speak unless asked a question. After this she might be able to make up her own brochure on how to handle dumbasses who didn't listen. She smiled and Luc gave her a quizzical look. She wanted to get up and bust a lamp over his head. Instead, she ignored him.

Thor picked up several folders. Cassie recognized them as the folders she had made on the people she had met or seen at Jimmy's apartment or around Julia.

"You gathered this information?"

"Yes."

"It's very thorough. We have someone trying to locate the people in your sketches and we're also looking into your theory about Julia's involvement with drugs in Chicago."

Cassie kept quiet. She could have told him her theory about Julia's father's involvement with the drug gangs of Chicago but why should she when he probably wouldn't believe her? She waited for several minutes. When Thor didn't ask her any further questions, she stood up, and then brushed off her jeans, deliberately drawing attention to them. "I'd like the battery to my car and my car key now. I'm leaving."

Thor sighed. "You can't go home to your apartment. It's not safe."

"I can't stay here. It will put Addison and Jenna at risk. Besides Addison and Cade just got married. I'm sure they have plans."

"You're going to stay at our house," Logan said.

"No." Cassie turned back to Thor. "I want my battery and my car key. I'm going home or you can put me in protective custody."

Thor grinned then pointed at Luc and Logan. "I'm putting Cassie in your custody. If you let anything happen to her, I'll kill you."

"No. I'll only agree to go into Federal protective custody."

"We don't know who else is involved with this and until we do we can't trust anyone else," Jackson said.

"I'll stay at Addison's house in town. Ben and Mac can stay with me."

"I've sent them back to Dallas," Thor said.

"Then, I'll stay at your house in Dallas. It's secure and you're not there."

"Cassandra, as your godfather and your employer, I'm ordering you to go with Luc and Logan until we figure out who's after you."

"I've been offered a job in Houston. I've decided to accept it. So, you're no longer my employer and I'm too old to need a godfather."

Luc stepped up on her left and Logan on her right. "Tonight you're going home with us. You're going to eat something and then get some rest, Cassandra. In the morning, we're going to figure out what you know that's got them so nervous. Do you understand?"

"I understand that as usual you're not listening to me," Cassie said.

"You told Marisol you were remembering things," Luc said.

"I lied," Cassie said, thinking they already thought she was a liar so she might as well lie to them now.

"Cassandra," Luc said, a clear warning in his voice. "What have you remembered?"

"The tattoo on the man's left hand. You have a copy of the sketch I drew."

"What else have you remembered?" Thor asked.

"You don't need to concern yourself with that anymore. I have someone else investigating this for me."

"Who the hell have you contacted?" Logan asked, his voice harsh.

"That's none of your business, Logan."

"Dammit, Cassandra," Luc said. "I'm going to blister your ass."

She smiled. "Red—to everything."

Luc crowded her. "You're staying with us, and you're going to tell us everything you know about Julia and her friends."

Cassie turned her back on him and walked away from both of them. "I'll stay until Ben and Mac can get back here. Then I'm leaving. I'll stay at Addison's house or if not there, anywhere away from all of you." She walked out of the room.

"A word of warning," Thor said. "Cassie can hotwire a car faster than you can catch her. Her father taught her all the tricks in the book. Don't ever underestimate her again."

"When did we ever do that?" Logan asked.

Thor laughed. "How'd the two of you end up zip tied and covered in ice cream? How'd we end up thinking she had hitched a ride with a trucker?"

"She got the jump on us the first time," Logan said, "and the second time she laid a false trail."

"Exactly. Because she's small and delicate, you both underestimated her skills and she got the jump on you not once but twice. If she hadn't slipped up and told Marisol she was driving a beige tank, we'd never have found her."

"She won't get away from us this time," Logan said before going after her.

Luc nodded then left the room. Instead of going in search of Cassie, he stepped out onto the porch. He heard Logan's footstep as he moved up beside him.

"Where is she?" Luc asked.

"In the kitchen with Addison, Jenna, and Marisol."

"Is she eating?"

"No."

"We fucked up."

"Yes."

"What do you think she's going to do?"

"I'm more concerned about what she's not going to do."

"Forgive us?"

"We've broken trust with her. We have to earn it back."

"That might take time we don't have."

Logan nodded. "Then we better get started."

As soon as they entered the house Jackson threw Cassie's backpack toward them.

Logan caught it by a strap and let it swing a few times before lifting it. "Damn, this is heavy. What's in it?"

Jackson laughed. "My advice to you—don't give it to Cassie. As soon as you get her home, do a full body cavity search and one of you stay awake at all times."

Logan opened the backpack and placed the guns, ammunition, knives, and other items onto the foyer table. "Damn, where the hell did she get all this?"

"Her dad." Thor stepped up and pushed several items aside before he picked up a small but lethal knife. "Damn, I haven't seen this in years. Ryan always carried it."

Cassie pushed her way between them and took the knife out of his hands. "That's mine." She dropped it back into the backpack then shoved the rest of the weapons and her clothes on top of it. She hugged the backpack to her chest. "Don't mess with my stuff and I won't have to use it on you." Giving them a fierce glare, she turned and walked away. At the open door she stopped and looked back. "Well, are we going or not?"

Logan hurried after her. "Sugar, promise me you won't shoot me."

"Of course, I wouldn't, Logan. Guns make too much noise."

Luc smiled. At the door he turned back. "We'll see you at breakfast if we live through the night."

Cassie jerked the door of the truck open, threw her bag in the backseat, and then climbed in after it. Logan started to climb in beside her and she placed her foot against the middle of his stomach and pushed him back. "No. You sit in the front with Luc."

"Luc and I know we fucked up, and you have every right to be mad at us, but we're willing to do anything to earn your forgiveness.

"I don't trust you and I don't want to be around either one of you, so do me a favor and keep your distance."

Luc climbed into the truck. "Sorry, sugar, but now that we know how easy it is for you to escape one of us is going to have to be with you at all times."

Cassie shrugged even though she felt like crying. "Whatever."

Luc started the engine and backed out. The tension in the truck matched the depth of the silence as they drove the short distance to Luc and Logan's home. Cassie stared out into the darkness beyond the window. The moon was barely up but she felt exhausted, as if someone had sucked all the energy out of her. Her nerves were humming and she had to force herself to keep from fidgeting. Luc pulled the truck to a stop and turned off the engine and she grabbed for her backpack but Logan got to it first.

"Sorry, sugar, but we're going to have to confiscate this." Logan opened his door and stepped out.

Cassie bit her lip then jumped down from the truck and walked by him. "Fine, but when I leave I want it back." She climbed the steps to the porch.

Luc stepped around her and pushed the door open and she stepped into the house. The memory of the first time she had entered the house swamped her and tears glazed her eyes. She walked toward the steps.

"We're going to eat first," Luc said.

"I'm taking a shower then I'm going to bed," Cassie said as she took the first step.

"I'll bring some food up," Logan said. "You go with her."

Luc nodded then followed Cassie up the stairs. He saw her enter the stairs to the third floor and followed her. By the time he got to the room she was already in the bathroom and the door was closed. He tried the knob. It was locked. He banged on the door. "Cassandra, unlock the door. I want to apologize to you and I want to see your face when I do. Please, sugar."

"I'm not your prisoner or your sub, and Logan already told me you're both sorry."

Luc leaned against the wall for a moment then moved to the chair and sat down and waited.

A few minutes later, Logan carried a tray into the room. "What's going on? I thought we were going to stay in the master suite."

"She came up here before I could catch up to her. She's not going to forgive us."

"If she wants to stay here then we'll let her. We'll stay with her."

Luc grabbed a ham and cheese sandwich and took a bite.

Logan pulled the second chair over to the table. After sitting down, he chose a sandwich and began eating it. "How long you think she'll be in there?"

Luc opened a chocolate pudding cup and took a bite then shrugged. "How many gallons of hot water do we have?"

Logan got up and went over and tapped on the door. "Cassie, we have sandwiches and chocolate pudding out here. Come out, sugar, and eat." His request was met with silence so he returned to his chair and poured himself a glass of sweet tea.

Luc sighed, put the empty container down, then got up and went over to the door. "Cassandra, we fixed the exhaust unit so it can't be removed again. You might as well come out here and eat."

A few minutes later the door opened and a wall of steam flowed out of the bathroom followed by Cassie still dressed in jeans and a T-shirt. She walked over to the bed and set the multi-tool she had been using on the bedside table before she slid into the bed. She fluffed the pillows and pulled the blankets up around her shoulders, then curled up on her left side. A second later she reached out and turned the lamp off.

Luc moved to the side of the bed, picked up the multi-tool, then set it back down. "I'll search the bathroom, Logan. You search this room."

Cassie snorted. They'd never find all the things she'd hidden in every other room of the house. She closed her eyes then took a deep breath, held it for a moment, and exhaled. Gradually, she managed to relax and quiet her mind by using the meditation methods her father had taught her.

* * * *

Several hours later, Luc opened his eyes and saw Logan looking back at him. Together he and Logan leaned up on their arms without removing their hands from Cassie's bare breasts. They could see her face in the dimmed light of the room. She moaned then cried out in her sleep as tears seeped from the corners of her eyes. She moaned again, then thrashed her legs as if she was attempting to kick something or someone away from her.

"Should we wake her up?" Logan asked, his voice soft.

"No." Luc slid his arm under her then gently pulled her against him as he rolled onto his back. He arranged her until she was lying half over him with her head on his chest.

Logan spooned her and pressed his chest against her back as he slid his arm around her waist and cupped her breast. He placed a line of soft kisses on her back and felt her settle between them. "She's remembering,"

"Yes," Luc said. "We need to talk to Doc Marshall in the morning."

"You think Doctor Carson is involved?"

Luc combed his fingers through Cassie's hair. "No, but what do you know about Thompson?"

"Other than the fact he's a Dom and a member of Club Mystique?" Logan asked. "He's on the drug task force."

"He probably knew Don Wilson. As far as I'm concerned that makes him a suspect. Plus, he's the person who sent Cassie to Doctor Carson." Luc stroked her hair again then sighed. "Cassie needs to start talking."

"Do you think she will?"

Luc adjusted his pillow then rested his chin on the top of Cassie's head. "No."

"She's going to be pissed off when she wakes up and realizes we undressed her," Logan said.

Luc smiled into the darkness. It had been easy to undress her without waking her. "I'd rather fight with her than have her ignore us."

Logan hummed an agreement. "Remember the rules in Maggie's brochure—*don't get angry or frustrated with your sub and have a plan.*"

"Bro, come on, you know that brochure is total bullshit," Luc said. "It's about horses, not subs."

"Jackson says subs are like horses."

"Jackson would live in the stables if Jenna would let him. Horses don't want to know what you're feeling. They don't cry if you don't call. They don't want attention during the big game."

"It's still good advice."

"Fine. We won't get mad and we've already got a plan. By this time tomorrow she'll have forgiven us and we'll be fucking her in the master suite."

* * * *

Three days later, Cassie slid sideways in the chair she was sitting in and slung her legs over the arm then swung her bare foot back and forth. She tipped her sketchpad toward the window and examined the drawing she'd just completed. She smiled then looked up and saw Luc talking on the phone, watching her with the same frustrated look he had worn on his face yesterday and the day before that. She swept her gaze across the room to Logan and he smiled at her. Their version of *good Dom, bad Dom,* she thought to herself, then gave them a big toothy smile before returning her attention to her drawing and doodling along the edge.

For the last three mornings, she had woken up in the bed in the playroom, naked, with Luc and Logan on either side of her. The first morning she had cussed them out then ignored them for the rest of the day. That night she had stubbornly curled up in the chair and had eventually fallen asleep. Sometime during the night they had undressed her and tucked her into the bed between them. When she woke up the next morning, she'd had a hard cock digging into her hip on either side of her. She'd grasped their cocks and squeezed them until their hazel eyes had popped open. Logan had looked alarmed but Luc had pumped his hips then smiled. She had released them then stood up and stepped over Luc, straddling his hips and giving him a good view of her pussy. When he slid his hands up her calves, she'd smiled at him then jumped from the bed and walked into the bathroom.

This morning she'd woken up sandwiched between them. Before she could stop herself, she'd wiggled her hips and a soft moan of pleasure had escaped her when Luc's cock had slipped between her legs. The temptation to squeeze her legs together and slide her clit over his cock had been nearly more than she could resist. Her body would still be humming with need if she hadn't taken care of the problem herself.

As long as she lived, she'd never forget the looks on their faces when she'd opened the bathroom door this morning after a very loud masturbation session in the shower. Luc and Logan had been waiting for her. Their hazel eyes had blazed with lust. Their erections had pointed in her direction. Logan's cock had jerked when she'd looked at it almost as if it was doing a happy dance because it had her attention. Luc's cock had remained still and pointed straight at her like a missile ready to be fired. Before she could take off, Luc had wrapped himself around her. Then with a deep growl he'd pulled her belly flush with his and he'd said, "If you don't want this say so now." She'd smiled, and wiggled her way down his belly, leaving behind a slick line of her cream, until she felt the head of his cock against her pussy. Then she'd slowly impaled herself on him.

Logan had pressed up against her back as she'd raised and lowered herself on Luc.

"Sugar, I'm going to play with your ass," he'd said right before she'd felt a lube-slicked finger begin to circle her rosette and then press into it.

She'd heard him go to his knees behind her while he'd slid his finger all the way into her. She'd raised and lowered herself onto Luc's cock and swiveled her hips and moaned when Logan had slid a second finger into her. She'd screamed with pleasure as sizzling hot waves of pleasure had rippled through her as Luc filled her with his hot cum. Logan had pulled his fingers from her ass then tugged her away from Luc. He'd laid her on the bed, on her back, with her legs hanging over the edge.

"Sugar, if you don't want me to fuck your ass you better say so now," Logan had said and she'd begged him to fuck her ass.

Luc had handed Logan a condom then he'd laid down on the bed beside her and kissed her before he'd lifted her and had pressed her back against his chest. He'd reached down and grasped her legs behind her knees then pulled them up to her chest and she'd been completely exposed to Logan. She'd sucked in huge gulps of air as she'd felt Logan press the head of his cock against her anus and begin to press inward. She'd wiggled as the pressure increased and he'd pulled away then pushed into her again.

"Oh, Logan, that feels so good," she'd said.

"Does it, sugar?" he'd asked as he'd pressed into her until his pelvis was against her ass.

"Oh, my god, that feels so good," she'd screamed. "Don't stop, please don't stop." She'd wiggled and felt him slip in deeper. The way Luc had held her had put them in total control of her movements and all she'd been able to do was wiggle her hips from side to side.

"That's it, sugar," Logan had said as she'd begged him to move.

Luc had chuckled then he'd reached down and stroked her clit before he'd slid two fingers into her pussy. "Is this what you want? Do you need my fingers in your pretty little pussy?"

"Yes, oh, yes, Luc," she'd said as her hand had wrapped around his cock. She'd heard him groan as she stroked him and had run her thumb over the head of his cock again and again.

Luc had fucked her with his fingers while Logan had fucked her ass and all she'd been able to do was enjoy their attention. When Logan had begun swatting her ass while he'd fucked her, she'd lost control and had been on the verge of an orgasm. Luc had pulled his hand away from her and she'd cried out in disappointment.

"Do not come, Cassandra," Luc had said, then a moment later he'd pushed his fingers into her again and circled her clit with his thumb.

Logan had fucked into her faster, then groaned. "Come now, sugar," he'd said as his hot cum filled the condom.

Luc had pressed on her clit and she'd screamed as an explosive orgasm had overwhelmed her. Luc's cum had spurted onto her belly then he'd leaned over and closed his lips around her clit and she'd come again. Luc had collapsed on the bed next to her while Logan had hung over her, panting. Several minutes later, he'd withdrawn from her and Luc had said, "Shower," then he'd lifted her and carried her into the bathroom.

After showering they'd gone to the kitchen where Luc and Logan had made her sit down while they'd tried to fix her breakfast. When the smoke alarm had gone off, she'd laughed then gotten the cereal from the pantry and the milk from the fridge.

Cassie glanced up and caught them watching her again. They had both apologized to her for breaking faith with her but she just wasn't sure she could trust them again. This morning had just been a one-off and it really hadn't changed anything. It had just been three consenting adults having sex. She added another line to the drawing then flipped over to a clean page and began drawing Logan. She grinned then added a few more strokes and held the pad up. Happy with the two sketches, she tore them out of the pad and moved to Luc's desk. She dropped a drawing on the surface in front of him then walked over to Logan's desk and dropped the second drawing on his desk. "Lunch," she said and walked away.

Behind her she heard Luc curse, and Logan laugh. "Luc, your head looks just like a smiling cock."

"Fuck off. So does yours."

Cassie hurried toward the kitchen with Luc a few steps behind her. She heard the scrape of a stool sliding across the tiles as she gathered the ingredients for peanut butter chocolate chip cookies.

Once the first baking sheet of dough was in the oven, she opened the fridge and got the bowl of salad out along with the roast beef and cheese. She made herself a sandwich, then sighed and made two more. Logan came into the room as she was getting the tea out of the fridge. She set it on the central island and got out three plates along with the salad dressing.

"Are you ever going to talk to us?" Logan asked after taking a bite of his sandwich.

"Probably not," Cassie said.

"We're not the enemy, Cassie," Luc said. "We can't help you if you won't talk to us."

"Someone else is helping me." The oven buzzer went off and she slid down from the stool and got the pan out of the oven. After sliding the second pan of cookie dough into the oven, she moved the hot cookies to a plate and walked toward the door carrying it. "Don't burn your cookies."

"How long do we leave them in there?" Logan asked.

"Figure it out, Sherlock," Cassie said before taking a bite of a cookie and walking out with Luc one step behind her. She could almost hear him salivating. Without thinking she threw a cookie over her shoulder and knew he had caught it when she heard him chuckle.

"Thanks, sugar. You know Logan is going to burn those cookies."

Cassie turned around and walked back to the kitchen. She waited a few minutes then pulled the pan out and put the hot cookies on the plate. She grabbed two and walked out. Logan grabbed the plate and he and Luc followed her back to the den. As she passed Luc's desk, she saw the sketch she had drawn of Logan with a big toothy grin on a cock-shaped head. She smiled then slid onto the couch and wrapped her arms around the pillow.

Luc picked her up and settled her on his lap before she could push him away. He pulled a light throw over her as Logan sat down at the other end of the couch. He pulled her feet onto his lap and stroked his fingers down her instep. She curled her toes then tried to pull her foot away. He held it tighter then smiled at her.

"Sugar, our brothers and Thor are coming over this afternoon," Luc said.

"Why?"

"We want to know everything about Julia. How you met and when she introduced you to Jimmy Martin. Don't leave out any details no matter how small," Logan said.

"It's my nap time," Cassie said.

"You can take a nap later," Luc said.

"I'm a creature of habit."

"Then I want you to get in the habit of forgiving me because sure as fuck I'm going to piss you off again and you're going to need to forgive me," Luc said.

"Me, too," Logan said, "and could you get in the habit of fucking us too?"

"Go back to Club Mystique," Cassie said as she pushed the blanket away, jerked her feet out of Logan's hands, and stood up. "I'm sure whoever the two of you played with the other night would be more than willing to give you a few more hours of her time."

Logan looked at Luc. "What's she talking about?"

"I'll tell you later."

"No. Tell me now."

When the doorbell rang, Luc jumped up. "I'll get the door."

Cassie sat down in the chair by the window, and curled her legs beneath her then planted her elbow on the arm of the chair. She glared at Logan.

"What? What did I do?"

Cassie snorted and looked away from him.

Luc came back into the room, followed by Cade, Jackson, and Thor. They each grabbed a couple cookies from the plate Luc had set on his desk earlier then dropped into chairs and made themselves at home. Luc walked over to her and reached down to pick her up.

Cassie pushed his hands away. "Hands off the goods."

Luc shook his head then sat down in the chair on the other side of the table.

"Having trouble with your sub?" Cade asked. "Maybe you should loosen the reins."

Cassie smiled because she had plans for the evening that didn't include the dominating duo. The temptation of all those lovely toys in the playroom had finally gotten to her. All she had to decide now was which one to use. Purple or pink? Pulsing, vibrating or both? It was a conundrum. Her smile widened when she thought it was a *hard* decision to make.

"Cassandra, you with us here?" Thor asked.

"Hmmm?"

"I've asked you a question—twice," Thor said.

"Sorry—I was thinking about something pleasant." She straightened up in the chair and hugged her sketchpad to her chest.

"First, I need to tell you Vincent Vitale works for me," Thor said. "He didn't tell us where to find you. We were listening in on your call to Marisol. As soon as you mentioned you had access to a beige tank we knew you were at Addison's house. You can be as pissed off as you like but we're all doing everything we can to protect you and prove you're innocent."

"Really? Well, your version of protection sucks considering it involves accusing me of selling drugs and trying to kill Julia."

"Logan and I have this," Luc said as he and Logan stood up and loomed over her. "Cassandra, you have two choices—you can answer our questions and then you can try to forgive us or you can answer our questions and refuse to forgive us. The one thing we won't let you do is make dangerous decisions because you're mad at us."

"We're doing everything we can to keep you alive, sugar, so we need an answer," Logan said. "Do you understand?"

Cassie lowered her eyes, chewed her lip, and thought about her options. She wasn't sure she could forgive them but she wasn't ready to lose them either. She didn't have any other options to prove her innocence but they were right when they said she was making poor decisions because she was angry. Decisions that might get her killed. She looked at them and wondered if she could play with them and keep her heart safe at the same time.

"We're waiting for an answer, pet," Luc said.

Cassie nodded as she made her decision. "I'll tell you everything I know about Julia, and I want to be *your* sub but only when we're playing."

"I don't want a misunderstanding here," Logan said, his face expressionless. "You're saying you no longer want to sign the contract we negotiated with Zane? You want us to treat you like any other sub we've played with at the club?"

"Yes, exactly," Cassie said, thinking she had them where she wanted them.

Logan glanced at Luc and then they both nodded and smiled. "Agreed, sugar."

Based on their level of satisfaction, Cassie knew she'd screwed up.

"Okay, then, let's get started." Thor held up the sketch of Julia. "Tell us everything you know about this person. Don't leave out any details no matter how small."

Cassie settled back in the chair and prepared herself for a long session of questions. Thor would hold up a sketch and she would tell him everything she knew about the person. Name, address, age, occupation and everything else she could remember.

After three hours Thor stopped her. "Did you ever feel as if Julia and Jimmy had made it a point to meet you, Cassandra?

Cassie shrugged. "Not really, although when I began remembering things I thought it was odd the way they included me in their business right away. When Julia had me take that box into Mike's house, I had only known her about four weeks or so."

"Do you remember the date?" Cade asked.

Cassie thought about it for a moment. "It was a few days before July fourth. Maybe the last day of June or the first day of July."

"When did Jimmy show you the video and threaten you?" Luc asked.

"July third. I remember because I tried to talk Julia into going to the police. She said she would think about it the next day when we were at the lake with her family celebrating the Fourth of July. That never happened because the three men broke into Velma's house that night and took me."

"Were you asleep when they broke in?" Logan asked.

"Yes."

"Tell us how they took you," Luc said.

Cassie looked down, and remembered the terror she had felt when she had woken up and seen three men standing over her bed. "Something woke me up. I don't know what—maybe a sound or something. I opened my eyes and there were three men standing by my bed. One on each side and one at the end. It was dark but there was some light coming in through the window. At first I couldn't move I was so scared but then I tried to fight them, to get away, but there were too many of them and two of them grabbed me. One of them held my back against his chest and another one had his hand around my throat, choking me. I couldn't breathe or scream. I was losing consciousness when the third one injected me with something. When I woke up I was blindfolded and tied up. I couldn't move but I could hear them talking." Her entire body was shaking and she felt so cold.

"Was the fourth man there?" Jackson asked.

"Yes. He was in charge. He scared me. The way he talked—like he was talking about the weather or something—he said 'your dad's going to regret fucking with me' and then he cut my clothes off with his knife and whipped me." She pulled her legs up and wrapped her arms around her knees. "I guess I fainted. When I woke up I was on a bed. He hurt me—raped me. So did the other two men but Tyson didn't touch me, at least not like that."

"Baby girl, did they say anything else about your dad?" Thor asked.

"No, I don't think so," Cassie said, feeling as if she was beginning to fade away, "but, I'm starting to remember things. Flashes. Images. I'm not sure if they're real."

"Things you saw when they drugged you and removed the blindfold?" Thor asked, then signaled the other men in the room to remain still.

Cassie nodded, then held still when the movement made her dizzy. "I got out of the room once," she said, her voice soft and distant, "but I couldn't escape from the house. I went into the den." She held out her fisted hands with her wrists together as if they were bound. "I found it and hid it."

Luc crouched down in front of Cassie. He touched her fists. "What is it, Cassie?"

"Proof. It's in the blue dragon." She dropped her hands, shivered, and then blinked her eyes as if she was just waking up from a trance.

Luc picked her up even though she tried to push him away. He lowered himself onto the couch next to Logan then pulled the blanket over her.

"Is this the blue dragon?" Thor asked, holding up a sketch of a dragon with blue and gold scales.

"Yes," Cassie said, then closed her eyes.

"Where is it now?" Thor asked.

"I don't know." Cassie closed her eyes and leaned against Luc.

"Go to sleep, sugar. You're safe with me and Logan."

A few minutes later when her breathing had evened out, Logan said, "Cassie's been having nightmares at night. We talked to Doc Marshall about them. He said that she's remembering more about what happened."

"Why now?" Thor asked.

Luc explained their suspicions about Thompson and Don Wilson being involved together in the local drug trafficking. "Logan and I think they've always kept an eye on Cassandra and that's why Thompson chose her at the May Day Masquerade at Club Mystique. He was checking to see if she'd remembered anything. When he put the cuffs on her and she freaked out he referred her to Doctor Carson. We've checked the doctor out and she appears to be clean but her office is so easy to break into a two-year-old could do it. If Cassie had told Carson any of the details about what had happened to her, she'd probably be dead right now."

Logan picked up where Luc left off. "Remember Cassie said she thought she heard the voice of one of the men who had kidnapped her in the hallway of your agency, Thor. She said she opened her door and looked out into the hall but it was empty. What if it wasn't? What if the man she heard saw her closing her door after she looked out? That might have spooked him enough to have someone go after her at her apartment."

Jackson leaned forward. "So, we have a solid connection between Thompson and Don Wilson. Tyson's dead. So we need to find Taylor and the third man."

"Taylor's dead, too," Logan said. "Luc's been on the computer and he found an article about Taylor. His body was found in an alley in Houston six years ago. The police said it was a robbery. He was shot then knifed in the back. Same way Cassie's dad died. Same way Tyson died. Luc and I think the killer was the third man. The one we haven't identified yet."

"I'll send Ben and Mac to watch Thompson, and I'll get Dania to start going through the security camera archives to see if she can find the footage Cassie described," Thor said, then he sent Luc and Logan a narrow-eyed frown. "Cassie said Thompson was nice and talked to her about getting some counseling. How do you know Thompson made Cassie *promise* to see Carson?"

"Shit," Jackson said. "You two have the private rooms at the club wired. Video? Audio? Or both?"

"Both," Logan said. "We'll tell you why at the next club meeting. Doesn't have anything to do with Cassie." He glanced at Luc. "At least we don't think it does."

Cade sat forward, an intense frown on his face. "I've heard something about dragons recently but I can't remember what."

"Well, when you remember let us know," Logan said. "Luc and I think the fourth man owned the house where she was taken."

"Marisol said I have a traitor in my agency," Thor said, "but so far she refuses to talk to me about it."

"Don't leave Vincent Vitale out of this," Cade said. "He and Marisol are cousins. He may know more than we realize since Marisol's father sent him here to watch over Addison when Mendez's men were after her."

"Logan and I think the central figure was Ryan Edwards," Luc said.

"What do you know that you're not telling us?" Cade asked.

Luc and Logan exchanged a few gestures then Luc nodded and Logan said, "Ryan Edwards was doing a few favors for some people who needed his particular skill set."

"Well, that might explain a few things," Thor said, rising and walking around the room, "and maybe why they went after Cassie." He picked up an interesting-looking rock, turned it over in his hands, and then set it back down. "What if Mendez is in control of the fourth man as well as Thompson and Don Wilson? Mendez has a reputation for holding the family members of his enemies' hostage. He may have given the order to take Cassie. We need to find out what Ryan was working on back then."

The room went quiet when Cassie moaned then her eyes popped open. In less than the blink of an eye, she went from sleep to alarmed wakefulness. Her body stiffened and she pushed away from Luc.

"It's okay, sugar. You're safe," Luc said.

Cassie glanced around then asked, "What time is it?"

"Three-thirty," Logan said.

"I'm going to start dinner," she said while trying to stand up.

"No, we're going to the club tonight," Logan said. "You're going with us."

"I don't want to go," Cassie said. "The club is less than five minutes away. If I need help—which I won't—you can be here in a flash."

Luc lifted her to her feet. "No, you're going with us. Be ready at six." He placed a hard pat on her bottom. "Get going."

"I don't need your permission to leave the room, Luc." Cassie stuck her chin in the air as she surveyed the five men in the room. "You all need to understand one thing—I hate what those men did to me and I always will, but I absolutely refuse to let them ruin my future. I may be having trouble coping with the things I'm beginning to remember, but I am coping and I'm still standing. I don't need or want you to protect me." She returned her gaze to Luc. "I chose to be your sub but only when we're playing. Outside of the playroom I'm your unwilling guest. Do you understand?"

Luc stood up and his large hands cupped her shoulders as he crowded her. She stepped back and came up against Logan. "You may no longer be *our* full-time sub, pet, but I'm still a Dom and you're still a sub and you will treat me, Logan, and every other Dom you encounter with respect. Do you understand?"

Cassie clenched her teeth to keep herself from telling him where he could put his request. After a few seconds she got herself under control and nodded.

"No," Luc said his tone hard. "Keep your chin up, eyes lowered and use words. Now, answer me—do you understand?"

"Yes, Luc."

"Not Luc—Sir."

Reminding herself that taking a swing at him was a bad idea, she decided to beat them at their own game. After all another one of her dad's favorite sayings was "fake it till you make it." "Yes, Sir, I understand."

"Good, now go get ready," Luc said. "Logan and I expect you in the entrance hall at six sharp."

Cassie turned to leave, but Logan reached out and snagged her wrist as she walked by him. Cassie froze.

"There's a list of the club rules in the top right-hand drawer of my desk. Get a copy and memorize them," Logan said. "Luc and I have been patient with you. From now on you're just another sub in our territory and all of the rules apply to you."

"Logan and I have decided to deliver the punishment you've earned over the last few days at the club tonight," Luc said. "Do you understand?"

"But that's not fair," Cassie said. "You and Logan broke our contract when you went to Club Mystique and played with another sub."

"That's the second time she's said that—what's she talking about, Luc?"

"I'll tell you later." Luc turned to Cassie. "Get going now, sugar."

Chapter Seven

Cassie entered the main room of Club Mystique, she looked around for Luc and Logan but didn't see them. Several Doms looked her way and she reached up and touched the collar around her neck. A medallion with Luc and Logan's initials hung from it and she traced them with her finger. She looked around again and saw a large man wearing a monitor's armband walking toward her. When he caught her looking at him, he frowned and she lowered her eyes.

"Sub, I'm David. You will call me 'Sir.' Logan and Luc requested that I escort you until they can join you. Follow me," he said, then turned and walked away.

Cassie stayed where she was, waiting for Sir David to realize she wasn't following him. When he noticed, he turned around, frowned, and walked back to her.

"May I have permission to speak, Sir?"

"Yes," Sir David said.

"Where are my Sirs?" Cassie asked.

"They were called away. They told me to take care of you and if anything happened to you they would do unspeakable things to me."

Cassie smiled, then lowered her eyes. "Oh," she said. "Okay. Thanks, Sir."

Sir David led the way across the room. As she walked behind him, she touched the medallion again while she wondered about the bruise she had seen on Luc's face when he and Logan had put it on her earlier. Lost in her thoughts, she was surprised when instead of escorting her to the subs' area, Sir David stopped in the middle of the room then pointed to the floor. She looked down and saw a small, round area rug. Turquoise, with a gold-and-black border. "Sir, permission to speak."

Sir David sighed. "You talk a lot for a sub," he said, then added, "Permission granted, sub."

"What am I looking for on the floor, Sir?"

"You're not looking for anything. This is where I'm putting you. On your knees."

"I thought I would be taken to the subs' area, Sir."

Sir David pointed at the floor again. "Luc and Logan told me to put you here."

"It's not safe." Her anxiety increased as she felt multiple pairs of eyes watching her. "Please take me to the subs' area, Sir."

"No. This is where you go," Sir David said.

"Sir, with all due respect, I have the right to protect myself and I'm exercising that right. Please take me to the subs' area."

"The Ramseys are in a meeting at this time but I'll pass your request on to them, sub. For the time being, remain here."

"Red, Sir," Cassie said then waited to see what he would do. A moment later another man joined them.

"What's the problem here?" he asked, his bass voice so deep it felt as if it resonated through her body, vibrating her bones.

"Luc and Logan told me to place this sub here, Lon. She refuses to stay here and has requested to be taken to the subs' area. I told her I would consult with them when they were available but she used her safeword."

"I see," Lon said. "Sub, why do you refuse?"

"It's not safe, Sir," Cassie said. "It's too open and I have no way to shield myself from harm."

"I see. Do you expect to be attacked?" Lon asked.

"I believe in being prepared for the unexpected, Sir," Cassie said.

"Did Luc and Logan say why they wanted her placed here?" Lon asked Sir David.

"No."

Lon nodded. "Then, escort her to the subs' area and they can deal with her when they're available."

"Thanks, Lon." Sir David motioned for Cassie to follow him.

Once they reached the subs' area, Cassie chose a large chair that faced into the room with Luc and Logan's personal booth behind her. To her left there were several stages along the wall where scenes were taking place and to her right was a long mahogany bar with several bartenders mixing drinks. The dance floor was across the room from her and an ornately carved staircase that led to the second floor was next to it. Cassie curled up in the chair. *This is more like it.* She smiled then planted her chin in her cupped hand and settled in for a long night.

She sneaked a few looks around the room but made sure not to look into anyone's eyes. The club was packed tonight with so many scenes going on that she was having trouble settling on just one of them. From the scene area closest to her, she watched as a Dom swatted the already blazing red bottom of his sub and felt her own arousal grow. A few feet away from her she heard the murmur of two masculine voices. She stiffened for a moment as one of them caught her attention then relaxed when she realized it was only similar to one of the voices she remembered. A little farther away, she saw cuffs being locked into place on a male sub. She glanced at his cock and saw it encased in a metal and leather contraption and couldn't help the lift of her brows. Her imagination filled in what was going to happen next as she saw the Domme pick up a riding crop and step to the side and slightly behind the sub.

Cassie shifted just a tiny bit before settling back into a more relaxed position. She didn't know how much time had gone by but it felt like it was way past her bedtime. For a moment she wondered if Sir Daniel had spoken to Luc and Logan yet but then her attention was pulled to a scene taking place to her left. She heard a soft humming sound then sharp moans of pleasure as the hum changed to a pulsing sound. The moans turned to begging as sharp slaps began raining down on the sub's bare skin.

She tipped her head a little bit, closed her eyes, and listened to the sounds of the other scenes to her left. There was the sound of hands swatting bare skin, then the sharp sound of a paddle as it contacted with a soft bottom followed by a moaned gasp. Cassie drew in a deep breath, and separated the different scents into cologne, perfume, sweat, sex, and the scent of her own arousal.

Someone bumped into her chair and she gasped then opened her eyes and froze. A Dom walked by her and her heart jerked then raced when the long slender length of a single tail whip uncoiled from his belt. It slid over her shoulder, then down her breasts and legs to the floor. It trailed behind the man's boots as he walked away from her. She watched it until it disappeared, then shuddered and locked her eyes on the spot where she'd last seen it. From one breath to the next, her sight narrowed to that one tiny spot on the floor and one image after another began flashing through her mind.

* * * *

Luc rushed into the security room, bent down, and adjusted the monitor. When he saw that Cassie wasn't where he expected her to be he frowned. "Where's Cassie?"

"She's in the subs' area. She said being out in the middle of the room wasn't safe and when David refused to move her, she used her safeword."

"She's smart and stubborn." Luc zoomed the camera in on Cassie. The dress she wore had ridden up and he could see the curve of her hip and her long slender legs. He scrolled the camera over her body, appreciating the silky golden skin that glowed through the lace of the dress he'd picked out for her to wear tonight. He paused on her nipples then moved the camera up to her face. "How do women curl up like that?" he asked, not really expecting an answer as he focused the camera on her face. He'd watched her every time she'd come to Club Mystique and he knew that the sounds and scents of the club had the tendency to spike her arousal. "Has anyone approached her?"

"A few have gone close but when they saw our collar on her they backed off," Logan said.

"Good, I don't want anyone else touching her." Luc zoomed in on Cassie's face. Her chin was up, and her eyes appeared to be half-closed.

"I don't like this. We shouldn't have left her alone." Logan leaned closer to Luc and adjusted the zoom. "We should have asked Cade and Jackson to watch for our drug dealer while we took care of Cassie."

"We need to catch the person who's leaving drugs in our private rooms," Luc said. "I've got one of my gut feelings that they're somehow connected to this mess with Cassie. Besides we've had eyes on her all evening." He adjusted the camera again. Something about her stillness bothered him. At first he thought she might be asleep, but then he saw the vein in her neck pounding the way it had when she'd had the panic attack by the pool. "Something's wrong." He rushed from the room with Logan one step behind him.

Luc pushed his way through the crowded room until he reached Cassie and crouched down in front of her. "Sugar?" He surrounded her face with his hands, and stroked his fingers down her cheeks. "Come on now, sugar. Wake up, Cassandra."

"How's she doing?" Logan squatted next to him and rubbed his hands over her bare legs. "Dammit, she's freezing cold."

"Logan, get a blanket. We need to get her to the hospital in Rendezvous."

Before he could pick Cassie up, Thor leaned over him, placed his thumb beneath Cassie's chin, and tipped her face up to the light. She didn't respond to his presence in any way. "What the hell happened?"

Luc brushed Thor's hand away then slid his hands beneath Cassie while Logan wrapped a blanket around her. "We don't know." He brushed by Thor, Cade, and Jackson.

Cade walked beside him for a few steps. "I'll call Doc and let him know what's happened. We'll be right behind you."

Luc nodded, then he and Logan headed for the private door they used. Once in the truck with Logan driving toward Rendezvous, Luc pulled Cassie up until her head was resting on his shoulder. He kissed her forehead and rubbed his cheek against hers.

"How's she doing?" Logan asked.

"Still out of it." Luc stroked his hand down Cassie's arm. "I should have had you keep her with you in the security room."

"She was only alone for about half an hour, and most of that time I was watching her on the security cameras.

"Then what the fuck happened?"

"I don't know but Doc will figure it out." Logan took the turn to the hospital emergency room entrance. Once he reached the brightly lit, covered entrance, he threw the truck into park and then jumped out and hurried around the front of the truck. Together he and Luc hurried toward the entry doors

Luc scanned the emergency room and saw Doc waving at him from one of the curtained-off areas and hurried toward him.

"Put her here." Doc patted the sheet-covered exam table.

Luc laid her down, made sure the blanket still covered her, then stepped back beside Logan and let Doc begin his examination.

"How long has she been like this?" Doc asked.

"Maybe fifteen minutes," Logan said. "No longer than twenty."

"Do you know what triggered it?" Doc flashed a small penlight over Cassie's eyes.

"No," Luc said. "Not yet."

Doc glanced at him, then turned back to Cassie. "After Cassie's episode a week ago, I consulted with a friend of mine in Austin who specializes in amnesia. She's read Cassie's medical records from the hospital eight years ago and she's also spoken to her neurosurgeon. Based on that information, she believes Cassie's amnesia isn't a result of the concussion but repressed memories from being abducted and raped."

"But, why did this happen now?" Luc asked. "She was fine at dinner tonight. Well, fine other than being pissed off at me and Logan."

Doc acknowledged Luc with a nod of his head, then ran an ink pen down the sole of Cassie's foot and smiled when she jerked her foot away. He pushed the call button for a nurse then asked, "Do you think one of the scenes upset her?"

"No," Logan said. "She was watching people and scenes but she seemed to be relaxed and enjoying herself."

There was the sound of a disturbance beyond the curtain then it was jerked back, and the metal rings screeched as it slid over the rod.

"Sir," the duty nurse said. "I've told you that you can't go back there."

"Yes, I can," Thor said. "That's my daughter in there." Thor stepped into the small exam area, and ignored the red-faced nurse when she tugged on his arm. He looked down at her then gently placed his hands on her shoulders and moved her back. "Woman, go away. Now," he said, and the nurse gasped, blushed, and then fled.

Doc chuckled. "Damn, Thor, I've been trying to get Betty to follow my orders for years and I've failed at every turn. You'll have to teach me how you do that."

Thor wrapped his hands around Cassie's blanket-covered feet and squeezed them. "Cassandra, wake up. Now," he said, then grunted when he didn't get a response. "She never was good at obeying."

A moment later, a young nurse came into the room and Doc said, "Jeannie, I need you to get the vitals, then I need an EKG and some blood drawn. I also want a CT scan, and let the ICU know I'm admitting her."

"Okay, Doc," Jeannie said. "I'll get her changed into a gown a—"

"No," Luc and Logan said, stepping forward. "We'll change her."

Jeannie shook her head. "That's against hospital policy."

"I don't think we'll worry about that right now." Doc placed his hand at Jeannie's lower back and urged her toward the curtain. "Let's step out here and Thor can fill out the paperwork for Cassie."

As soon as the curtain closed behind them, Luc pulled the blanket away from Cassie then stopped.

Luc ran his finger over the collar he and Logan had placed around Cassie's neck earlier, then removed it and shoved it into his pocket. "We need a gown."

"I'll get one," Logan said.

When Logan returned, they removed the sheer gown Luc had chosen for Cassie earlier, then dressed her in the hospital gown. Luc held her on her side while Logan snapped the back snap at the neck then tied the straps together.

Luc almost smiled when Logan pulled a pair of socks from his pocket and held them up. "Her feet always get cold." He tossed one of the socks to Luc and they put them on her. Logan held Cassie's foot up then closed his hand around it. "Her feet are so tiny."

"She may be tiny but she's fierce. I could tell she wanted to tell me to fuck off earlier today. I think I heard her grind her teeth."

Logan picked up Cassie's hand, compared it to his, and then held onto it. He leaned over the bed and said, "Come on, sugar, wake up." When she didn't stir, he stood up. "We need to find out what happened."

The curtain slid back and Doc and Jeannie entered. Thor stood behind them with Cade and Jackson at his side.

"Come out here and let Doc and the nurse take care of Cassie," Cade said.

Luc and Logan stepped out of the exam room and followed Cade to the waiting room. Once there, Cade pulled out his phone and brought up a video.

"This is what we think triggered Cassie's episode," Cade said. "It's from the security cameras at the club."

Luc and Logan moved closer, their eyes on the screen. In the center of the picture they saw Cassie curled up in a chair, her chin resting on her palm. Then suddenly a slender man dressed in a black shirt, black jeans, and heavy boots with short brown hair and a trimmed beard and mustache walked by her. As he stepped past her, the single tail whip on his belt uncurled and fell across her shoulder. On the screen, Cassie jerked to the side, her eyes wide and startled as the whip fell over her breasts and down her legs. Her focus remained on the whip as it was dragged out of sight by the unknown man.

"Damn," Luc said. "Look at her. She's terrified."

"I don't recognize him," Logan said, reversing the recording then pointing to the man on the screen. "Do you?" he asked, looking at Cade, Jackson and Thor.

"None of us could identify him," Cade said. "We looked for him in the club and couldn't find him. We asked around and nobody seemed to know him—not even Carly and she knows everyone. He appears on several other cameras but he always turns his head away or down."

"Then he's familiar with our security and where our cameras are located," Logan said.

"Not only that, watch what he does right before he steps by Cassie," Thor said.

"He deliberately bumped into her and loosened the whip so it would trail over her shoulder," Logan said. Jackson stepped closer and tipped the screen toward him. "Play it again, Logan." After watching it several more times, Jackson shook his head. "Something's not right with that guy."

Luc said, "I think he's in disguise. If Carly doesn't remember seeing him, then he entered the club another way or he didn't look like this when she saw him in reception."

Jackson pulled out his cell phone and made a call. A couple minutes later he said, "Security is going to check the video and see if they can spot when this guy first showed up."

"If they don't see him entering or exiting then we'll start counting heads," Cade said. "See who disappeared and came back in disguise."

Luc nodded. "Logan and I are going to stay here with Cassie."

"We'll bring you a change of clothes in the morning," Cade said. "Are you armed?"

Logan grinned and Luc nodded. "We've got it covered," Luc said.

* * * *

Cassie shivered then froze. She cracked her eyes open just far enough to be able to see the blinking lights of some kind of machine to her right. Inhaling a soft breath, she recognized the scents of a hospital then heard hushed voices to her left.

She listened to Luc and Logan as they speculated about what they thought had happened to her at the club. Apparently, they knew about the whip touching her and throwing her into one of her black outs. She could've told them they were right on the mark although they had no way of knowing about the memories that had overwhelmed her right before the world had faded away. There was no way she could ever tell them, or anyone else, what she'd remembered the fourth man telling her—that her dad had been a part of the cartel and he'd betrayed his team for money. She closed her eyes, and refused to let her tears fall.

Hearing another voice, Cassie held still and strained to hear what was being said. She wasn't sure who the unknown speaker was until she heard Logan call him Doc. She listened as Doc explained to Luc and Logan that her memory was returning now because she was finally able to deal with the truth. He added that there was no way to know what she had remembered until she woke up and told them.

Cassie felt a fleeting moment of hope then knew she couldn't live with herself if something happened to one of her friends because she withheld the truth. But, what if she *remembered* just enough to point them in the right direction? The only way she could keep her dad's memory intact was to avoid being questioned. That left her with *confessing* and trusting them to believe she was guilty of all the things they had accused her of doing. That way they would never know that her dad had betrayed them, and Thor and the Ramseys would have the information they needed to find an enemy who was out to kill them all.

Closing her eyes, she wondered if there were still other things she would remember in the coming days and shivered. What she had already remembered was just about more than she could bear and knowing they would hate her after she confessed would take all the energy she had left.

* * * *

"Sugar, time to wake up now," Luc said.

Cassie moaned then opened her eyes and saw Luc hanging over her. She reached up and slid her hand behind his neck then tugged him down and placed a little kiss on his lips. She smiled into his eyes, then blinked and looked around as she remembered what had happened and what she had decided to do. "What happened?"

Luc brushed his hand over her hair. "You're safe, Cassandra. You're in the hospital in Rendezvous. How are you feeling?"

Cassie scooted up and Luc adjusted the pillows beneath her head. "I'm thirsty."

Luc reached for a clear cup with ice water in it then held the straw to her mouth. "Not too much, sugar."

Cassie drank then asked, "Did I fall down? Did I hit my head?" She reached up and felt her head.

Luc took her hand and held it. "No, you didn't hit your head. Do you remember what happened last night?"

"Last night?"

"Yes." Luc narrowed his eyes. "What do you remember about last night?"

Cassie wrinkled her brow and pursed her lips. "I, uh, remember going to dinner at the hotel and I remember we went to the club."

"That's right. What else do you remember about going to the club?"

"Well, you and Logan went off and did 'important things' while I sat by myself and thought about my behavior."

Logan had heard what she said as he entered the room. "Sugar, we were giving you time to think about why you were going to be punished. We let you watch other scenes while we worked. We could have locked you in a cage until it was time for your punishment."

"I wish you would have, then that horrible man wouldn't have dragged his whip over my shoulder and scared me half to death," Cassie said before bursting into tears.

Luc and Logan surrounded her while she cried. The more they tried to comfort her the harder she cried until finally she got the hiccups and leaned against them. Then, she thought about how she had decided to lie to them and she began to cry again but this time soft hopeless tears.

"Cassie, it'll be okay," Logan said.

Cassie shook her head. "No, it won't. I can't do this. I just can't." She struggled to get away from them, but they held her tight. "You don't understand. You don't know what I know."

"Then why don't you tell us what you know, sugar?" Logan asked.

Cassie shook her head. "No, I want everyone to hear what I have to say. I only want to have to say it once before you have me arrested."

"Cassandra, we'll decide what Thor and our brothers need to know," Luc said.

"No. I want to tell them now," she said.

Luc pulled out his phone, dialed a number, and then said, "Cassandra is ready to confess." He held out the phone so she could see it was connected to Cade.

Cassie straightened the covers, then picked at a loose thread as she gathered her courage. Finally, when she looked up she knew this was the last moments she would ever spend with them. She gave herself a minute to look at them and filed the memory away in her heart where they would live forever. Her two fierce warriors. So much alike and yet so different. Logan with his laughter and sweet caring ways, and Luc with his fierce frowns and the moments of surprising gentleness when his guard was down. She felt tears glaze her eyes and quickly lowered them. She cleared her throat, swallowed, and then said, "Everything Julie said I did was true. I lied to you."

"What?" Logan asked, his voice clearly puzzled.

Cassie glanced up, saw Luc's narrowed eyes, then looked back down and watched as she smoothed her hand over the sheet then let her hands drop to her lap. "I did all those things Julie said I did. We sold drugs to lots of people, and Tyson was my, uh, boyfriend."

"I see," Luc said. "So, you and Tyson were lovers?"

Cassie nodded then remembered the men listening on the phone and said, "Yes."

"And, you sold drugs," Logan said.

"Yes. I don't know the name of the leader but I could identify his house if I saw a picture of it. It's huge. Like a private estate and it has a huge garden and the bushes are trimmed into shapes, like animals and things like that. There's a large maze with a fountain in the center."

"When you say leader do you mean the fourth man?" Luc asked. "The one who used his whip on you?"

Sensing a trap, Cassie hesitated then shook her head. "That was just an accident when, uh, Tyson got carried away. You know how it is?" She cleared her throat and swallowed to keep from throwing up. "It doesn't matter now. What matters is that I can help you find the leader and I remembered something about my Aunt Velma's boyfriend Chuck. He showed up around the same time I met Julia, and there was always something suspicious about him. After my aunt died I caught him in my house searching it."

"Was he looking for the blue dragon?" Logan asked.

Cassie's head went up in surprise. "No, that doesn't make sense. The dragon is enameled gold and too big and heavy."

"How big?" Luc asked.

"About the size of a cat," Cassie said, holding her hands out and showing them the dimensions. "There's a picture of it in the file Thor has."

"What room was the dragon in?" Logan asked.

"The den," Cassie said. "On the mantel with two other dragons. A green one and a red one."

"Describe the room to me," Logan said.

"It was large with bookshelves on all four walls but windows on the two outer walls. There was a large desk across from the door. Between the door and the desk there was a large, dark red leather couch facing the fireplace and two chairs on either side of it. There was lots of dark wood including the floor but it had one of those really expensive-looking area rugs in reds and blues. The three dragons were on the mantle, and above the fireplace there was a painting of a woman in a cream-colored dress. She's really beautiful and has long black hair and gray eyes. She looked sad."

"How long were you in the room and how did you get there?" Luc asked.

Cassie didn't dare tell them the truth—that she'd fought the third man and managed to escape from the room and down the two flights of stairs to the first floor. She'd been looking for a way out of the house when she'd stumbled into the den and had seen the computer. She'd managed to grab the flash drive and hide it in the blue dragon before she'd run from the room and been caught in the hallway. If the beating she had taken was any indication, whatever was on that flash drive was important to its owner.

Cassie fisted her hands, determined to tell them everything she could to help them find the leader and the third man. "Tyson took me to the house but I was blindfolded so I don't know where it is. It can't be too far away though because it only took us about thirty minutes to drive there. I think it was east of the lake. It had a large entry hall with double doors and it had two staircases going up to the second floor. One on each side of the entry that curved toward each other at the bottom. The floors were wood and there was a large chandelier in the entry. I was only in the house for a few minutes."

"You said Tyson got carried away when he was playing with you," Logan said. "Did that happen at that house? In the den?"

"Uh, no, that was upstairs. In a room on the third floor," Cassie said. "It has a black door and an electronic lock. It takes up most of the top floor." Cassie pleated the edge of the sheet then dropped it and looked up and wished she hadn't. Luc and Logan looked absolutely enraged. Logan's eyes were a burning golden color she had never seen before and Luc had a tic next to his lips—lips that were white with rage.

"Go on," Luc said.

"I remember a little bit about the third man," Cassie said. "I might be able to sketch him. At least enough that you might be able to identify him."

"I'll go find Doc," Luc said. "You get her dressed."

"No, I'll go find Doc," Logan said.

Cassie watched as the two of them held a long and drawn out silent conversation and she realized they were fighting over which one of them had to stay in the room with her. She took several deep breaths to hold off the tears that wanted to fall. "I understand that you don't want to be around me now. You can both leave and I'll take care of myself." She swung her legs over the side of the bed. "If I remember anything else I'll call you."

When Luc and Logan turned to look at her, she cringed then slid her feet to the floor.

"Is there anything else you want to say at this time, Cassandra?" Luc asked.

"No," she said, shaking her head.

"Good, then while you can still sit down be quiet," Luc said. "I'll be right back."

Cassie heard laughter coming from the phone Luc held before he stabbed the disconnect button and shoved it into his pocket. She waited until Luc left the room then opened her mouth to tell Logan he could leave, too. He stopped her by putting his fingers over her lips and shaking his head.

"You're in enough trouble. You have ten minutes to shower and get dressed, then we're leaving." He stepped back and waved her toward the bathroom. "Get going."

"But, don't you want to leave me here?" she asked, then squeaked with surprise when Logan grabbed her, sat down on the edge of the bed, and pulled her over his lap. He shoved one leg between her legs and forced them apart. She grabbed for the sheets on the bed to keep from sliding off his legs. "Logan!"

"I told you to be quiet." He swatted her ass six times, once for each word he gritted out. He put her on her feet, made sure she was steady, then said, "Get out of my sight, sugar. Now."

Cassie backed away from him then turned and ran into the bathroom. She slammed the door behind her. Once alone, she rubbed her stinging ass then wiped the tears from her face. Logan couldn't even stand to look at her now. Before she could turn the shower on, the door flew open and Luc stood there, staring at her with cold eyes.

"Get in the shower, Cassandra, or we'll take you home the way you are."

"Logan spanked me." Cassie sniffled, still shocked at how quickly he had grabbed her and turned from her sweet Logan into another version of Luc.

A dark brow rose over narrowed eyes, then Luc smiled and glanced at Logan before turning back to her. "You have five minutes to shower." Luc tossed some clothes on the counter, dropped a pair of sandals to the floor, and then leaned against the doorframe.

Cassie waited for a moment, realized he wasn't leaving, and moved to the shower. She adjusted the spray then stripped off the hospital gown and stepped into the stall. She washed as quickly as she could then dried off and struggled into her clothes

"Let's go," Luc said and turned away. "Doc's waiting to take a look at you before he discharges you. Then, we're going home."

"I'll just get my things and my car then I'll leave," Cassie said.

Luc stopped, pointed to the bed. "Sit down and be quiet."

Cassie shivered then hurried to sit down. She watched Logan's back as he stood at the window looking out. He wouldn't even look at her now and Luc was standing next to him and they were having a quiet conversation. Too quiet for her to hear what was being said.

Doc entered the room, smiled at her, and then asked, "How are you feeling today?"

"Better," she said, watching Luc and Logan as they turned to watch Doc examine her.

After a few minutes, Doc stepped back, frowned and rubbed his chin. "I don't feel comfortable releasing you unless I know someone is going to be with you." He turned to Luc and Logan. "Will she be staying with you?"

"No," Cassie said.

"Yes." Logan stepped forward and held out a paper and pen to Cassie. "Sign this."

Cassie took the paper, glanced at it, then looked up in surprise. "But this is our contr—" she stopped herself before she could blurt out their business in front of Doc. Shaking her head, she said, "I can't sign this."

"If you don't have anyone to take care of you, Cassie, then I'll have to keep you in the hospital for a few more days for observation,"

Doc said. "Just let the nurse know your decision." Doc gave Luc and Logan a stern look, then left the room.

Cassie held the contract and thought about how hopeful she had been when they had negotiated it. Now, it represented something she could never have. She looked up, met their gaze, and lowered her eyes again, hiding her devastation from them. She needed to get moving to stay ahead of the men hunting her but she couldn't sign the contract knowing she didn't intend to keep it. She also couldn't stay in the hospital where she would be a sitting duck and endanger the lives of the nurses and other patients.

"Sign it," Luc said. "We've already signed it."

"I can't," Cassie said. "I can't sign a contract I don't intend to keep."

"Really, sugar," Logan said. "You just confessed to being a drug dealer and a killer. Surely signing a contract you don't intend to keep can't matter to you. Not if it gets you out of here."

When she didn't answer, she heard Luc tell Logan, "Let her stay here. Come on, Logan, we have things to do."

Hearing their footsteps leaving, she panicked, knowing she would never see them again if she let them go. "Wait, wait," she said, jumping to her feet. Without giving herself time to change her mind she scribbled her name on the contract. Logan grabbed the paper and stuffed it in his pocket as Luc stalked toward her. She put her hands up as she backed away. "Wait." She squealed in surprise as he shoved his shoulder into her tummy and gave her a hard swat.

"We've got you now," Luc said, "and your ass belongs to us."

Chapter Eight

As soon as they entered the house, Thor stepped out of the den, frowned at Cassie, then said, "Cassandra, get your ass in here now."

Luc and Logan ignored him as they headed for the stairs. "We've got something to do right now. We'll be down in an hour or so," Logan said.

"Can't it wait?" Thor asked.

"Nope." Luc took the stairs two at a time with Logan a couple steps below him.

Once in the playroom, Luc dropped her to her feet then pulled her shirt over her head as Logan worked on undoing her pants. In seconds they had her naked and Luc had her over his lap.

"Your confession was bullshit and you will never again lie to us," Luc said as Cassie struggled and tried to get away. He rubbed his hands over her ass, then down her legs and over her back. Cassie kicked her legs and a hard arm pressed down on her lower back, and held her still just before a large hand snapped a stinging swat against her ass cheeks. Followed by another then another. They rained down so rapidly she couldn't distinguish one from the other.

"Stop, Luc, stop." Tears fell from her eyes as the stinging swats increased in intensity on her ass.

"Be quiet." Luc's hand snapped against her ass.

From that point on it was a long series of sharp slaps that ran over her ass and down the backs of her thighs. Cassie continued to scream and struggle but it was no use.

"Oh, yes, sugar, now we're getting some color on this ass," Luc said.

Cassie sobbed then felt Logan lift her from Luc's lap. He turned her into his arms and she hugged her arms around his neck, and hiccupped and cried, but thankfully it was over. Her ass was on fire and she wanted to sink into a tub of cold water and ease the pain. Instead she screamed, "No, no," when Logan sat down, pulled her over his lap, rubbed her ass a couple times, then began swatting it. When she kicked her legs, he slapped the backs of her thighs then squeezed her ass cheeks.

"You can be still and take your punishment, or I can restrain you, Cassandra, and then punish you," Logan said.

Sniffling, Cassie said, "I'm sorry...sorry," then hiccupped and tried to reach back to cover her butt. Logan brushed her hand away.

"Not good enough." Logan began swatting her ass again. Eventually, he stood up and dropped her onto the bed between Luc's legs.

"Hands and knees, sugar," Luc said as he sat up from his lounging position against the headboard. He wiped her red face with the edge of the sheet, then guided her to his cock and rubbed the mushroom head against her lips.

Cassie sniffled then opened her mouth and licked the slit. She swallowed the drops of pre-cum she found there then worked to get him into her mouth. Logan moved behind her, and pulled her hips up before he rubbed his cock against her slit and pushed into her. He gave her only a few seconds to adjust before he began a pounding rhythm.

"No coming or the punishment starts over," Logan said.

Cassie was so close to the edge of an orgasm, she knew if she moved she would explode into flames. Her ass was on fire but her clit was swollen and hot and ready to explode. She didn't know whether to move into Logan's thrusts or try to pull away from them as she licked and sucked and hummed around Luc's cock. She ran her hands up his chest and felt his fingers slide into her hair.

"That's it, sugar, suck on my cock, baby."

Cassie hummed with pleasure and Luc's cock grew harder in her mouth and Logan slid his cock out of her then back in. The head of his dick scraped the sensitive walls of her cunt. Little cries of need hummed over Luc's cock as her need to come grew.

Luc gripped her head, then said, "Swallow, sugar."

Cassie lashed his cock with her tongue then took him to the back of her throat and swallowed as the first splash of hot sperm erupted from him. She swallowed and gently cupped his balls and another spurt of cum filled her mouth.

Logan grasped her waist and thrust into her deeply, then began a series of sharp little thrusts until she felt him stiffen and groan. Hot cum pooled inside her and she shivered, then wiggled as she released Luc's cock and rested her head on his thigh. "Please, please," she begged, her body aching with need as Logan pulled out of her and she just knew she wasn't going to get to come. A sob left her lips as she collapsed between Luc's legs.

"Sugar, are you ever going to lie to us again?" Luc asked.

Unable to speak, Cassie shook her head then remembered they demanded words and said, "No, Sir."

Luc pulled her up and kissed her forehead. "All is forgiven, sugar," he said. "Let's get you in the shower and dressed. We have a lot of talking to do."

Logan picked her up, planted a little kiss on her lips, and then patted her hot bottom. "You're forgiven, sugar, but if you ever lie to us again we're going to take a riding crop to your ass. Do you understand?"

"Yes, Sir." Cassie let him lead her toward the bathroom. She ached but was strangely relieved that they hadn't believed her lies.

Once out of the shower, Logan dried her off while Luc opened drawers and got out several items. When Cassie saw them, her first instinct was to run. Instead she let Logan hold her over his lap and spread her legs as Luc began coating her back hole with lube. The need to come increased with every little press of his finger into her and she found herself rocking back and forth while little moans of pleasure echoed around them. Little by little his finger breached her and she lifted her ass to him, hoping he would give her more, which he did when he added a second finger. When he began penetrating her and twisting his fingers at the same time, her moans turned into sharp cries of need and begging.

She wiggled, and tried to move forward on Logan's lap to get her needy clit against his jean-covered leg. Before she could move into position, she heard him chuckle then slide her away.

"None of that," Logan said, then patted her hot bottom. "We're going to get this tight little ass ready so we can fuck you at the same time. So, be still and let Luc get that big plug in your ass."

Cassie groaned then froze as Luc pressed what felt like a huge plug against her overly sensitive hole. He pushed it into her then pulled it back, and gave it a little wiggle and twist as he worked it in deeper. She felt Logan slide his hand down to her ass and use his fingers to stretch her cheeks farther apart so Luc could work on getting the plug past the tight muscle keeping it out. Without thinking she pushed back, opening herself to the pressure on her anus, and felt the plug slip into her.

Luc and Logan moaned just before she felt a little kiss and nip on her ass cheek and Luc said, "Sugar? That is one beautiful sight."

Logan lifted her to a sitting position then bent her back over his arm and kissed her. "If we don't get you dressed and out of here, Thor is going to come up here and kick the door down."

* * * *

Cassie shifted in the chair, glared at Luc's smirk, then looked at Logan for sympathy—something he wasn't willing to give to her. Instead he winked and grinned. She settled back and the plug in her ass shifted, causing her to give a little squeak of distress and drawing the eyes of the other five men in the room her way. Blushing, she focused on her clenched fists, knowing they probably had a good idea what was causing her discomfort. *Damn Doms.*

"Cassandra, would it help if I told you Logan and I knew your dad and that he was a good man trying to do an impossible job?" Luc asked.

"What?" Cassie looked at him. "You knew my dad?"

"We can't tell you how we met him," Logan said, "but we can tell you we're absolutely positive Ryan Edwards never did anything to betray his oath."

"Are you sure?" She sat forward and pushed aside her discomfort.

"Yes." Luc surrounded her face with his hands and made her meet his eyes. "Your dad was a good man, sugar. We think someone blew his cover and the fourth man, the one you think was in charge, was going to use you to control him."

"But, then it's my fault he was killed," Cassie said. "Because I told him what they'd done to me."

Luc shook his head. "They didn't have any way of knowing you'd told him, sugar. Velma wouldn't have told them. That means they'd already decided to kill him."

"Julia knew, and I think her parents knew, too," Cassie said. "Chuck knew, too. He had taken my aunt to his house the night I was abducted. After I was returned he helped her take care of me."

"Do you know where Chuck is now, sugar?" Luc asked.

Cassie shook her head. "After I caught him in my house he left and I never heard from him again. His picture is in the file Thor has."

Thor dug through the file and held up a picture of a man with dirty blond hair and a goatee. "Is this Chuck?" he asked.

"Yes, that's him," Cassie said. "He was a little under six feet, medium build, not buff like Luc or Logan. He has a mustache and goatee, and brown eyes. He spoke with a northern accent and he said he was a truck driver. He liked to play pool and he would take Velma to the local bars and play for money."

"What do you think he was looking for in your house?" Luc asked.

"The flash drive," Cassie said, her brows drawn down as she rubbed her temples. "I hid it in the blue dragon."

Luc and Logan looked at each other over Cassie's head then Logan nodded and said, "Where'd you get the flash drive, sugar?"

"I took it from the computer on the desk in the den. They were looking for me so I didn't have much time to hide it. I put it in the mouth of the blue dragon." Cassie wrapped her arms around her waist and comforted herself as she told them about the beating she had taken from the fourth man when he realized the flash drive was gone.

"God," Luc said, as he sat down next to her and cuddled her. "Sugar, he's never touching you again."

Logan slid closer to her, sandwiching her between them as Jackson handed her a sketchpad and box of pencils.

"Try to sketch the third man, Cassie," Jackson said.

Cassie sketched while the men discussed the information she had been able to give them. At first she just drew a series of lines and curves but then they began to form into a face.

Thor leaned on the back of the couch and watched her. Then, suddenly he cursed and reached over her shoulder. He grabbed the sketchpad and held it up and showed it to Cade.

"Son of a bitch," Cade said. "That looks like Dale Miller."

Cassie cried out then slid onto Luc's lap and tried to disappear into his chest. Discovering that she had been working with, speaking to, and even laughing with the man who had abused her terrified her. Miller's office was only two doors down from hers. He had spent time in her office, leaning on her desk and joking with her.

"It's okay, sugar," Luc said, rubbing her back and holding her close.

"I spoke to him all the time at the office," Cassie said. "I didn't recognize his voice."

"Describe the third man's voice to us, sugar," Logan said.

"It was raspy. Really deep, like he had to strain to talk," Cassie said.

"I think he disguised his voice deliberately then," Luc said. "Plus, they drugged you, sugar. That would make a difference as well."

"What about the fourth man?" Cade asked. "Do you remember his voice?"

Cassie nodded. "Soft with an east coast accent, maybe Boston. He sounded arrogant and pompous. Whenever he spoke I always thought he talked really big for a little man and I thought if I could get away I could have kicked his ass."

"He was short?" Thor asked.

Cassie nodded. "Not too much taller than me. When he held me down I could feel him against me and he was heavy. Overweight and a few inches taller than me. Maybe five feet eight or nine. He wore too much cologne. The same kind your accountant wears, Thor. That's why I can't stand to be around him."

"That's it," Cade said. "That's where I heard about dragons." He looked at the rest of the men in the room. "When I had lunch with Zane two weeks ago, he told me that Ravyn Dolman has a collection of gold-enameled dragons that her husband was demanding she give him in their divorce case."

"Isn't he the guy who was arrested for trying to have his wife killed?" Thor asked.

"Yeah, but he claims she's been laundering drug money through her father's company and that she had hired someone to get rid of him so he hired someone to kill her first," Cade said. "Dolman claims his wife's father was in partnership with a Colombian drug cartel."

"Let me guess," Thor said. "Mendez."

"That's right," Thor said. "Dolman says after Ravyn's father died and she took over the business, she continued to launder money for Mendez. He claims when she decided she wanted out she tried to frame him."

"What does Zane say?" Luc asked.

"He's not sure. It doesn't look good for Ravyn Dolman. All the evidence leads back to her," Cade said. "I think Zane has a thing for her but you know how he feels about the justice system. If she's guilty, he won't save her no matter how much he wants her."

"You mean the same way everything led back to me," Cassie said, sitting up on Luc's lap and looking at the other men in the room. "Think about it. This is how they operate. Put the blame on someone else and then they walk away and continue doing what they do. Eight years ago they framed me and took me so they could control my dad but when I got away they killed him. Then they took Marisol's sister so they could control Juan Rios. Then they took Hank Stewart's sister to try to control him and he helped Mendez kidnap Addison. They took Addison to teach you a lesson, Cade. Earl Baume wanted to take Jenna and Jackson for revenge but I'll bet if you check you'll find he was involved with Mendez in some way. And now Ravyn Dolman is right in the middle of this. If she still has the blue dragon then we need to get the flash drive from it and see what's on it."

Cade already had his phone out and was talking to Zane telling him what they had figured out. "No, just get the flash drive," he said, "and bring it to the ranch. Once we look at it we'll decide what to tell Ravyn Dolman, if anything." He listened for a moment then rolled his eyes. "Well, Zane, I don't know what we'll do if it proves she's guilty. We'll figure out what to do after we've looked at it, and no, we don't want to get a search warrant right now. If we have to we'll put it back and then get one and find it again." He hung up and sighed. "I swear sometimes I want to kick Zane's ass. I don't know where he got this honest streak but its damn irritating when I'm trying to get something done."

Jackson snorted, then chuckled. "We'll have to watch him or he'll have that poor girl behind bars and then he'll be moping around. Anyone with eyes in their heads can see he's got a hard-on for her."

Logan reached over and took Cassie from Luc's lap and pulled her onto his lap. "My turn," he said as he cuddled her close. "You okay, sugar?"

"Yes, Logan," Cassie said.

Thor drew their attention as he moved around the couch. "Cassandra, I've put a tail on Miller so you don't need to worry about him. Hopefully, he'll lead us to the fourth man."

Cassie nodded then narrowed her eyes. "Do you have a picture of Ravyn Dolman?"

"Why, sugar?" Luc asked.

"Just a theory I have," Cassie said.

Luc pulled out his phone and pulled up a picture of Ravyn Dolman then turned the screen to her.

Cassie nodded then rubbed her forehead on Logan's chest. "That's the lady in the portrait. The one above the fireplace in the den."

"Dammit," Thor cursed. "We need to find out if Charles Dolman moved into Ravyn's family home after he married her eight years ago. Her father, Douglas Benson, died seven years ago, so the fourth man might have been her father or her ex-husband."

"Or both," Cade said. "I think they were both involved with laundering money for the drug cartel. We need to get descriptions of both of them."

"We need to get in that house and see what's on the top floor," Logan said.

"Let's take this to your house," Luc said to Cade. "Call Zane back and see what he knows about Ravyn Dolman's house. She probably has a security system and housekeeper. Find out her schedule. Logan and I will retrieve the flash drive tonight."

"I want to go with you," Cassie said.

"Sugar, we can't take you." Logan rubbed her back. "We want you to stay with Addison, Jenna, and Marisol."

"No. I need to go," Cassie said. "That room haunts me. I need to see it." She waited while Luc and Logan decided then breathed a sigh of relief when Logan nodded.

"You'll do exactly what we say, no hesitation," Logan said.

"Yes, Logan," Cassie said. "I promise. Can we stop by my apartment? I'd like to check it and change into some dark clothes."

"We can do that," Luc said. "While we're there you need to grab some more clothes. You're going to be staying with us for a long time now, sugar. In fact, we need to have your apartment packed up and your things moved to our house."

"But, what about my school and stuff?" Cassie asked.

"Sugar, do you really want to be a forensic psychologist? Or did you just choose that to try to find the people responsible for your dad's death?" Luc asked.

"My dad's death," Cassie said, then looked at Thor. "Sorry, Thor."

"That's okay, baby girl. As long as you're happy I'll be happy." Thor rubbed his hands together. "Okay, let's get going."

* * * *

Off in the distance a dog barked and Luc held up his fist, signaling Logan and Cassie to stop. Cassie knelt down in the shadow of a large bush and waited for the signal to move. Dressed in dark, body-hugging pants and a shirt along with black, soft-soled boots and a dark hoodie to cover her hair, Cassie tried not to smile. Luc and Logan had painted her face with camouflage paint and she knew she looked like something out of a horror movie. Luc had kissed her and said she looked cute then Logan had kissed her and when he pulled away, he'd had smears of black and gray all over his face. Then he'd told her to hold on a moment and he had smeared more stuff on the tip of her nose and smiled. Luc had given her backpack back to her and she'd armed herself from it with two guns and her dad's knife as well as several zip ties just in case.

Logan drew her attention back to their mission when he knelt down behind her. She turned to him and asked, "What's he doing?"

"Disarming the alarm system," Logan said. "Give him a couple seconds."

"I want some of those goggles," Cassie said, talking about the night vision goggles Luc and Logan wore.

In her ear she heard Luc snort then say, "Move now," so she stood up and ran, half bent over, to the side of the house, and stopped next to him. Logan was one step behind her and crowded her against Luc. She glanced over her shoulder, and was barely able to make out his shape against the darkness cast by the house.

A few seconds later she watched as Luc disappeared through a dark window then held his hand out and shook it. Logan urged her forward and she took Luc's hand and let him pull her up through the window, and into the room. She looked around and caught her breath when she realized she was in the den from her memories. Without thinking, she got up and walked over to the fireplace. In the small amount of light shining into the room through the window she could see the three dragons on the mantle.

She reached into the mouth of the blue dragon and felt the flash drive where she had left it, trapped between the teeth of the dragon. She picked at it with her fingernail until it popped loose then held it up to show it to Luc and Logan. Luc took it from her and slid it into a small envelope and stuck it in a pocket. He leaned over until his lips were against her ear then said, "Follow me. Stay between us."

Logan's hand pressed against her lower back, and urged her forward toward the open door. Luc paused then looked around the edge and signaled them to follow him into the hallway. They climbed the stairs, keeping to the carpet runner to muffle their steps. At the top, Luc looked at her and she pointed to the small sitting area straight ahead of them. When he looked at it then back at her, she stepped around him and crept to the wall at the left side of the sitting area and pushed on the paneled wall. A hidden door popped open, revealing another staircase.

Luc pulled her back then went up the steps first. She and Logan followed behind him. At the top of the stairs was a short open hallway with a door on the right and a door on the left. Cassie pointed to the door on the right. It was just as she had described it—black with an electronic keypad next to it. She reached around Luc and keyed in the four digit number she remembered seeing the third man key in and they heard a snip as the lock disengaged.

Luc opened the door and stepped into the room then cursed and pulled her into the room. As soon as Logan stepped in behind her, Luc covered her mouth with his hand and turned on the light.

Cassie screamed, the sound muffled by Luc's hand. The walls were covered with large pictures of naked girls, including her. Luc picked her up and cradled her in his arms. He whispered assurances to her while Logan walked around the room. He filmed the room and the pictures on the walls. Miller, Tyson and Taylor were in the pictures but the fourth man wasn't in any of them.

Cassie was crying, sobbing, her body curled into Luc as he leaned back against the door with his eyes closed.

"Sugar, I've got you." Luc said, nuzzled her neck. "Let Logan finish and we'll get the hell out of here."

"The pictures," she said, "take them down. Take them down."

"We can't. We have to leave them here," Luc said. "If Dolman's the fourth man and he gets in here and sees they're gone he'll know someone knows and he'll run."

A few minutes later Logan took her out of Luc's arms and they left the room with Luc in the lead. When she wiggled, Logan told her to be still so she let herself relax in his arms until they reached the truck where he climbed in then kept her on his lap. She settled her cheek into the curve of his neck and let her thoughts drift while he and Luc spoke in soft voices. She breathed in Logan's scent and let it calm her.

* * * *

Cassie snuggled her nose into the middle of a hard, warm back as she slid her hand over a tight waist and fanned it back and forth over the hills and valleys of hard abs. Luc moved up close behind her and pressed his chest to her back as his hand wiggled between her arm and side and his hand cupped her breast and plucked at a hardening nipple.

His arms tightened around her as he pulled her back then slid her onto her tummy. In seconds he was lying over her. He nibbled on the back of her neck as he slid a knee between her legs and spread them. His hands cupped and squeezed her breasts before he ran them down to her pussy and gathered her juices, spreading them over her clit.

"Sugar, you've been having a really interesting dream." His hot breath fanned across her neck as he pushed his cock through her slit and began stroking his way into her.

Cassie raised her ass, giving him better access, then moaned as he slid home, his weight flattening her against the mattress, restrained yet still free to move.

A second later his hands slid back up to her breasts. He palmed them as he fucked into her. Next to them Logan rolled over and opened his eyes. He went from drowsy to completely awake in less than a second.

"Damn, that's hot," Logan said. "I love watching Luc fuck you, sugar. Spread those legs a little wider so I can see your sweet little cunt taking his cock."

Luc pushed his knees out, forcing Cassie's legs wider before he thrust into her harder. His pelvis slapped against her ass with each deep thrust and Cassie lifted her ass a little higher then moaned.

"Cassandra, I want in your ass," Luc said. "Are you ready for that, baby?"

"Yes, oh, yes." Cassie wiggled her ass, and moaned again.

He pulled out of her. Logan handed him a tube of lube and then pulled Cassie on top of him and thrust his hard cock into her pussy. "Sugar, your cunt is so hot and wet."

Cassie wrapped her arms around Logan's neck and nibbled on his chin. His hand slid into her hair, and held her in place while Luc spread cold lube over her dark hole. His fingers sank in a tiny bit then more as he made sure she was ready for him. She looked over her shoulder and wiggled again and he swatted her ass. A second later he drizzled a line over his hand then grasped his cock and pumped it several times until it was slick. His eyes met hers while he began rubbing the head of his cock against her rosette.

"Oh, god, oh, Luc." Cassie felt Logan's cock shift inside her. "Don't stop, Luc. Don't stop."

Luc held her hips while he slowly entered her. "Oh, sugar, you feel so good. So tight and hot."

Luc ran his hands over her ass cheeks to her waist as he slid deeper into her. She rested her weight on Logan, totally incapable of movement as she concentrated on the feeling of having both of them inside her. Waves of pleasure shivered through her as goose bumps popped up on her arms. She wiggled her hips, lighting up more nerves, then moaned and panted as they began to move.

"More," she begged. "More, Luc, please, please."

"Just about there, sugar." Luc slid the last inch into her, then paused before pulling out, drawing another little scream of pleasure from her at the same time.

Cassie squirmed then held still as Luc and Logan began a rhythm of in and out—Luc slid in as Logan pulled out then Logan slid in as Luc pulled back. Sandwiched between them, all she could do was feel as pleasure swamped her and she pressed down, feeling her clit slide over Logan's pelvis with each thrust. Her belly began tingling and she stiffened her legs, reaching for an explosive pleasure that was just out of reach. Luc pressed her down, hard, against Logan and fucked into her several times then slapped her ass and she exploded, screaming their names. A few seconds later she heard Logan groan as he filled her with his hot cum. Luc drew his cock out then thrust back into her and she felt his cock jerk inside her as he came.

Luc rested his forehead in the center of her back, between her shoulder blades, and his hot breath flowed over her skin. He got control of his breathing then four hands ran over her, soothing her. When Luc tried to pull out of her, she tightened around them. "No," she said, too tired to move.

"Our girl likes us where we are, Logan."

"I vote we stay here all day," Logan said, too sated and comfortable to even think of moving. He gripped Cassie's wrists and pulled them above his head and held them there. "What do you say, sugar? Want to stay home and fuck all day?"

Cassie smiled then licked Logan's nipple and gave it a little kiss. "Yes, I want to suck your cocks in the shower, and I want to fuck you both in the kitchen, and later in the living room on the couch and in the truck on a bumpy road." She smiled when she heard them groan. "I want one of you to have your big hard cock inside me, fucking me, until I can't speak or think. Until we're so worn out we can't move."

Every word she spoke had their cocks growing harder until Luc was pumping into her again and Logan was sliding his cock in sync with Luc's.

"Sugar, talk like that will get you fucked every time," Logan said.

"I was counting on that, Sir." Cassie giggled and settled in to enjoy their attention. Logan slid his hand down her belly and grasped her clit, then pinched it.

"Come now, sugar."

Cassie sucked in a breath then screamed her pleasure against his neck. Her body quaked as Luc and Logan came inside her.

After a few moments of heavy breathing and pounding hearts, Luc swatted her ass and pulled out of her.

"Shower then breakfast and fucking in the kitchen," Luc said.

Before Logan or Cassie could respond, a cell phone rang and the three of them groaned, knowing their plans for the day were about to be changed.

Luc answered the phone, listened for a minute, then Cassie heard him say, "We'll be there in thirty minutes." He looked at her and Logan, then sighed when he hung up. "Change of plans. Cade wants us at his house as soon as possible."

"What's going on?" Cassie trembled. "Is something wrong?"

Luc picked her up, and cuddled her. "It's okay, sugar. We'll never betray you again. No matter what." He carried her into the bathroom and Logan turned on the shower.

"Cade and Thor have looked at the flash drive. They want to discuss it with us," Luc said as he grabbed the shampoo. He waited while Logan tipped her head back and wet her hair before running it through the soft strands.

Cassie grabbed the shower gel Luc and Logan used and divided her attention between them while the two of them gave her their full attention. Eventually they ended up clean and rinsed and ready to dry off with hearts pounding and lungs straining for the next breath. Cassie giggled then fell against Luc and Logan as they tried to dry her off.

"We'll never get there if we don't stop touching each other," she said.

Logan chuckled and ruffled the towel over her hair. "Okay, sugar. Just let us comb the tangles out of your hair and then we'll get dressed."

Cassie smiled into the mirror as Luc and Logan moved behind her, and each of them ran a comb through her hair, starting at the ends and moving up to the crown. Eventually her hair hung down in shiny strands, still damp. Luc and Logan leaned down, kissed her shoulders, then their eyes met hers in the mirror. She looked at the two of them standing behind her and said, "I love you. Both of you so much. More than I ever thought I would love anyone."

Logan whooped and grabbed her. His mouth covered hers as he kissed her. His tongue dueled with hers. Cassie wrapped her arms and legs around him, and kissed him back, so happy that tears flowed from her eyes and down her cheeks. When Logan lifted his mouth from hers, she expected Luc to be grab her. Instead Logan held her tighter. His hand ran up and down her back.

"It's okay, sugar. Luc's just scared."

"He doesn't want me. He doesn't love me."

"No, sugar, that's not true. We just never believed we would find anyone like you. Someone who would love both of us. I love you, Cassie, and Luc does, too. He just needs time to be able to say it."

Cassie shook her head and moved back from Logan. "He said he wouldn't, Logan. He meant it." She looked around, realizing she didn't have any clothes in the bathroom, and moved quickly into the closet area. She grabbed the first dress she found and struggled into it, then smoothed it down her body and slipped her feet into a pair of flats. She could hear harsh whispering coming from the far side of the closet and knew Logan and Luc were arguing about her.

Heartbroken, thinking that the past days had meant nothing to Luc, she realized she couldn't face him and hurried from the room and down the stairs. She would drive herself to Cade's and ask Addison to let her stay there until she and Logan could talk about what they were going to do. Luc may not want her but Logan did and she was keeping him if she could.

Once she reached the front porch, she glanced at her car, remembered she didn't have the key, and ran to Logan's truck. He always left the keys in it no matter how many times Luc told him not to. She opened the door, jumped in, and started the engine. She could barely reach the gas pedal so she scooted up until her tummy was against the steering wheel and took off, clipping the edge of the flower bed on her way around the circular drive. She made it to the main road and the truck bounced up then down and she went flying.

The top of her head hit the roof of the truck before she landed on the seat again and bit her tongue.

She cursed then tears glazed her eyes as she remembered how she had said she wanted to fuck Luc or Logan on a bumpy road. She reached for the brakes, intending to stop and have a good long cry, but before she could a truck passed her then slammed on its brakes in front of her. She barely had time to jerk the wheel to the side and drive down into the ditch and then back up on the road. Before she could stop the truck and give the other diver a cussing out she was bumped hard from behind. She glanced in the rearview mirror and saw at least four men in the truck behind her and knew the men hunting her had caught up to her. She increased her speed to keep from being hit again.

She was going so fast she missed the turn to Cade and Addison's house. The truck behind her forced her to drive farther from Luc and Logan as it came up behind her again. She held the steering wheel with one hand while she reached for the gun Logan kept in the glove box. It took her several tries before she got it open and managed to get the gun in her hand along with an extra magazine. Ahead of her, she saw the entrance to the Ramsey cemetery and without hesitation she turned into it. Gravel sprayed out behind her as she crashed through the gate guarding the entrance. The large truck followed behind her but she managed to put some distance between them as she turned off the road and headed for the river.

Once there she bailed out of the truck and ran for the cover of the trees and bushes. She heard the sound of truck doors slamming behind her as she ran. She dodged bushes and fell several times as her feet got tangled up in the vines on the ground. Once at the river, she stepped into the mud, deliberately leaving a smeared track. She jumped back toward the shore, stopping only long enough to clean up her trail as she made her way back into the bushes along the shore.

Cassie knew her bright colored hair would give her away, but the green dress she wore would blend into the bushes. At least it would in a moment, she thought, as she took it off and rubbed it in the dirt, dulling its color. Then she put it back on and left her hair inside her dress. She gathered a handful of dirt and rubbed it into her hair then wove leaves and twigs into the strands. She scraped up some dirt and smeared it over her face, arms and legs until she disappeared into the background of the forest.

The black barrel of Logan's gun wouldn't reflect the light and she placed the extra magazine in the pocket of her dress. Around her the sounds of the forest resumed, and she hid a grin. The men hunting her, at least four of them, were obviously unaware they were playing a game her father had taught her long ago. She crept from her hiding place, staying in the shadows and pausing often as she moved in the direction of Club Mystique.

She heard steps coming her way and slid into a clump of bushes, then narrowed her eyes as Miller walked by her. He carried a large knife and he had a scoped rifle over his shoulder. He never bothered to look behind him as he spoke into a small mic. She saw him signal to someone on his left then someone to his right. So, three hunting her and maybe the fourth one was in front of them or trailing behind. Her father had always said making assumptions about the enemy would get you killed so she stayed hidden.

After a few moments, she wondered if she could make it back to her truck and quickly decided not to try. They may have left the fourth man there just in case she decided to do that. She built a map in her mind of her location and realized she had three options. Cade and Addison's house to the east, Club Mystique to the west, or Luc and Logan's to the south. The only thing across the river was more land and the highway.

Wondering if Luc and Logan had realized that she was missing and if they were on their way, she decided her best bet was to stay put and let them find her. She settled in for a long wait, knowing when Logan found her she wouldn't be sitting for a very long time. When something crawled up her leg, she let out a little squeak of distress then froze, hoping whatever it was it was alone and not a colony of ants. She squeezed her legs together, determined to keep it away from her vulnerable pink parts and breathed a sigh of relief when it dropped off of her.

A second later two hands grabbed her and jerked her from her hiding place. She kicked and punched out, landing several blows and hearing her captor's grunt of pain before his arms surrounded her then shoved her to the ground. He dropped down onto her, forcing her face into the debris on the ground. Fighting to get loose, Cassie turned her head to the side and screamed, hoping Luc and Logan were close enough to hear her.

A second later, her arms were jerked behind her back and a pair of cuffs snapped around her wrists. She was jerked to her feet. Miller stood in front of her, smirking, then without warning his hand shot out and he slapped her, then backhanded her. Blood flooded into her mouth and without thinking, pissed off that she had let them catch her, she spit in his face. He fisted his hand and punched her in the belly. She screamed as loud as she could before she bent over with pain.

"Bitch." Miller wiped the bloody spit from his face. "I'm going to enjoy killing you."

Cassie looked up and smiled. "I'm going to enjoy watching Luc and Logan kill you."

Miller laughed then grabbed her arm and began dragging her back toward the trucks with his two companions a couple steps behind them. When she stumbled, he jerked on her arm, causing the cuffs to dig into her wrists as her shoulder ached with the pressure he was putting on it. At the edge of the trees, Miller didn't hesitate to step out into the open and tug her toward his truck.

* * * *

"They're coming out of the trees," Logan said, knowing Luc was up at the monument waiting for him to report.

"I've got them," Luc said while watching the tree line through the scope on his rifle. When he got his hands on Cassie, she wasn't going to be able to sit for a week, he thought, deciding this called for more than a hand on her bare ass. When he and Logan had realized she had taken off, he had cursed a blue streak. Finding out she was being chased had shaken him like nothing else ever had. Even now his hands wanted to shake with pure terror and he had to use every ounce of his control to steady them. If he didn't clear his mind and calm down he wouldn't be able to make this shot. He forced himself to take several deep breaths and focus on the job at hand. "Get ready to grab her when she runs back into the trees, Logan. Do you recognize any of the men with Miller?"

"No. I don't' think they're military," Logan said. "What if Cassie takes off for the truck?"

"She won't. Her father taught her better than that," Luc said as he lined up the shot. "Dammit, Cassie's in the way. I can't get a clear shot at Miller."

Beside him Jackson looked through his scope and said, "The truck's blocking me. I can't get him either." Next to them Mac acted as their spotter. He took a look and shook his head.

Luc took a breath, held it, and then fired twice as Jackson fired at his two targets. Three men went down and wouldn't be getting up but Miller spun around and dropped to the side. Luc knew he was only winged. Luc fired again, laying down a line of shots and giving Cassie time to run, which she did, although from the position of her right arm, the move had cost her.

"I'm going," Luc told Jackson. "Keep an eye on the trucks in case Miller tries to escape."

"I've got it," Jackson told him as Luc slipped away and Mac picked up his rifle Pretty Patty and began scoping the area.

"Two guns are better than one," Mac said, and Jackson nodded in agreement.

* * * *

When Cassie heard the shots being fired and saw three of the men fall she jerked away from Miller. Her shoulder popped, but she gritted her teeth and ran back into the trees. She ducked under a low-hanging branch, and ran as fast as she could in the direction the shots had come from—the monument on the hill.

Behind her she heard several more shots, and then the sound of someone in pursuit. She looked around, desperate to find a place to hide, and saw a fallen log with bushes and vines growing over it. Hoping there were no snakes or creepy crawlies nesting beneath it, she lay down by it and tried to muffle her breaths.

Cassie felt something touch her leg and froze then smothered a scream when a set of blazing hazel eyes slid into view followed by a set of relieved hazel eyes. Logan smiled at her and gave her a thumbs-up before Luc glared at him then knocked his hand aside.

Luc clenched the hair at her nape then his mouth slammed down on hers. The kiss was brutal, his teeth nipping her cut bottom lip just before his tongue swept into her mouth and took possession of her. He licked the inside of her mouth, tangled his tongue with hers, then ended the kiss with another little nip on her bottom lip before he kissed his way to her ear. "I'm going to blister your ass." Then with a little nip on her earlobe, he smiled into her eyes, and she shivered with fear and excitement. Maybe she had jumped to the wrong conclusion. Maybe Luc felt more for her than she realized. Before she could decide, he tapped her cheek then signaled her to follow him.

Cassie eased out of her hiding place, and Logan removed the cuffs from her wrists. Luc turned in the direction Miller and his friends had taken her. She tapped him and when he turned to her, she shook her head then mouthed "Miller" and pointed in the opposite direction.

Luc shook his head then gave her a look that let her know he was in charge and her best chance of avoiding even more punishment was to keep quiet and follow his directions. Cassie lowered her eyes.

Apparently a move that satisfied Luc's need to dominate her as a moment later Logan nudged her to get her moving.

They moved through the forest, staying to the shadows until Luc signaled them to drop to the ground. Cassie kept her face down and listened to the sounds around them. A twig snapped somewhere ahead of them. Logan pushed her closer to the ground then pressed down on her back, signaling her to stay put. A few seconds later he pulled her up into a running crouch and they moved to another mound of bushes by a large tree. Ahead of them, Miller entered a small clearing. Logan signaled her to be still then he and Luc moved off in opposite directions.

Cassie waited until she heard Luc's voice telling Miller he had him in his sights. Miller fired in Luc's direction as he dove for the nearest cover and right into Logan. She heard a grunt then the sound of fists hitting flesh and Miller stumbled back into the clearing, followed by Logan.

Miller had his knife out and Logan wore a smile on his face as he motioned to him, inviting him to come after him. Miller attacked and Logan slugged him several more times as he swept past him, then grabbed him and threw him into the center of the clearing.

Luc stepped into view and said, "My turn," then blocked Miller when he made a break for the trees and punched him in the face once, then again until Miller was on the ground, cursing and spitting blood.

"You're going to die," Miller said, then spit again. "But before you do you're going to watch me fuck your bitch and cut her up."

Luc jerked Miller up then punched him and Miller crumpled to the ground as Thor and Cade stepped into the clearing.

"Is he still alive?" Thor asked.

"Alive enough to answer questions," Logan said as he watched Luc pat Miller down and remove several more weapons before holding up a handcuff key.

Cassie moved into the clearing and stopped next to Logan while avoiding Luc's glance. Logan carefully hugged her and she started crying. "Are you mad at me?"

Before Logan could answer, Luc walked over to her and pulled her back against him while he carefully moved her arm and Logan used his belt to make a temporary sling.

"The answer is hell yes, sugar," Luc said. "I'm madder than hell at you for risking your life like that and because I love you I'm going to blister your ass red."

"You love me?" Cassie asked, ignoring his threat to punish her. "Are you sure?"

"Sugar, if you'd stuck around you would have known I left the room because hearing you say you loved us, loved me, got to me. I didn't know how much I wanted to hear those words until you said them."

"Oh, Luc, I love you and Logan so much," Cassie said, tears in her eyes. "I'm sorry for leaving."

"I know you are, sugar, but I'm still beating your ass," Luc said and smiled.

"After we get you to the emergency room and back home," Logan said then added, "I think we should do it at the club."

"No," Luc said. "I want to put some restraints on her and see how she handles them. Better do it at home."

Cassie watched the two of them walk off, arguing. She smiled at Thor and Cade and had taken a step to follow them when they stopped and turned around.

"Sugar, are you coming?" Logan asked.

Cassie laughed then hurried to catch up to them and took her place between them where she belonged.

* * * *

That evening she stepped out of the shower, rubbed herself dry then opened the bathroom door. She wandered into the bedroom and found Luc and Logan sitting in the chairs by the fireplace. They were relaxed with their legs stretched out in front of them and bare feet crossed at the ankles. They were naked.

Cassie smiled then licked her lips before she moved to the rug between them. She knelt between their feet and spread her legs as she rested her hands, palms up, on her knees.

"Look at me, Cassandra." Luc pulled his legs back then leaned forward and rested his elbows on his knees.

Cassie met his eyes and her bottom lip trembled. He was disappointed in her.

Luc reached down and pulled her up onto his lap. "Sugar, don't cry. Logan and I have talked about this." He wiped the tears from her face with his fingers. "We didn't trust you and we let you down. You didn't trust me and I let you down."

Logan crouched down next to them and ran his hands over her bare legs. "And, I let you down, sugar. We've got the love thing down but we need to work on trusting each other."

Cassie nodded. "I'm sorry I ran away."

Luc smoothed her hair. "I'm sorry I didn't trust you and I'm sorry I walked away without telling you how much I love you."

Logan chuckled. "I love you, too, sugar, and I'm sorry for not trusting you."

Cassie smiled but her lip still trembled. "Do you want me to bend over the bed now?"

Luc patted her bottom. "No. It's been a rough day and you need to get some rest."

Cassie scooted off his lap. "Are you tired, Luc?"

Luc shook his head. "No, sugar."

"Are you tired, Logan?"

"No, sugar."

Cassie smiled then swiveled on her bare toes and strolled toward the door. "If you can catch me"—she turned at the door and smiled at them—"you can have me." She took off for the stairs leading down to the first floor. A second later she heard their footsteps pounding behind her. She made it to the first floor and ran through the kitchen and up the back stairs. Luc was waiting for her at the top of the steps. She screamed then laughed and ran back down and right into Logan.

"We're beginning to understand how you think, sugar," Logan said.

He carried her up the stairs. Luc pointed to the third floor and several minutes later Cassie found herself standing by the spanking bench. She laughed then climbed on and did a reenactment of the first time they had spanked her after the ice cream attack. She wiggled and stretched and ran her hands over her breasts and her belly then swiped her fingers over her pussy and held her wet fingers up to her lips. She licked them then smiled. "I've been a very, very bad girl, Sirs."

"What do you think we should do about it, sugar?" Luc's eyes glinted as he stroked his cock.

Cassie leaned forward but reached back and ran her hands over her butt cheeks. "I think you should restrain me and spank me." She slapped her ass and moaned, "Then fuck me really hard and deep."

Logan chuckled. "You don't need to spank yourself, sugar. We're happy to do that for you."

Luc and Logan stepped forward and slipped wide wrist cuffs around her wrists then hooked them on the bench. "Okay, sugar?" Luc asked as he tested the tightness.

"Yes, Sir."

Luc kissed her then Logan kissed her. Together they restrained her legs then stepped back. She watched them in the mirror. Luc opened the doors to the cabinet and rummaged around. A second later he returned with two paddles and handed one to Logan. He moved to her left and Logan moved to her right.

The each rubbed her butt with their paddles, moving them in circular motions until her skin felt alive and tingling.

"You don't need to keep count, sugar," Logan said. "We're not going to stop until we feel like it."

"Brace yourself, sugar," Luc said just before he swatted her with the paddle. It made a sharp thwacking sound and she cried out then wiggled.

Logan swatted her and she gasped. They took turns, back and forth, and Cassie wiggled and cried out and gasped then moaned when her arousal built and her clit throbbed.

"Please, please, fuck me," she said. "Oh, oh."

Luc and Logan gave her one more swat each then dropped their paddles. "You get her legs," Logan said, "I'll get her wrists."

Half a minute later Logan lifted her from the spanking bench. "Wrap your legs around me, sugar."

Cassie did and Logan slid balls-deep into her pussy. He sat down on the edge of the bed and fell back, pulling her down on his chest. Luc moved behind her, spread lube on her rosette, then slid one finger into her. He moved it in and out then added a second.

"Oh, Luc," she said. "That feels so good. So good." Cassie rubbed her forehead on Logan's chest then kissed his neck as she felt Luc press the head of his cock against her.

Luc ran his hands up her back then gripped her shoulders as he slid into her and she cried out with pleasure.

"Ready, sugar?" Luc asked, as he pulled out.

She felt Logan shift beneath her and then they began fucking in and out of her. She wrapped her arms around Logan's shoulders and rested on his chest and absorbed the feel of them in and around her.

"Oh, I love you," she said, "so much, so much." She felt Logan's hand slide between their bodies and over her clit.

Logan stroked her clit then pressed on it. "Come now, sugar."

Cassie panted out her pleasure against his chest as she trembled and pleasure rushed through her. She felt them come inside her and she came again.

Their arms surrounded her and hugged her tight.

"I love you, Cassandra," Luc said. "I want you to marry me." He kissed the back of her neck. "Will you?"

Cassie tried to turn so she could kiss him but couldn't quite twist far enough around. Luc leaned down until their lips met. When he pulled away she licked his lips then said, "Oh, yes, I'll marry you, but only if you'll tango with me at the wedding."

Logan chuckled and Cassie looked at him. He smiled at her. "I told you we'd win, sugar."

Epilogue

The next day, Luc, Cassie, and Logan got comfortable on the couch in Cade's den while Thor, Ben, and Mac slouched in chairs placed around the room. Ben and Mac had their phones out and were obviously passing the time playing some kind of game while Cade talked on the phone. His voice too quiet to hear what he was saying.

"What are we waiting for?" Cassie asked.

"Zane," Luc said.

"Uh, do you think that's wise?" Cassie asked. "Shouldn't we discuss what's on the flash drive before we bring him into this, and what about Miller? Has anyone questioned him?"

"Thor's taking care of Miller," Logan said. "Zane needs to know what's on the flash drive so he can protect Ravyn Dolman."

"But you said he wouldn't protect her if it had information on it that proved she was guilty," Cassie said.

"Yes, but we have information that may help him prove she's innocent," Luc said. "Zane's going to have to be prepared to defend her from the accusations Charles Dolman and his attorney are going to make against her."

Cade drew their attention when he slammed the phone down. "That was Muldoon. He just got back from taking his wife on a two month tour of Europe." He grimaced then shook his head. "Poor bastard. Anyway, he said he had our dad's car but sold it off for scrap a long time ago. He also said our parents were burned up in the fire. Guess that's why there's only a plaque at the cemetery and no graves."

Jenna leaned against Jackson's chest then hugged him. "That explains how the Ramseys were able to adopt the five of you so quickly. I guess the courts didn't think you had any other family to take you."

"I didn't know you were adopted." Cassie looked at Luc then Logan. "You guys have got to spend more time talking to me."

Before they could respond, the den door flew open and Addison stepped in looking very pleased with herself.

"Guess who's here?" Addison asked, then before anyone could answer, she stepped aside and waved a dark-haired, voluptuous woman with soft gray eyes into the room. "Ravyn Dalmon. The press is giving her a really hard time so I invited her to hide out with us for a few weeks."

"I appreciate the invitation," Ravyn said, her voice soft and breathy.

Cade stood up and moved forward.

"Ravyn, this is my husband, Cade," Addison said as Cade slid his arms around her waist.

"You're welcome to stay as long as you like, Mrs. Dolman," Cade said.

"I've taken my mother's maiden name, but please call me Ravyn," she said, as she looked around the room. "Zane said he had a large family."

Addison laughed. "Oh, yes, very large and I have to warn you— we're all meddlers."

Jenna slid off Jackson's lap. "Speak for yourself, Addison," she said as she walked toward Ravyn. "I'm Jenna Parnelle, Ravyn, and I'm definitely not a meddler." Jenna waved toward Jackson. "This is my fiancé, Jackson Ramsey."

Ravyn stepped closer to Jenna. "It's a pleasure to meet you, Jenna," she said. "Zane has mentioned all of you so often I feel I know you."

Luc and Logan stood and pulled Cassie up between them. "I'm Cassie Edwards"—she pointed to Luc—"and this is my fiancé Luc

Ramsey." Then she pointed to Logan. "And my fiancé Logan Ramsey."

Thor moved forward. "Ravyn, I'm Thor Larkin. Cade and I are partners in The Larkin Agency." He pointed behind him to Mac and Ben. "This is Mac Malone and Ben Harrington. They work for Cade and me when they aren't gambling and drinking."

"Hey, boss, don't forget the chasing women part." Mac stepped forward and smiled down at her. "In case you didn't catch my name it's Mac. I know how hard it can be to get back in the dating scene after a divorce, and I'd like to help you with that, darlin'. How do you feel about spankings?"

Before she could answer him, Ben shouldered him out of the way. "You don't ask that yet, Mac. You wait until after the first date." He smiled down at her. "I'm Ben Harrington. Do you like to dance, honey?"

Ravyn laughed, but before she could answer they heard the sound of the front door being slammed and then footsteps coming toward the den. A moment later Zane appeared in the doorway. He glared at Addison then said, "Cade, if you don't take a crop to Addison's ass I'm going to," before he turned to Ravyn and said, "You can't be here. Your presence puts me in an impossible position."

Ravyn smiled then put her hand on her hip. "Well, hello to you, too, lover."

THE END

WWW.MARDIMAXWELL.COM

ABOUT THE AUTHOR

I love writing erotic romance combined with adventure and a lot of hot sex. And, don't forget an element of BDSM. I'm a firm believer in happy endings. I also create the kind of hero we would all like to meet and fall in love with so please feel free to fall in love with mine. Did I mention I like to have my characters pop up in other books? Well, yes, I love that. It's like running into an old friend at the grocery store and taking a moment to catch up on their lives.

What is my life like? Busy. When I'm not writing, I'm researching or reading, spending time with my family and friends, making plans to travel, gardening and appreciating the interesting and constantly fascinating people and places around me.

I hope you enjoy reading my books as much as I enjoy writing them for you. If you'd like to know what I'm working on now, check me out at www.facebook.com/MardiMaxwellRomance or www.twitter.com/MardiMaxwellRom.

For all titles by Mardi Maxwell, please visit
www.bookstrand.com/mardi-maxwell

Siren Publishing, Inc.
www.SirenPublishing.com

CPSIA information can be obtained at www.ICGtesting.com
Printed in the USA
BVOW11s1250211114

376169BV00023B/272/P